BLOOD
of the
DEMON

DEMONS OF INFERNUM

BOOK ONE

BLOOD
of the
DEMON

DEMONS OF INFERNUM

BOOK ONE

ROSALIE LARIO

Entangled Publishing, LLC
2614 South Timberline Road
Suite 109
Fort Collins, CO 80525
Visit our website at www.entangledpublishing.com.

Edited by Libby Murphy and Heather Howland
Cover design by Heather Howland

Print ISBN   978-1-62061-039-8
Ebook ISBN   978-1-62061-040-4

Manufactured in the United States of America

First Edition July 2012

The author acknowledges the copyrighted or trademarked status and trademark owners of the following wordmarks mentioned in this work of fiction: Disney World; Jacuzzi; James Bond; New Orleans Saints; Four Seasons; Taj Mahal; Wizard of Oz.

To my parents, Gladys and Ramiro, who instilled in me the belief I can accomplish anything I put my mind to; my sisters, Dixiana, Rebecca, and Jeannette, for always believing in me—no matter what; my Titi Annie, who taught me that a strong woman may fall, but she never stays down; and last but certainly not least, to Joel and David. You are my heart, my life, my inspiration. Accomplishments mean little without loved ones to share them with. This one's for all of you.

CHAPTER ONE

She wasn't what he'd expected.

Keegan crouched on a nearby roof, watching, waiting for her gallery to clear out. A stray gust of cold wind whipped through the night air, ruffling his jacket. It didn't matter. Considering where he'd come from, the cold was a welcome relief.

The woman had looked fragile when he'd caught a glimpse of her through the store's large window front. Undeniably beautiful, with her long honey-brown hair falling in waves around her heart-shaped face—but fragile nonetheless.

It was the perfect cover. No one would ever believe what she truly was, what lived inside her. But the blood never lied. She wasn't what she seemed.

Despite the gravity of the situation, Keegan had felt a stirring of lust rise within him at the sight of her, blindsiding him with its unexpected force. It had simply been too long since he'd gotten laid, something he'd have to remedy soon. Didn't have anything to do with the woman. It couldn't.

After all, she might very well be dead by the end of the day. Because if he received the order, he'd have to kill her.

He fished his cell phone out of his jacket pocket and called his brother. As expected, Taeg answered on the first ring. Skipping the useless chatter, Keegan said, "I've got an eye on the target."

"That's perfect." Even over the phone, the relief in Taeg's voice was palpable. "What now?"

"As soon as she's alone, I'll grab her."

"You don't think Mammon has managed to find her yet, do you?"

Keegan gave a short laugh. "If he had, he would've taken her already. Waiting's not his style."

"Yeah, right," Taeg muttered. "Don't I know it?"

"I'll keep you posted." He hung up without waiting for a reply.

Even though he couldn't see her from this vantage point, he wasn't worried about losing her. Not after he'd tagged her scent. He closed his eyes and inhaled, giving himself over to his sense of smell. Sorting through the various odors he'd picked up—the rich aroma of coffee, the ashy smell of a discarded cigarette, the pungent stench of rotting food—he discarded them, one by one.

Yes. There she was. Her scent was unique. Like strawberries and cream. Something he'd tried only recently and discovered he loved.

Would she taste just as sweet?

Shit. What was he thinking? She wasn't a potential lay, but a dangerous and powerful weapon. Maybe even the enemy. He'd do well to remember that.

Finally, the store emptied of everyone but her. He supposed

the right thing would be to go in and question her. But what if Mammon was no more than a few steps behind him? He couldn't take that chance. Not when the stakes were so high.

He would take her back to the apartment with him. There, he could question her at leisure and decide what to do without having to worry about Mammon or his henchmen discovering them. But what were the odds of her going along with him willingly?

Well, he couldn't worry about that now. He'd simply take her.

The night had grown dark enough that he didn't bother heading for the roof exit. Instead, he walked to the side of the building facing the narrow alleyway and stepped off. He landed the six-story fall with a *thud* that shook the ground. A cracking sound, followed by a twinge of pain shooting up his right leg, made him pause, but he ignored it as the fissure healed itself. The homeless man lying unconscious in a puddle not ten feet away mumbled and stirred before growing still once again.

Keegan crossed the street, his gaze single-mindedly locked on the figure of the woman visible through the window as she buzzed about the front of the gallery. A ray of light from a small lamp decorating the window caught her hair, spinning it into a web of gold. In that lighting, she looked almost like an angel.

But why was he thinking about the color of her hair? She wasn't an angel—not by a long shot.

And her luck was about to run out.

ജ

Brynn Meyers stifled a yawn as she tidied up the eclectic space of her showroom floor. With its old furniture and traditional chandeliers, the space more closely resembled an antiques shop than an art gallery. She'd started it several years ago with the inheritance she received following her father's death from a car accident, just a short time after her mother died of breast cancer. It seemed like she spent every waking moment there. If she wasn't working, she was painting in her small studio located in the back.

"Just two hours of painting tonight, then I'll go to sleep early for a change," she told herself. "This time I mean it."

God, how pathetic was she? Was she so lonely that she had to start bargaining with herself?

No, not lonely, Brynn. Just a loner. There's a difference.

Really, there was. Even if deep down inside, part of her wished she wasn't quite so alone. So unique.

Her hand grazed the easel holding the painting that had arrived earlier today. She turned to examine it more closely. Created by her favorite artist, it drew her in because of the artist's tendency to incorporate unusual materials into his work, such as the tattered pieces of muslin glued to this painting. It was an amazing work of art, and the cloth was obviously old and worn.

Brynn brushed her hand against the gathered fabric. Closing her eyes, she focused on the feel of it at her fingertips, on the shadows of memories that whispered to her, begging her to uncover them.

The muslin yielded beneath her touch, revealing its deepest secrets. Her vision narrowed, focusing in on the fabric as its memories hurtled toward her. Several hundred years old, the painting began its journey to her as part of an elegant dress worn by a Frenchwoman. Images of the woman's trembling fingers flowed into Brynn's mind, and she smiled at the impressions of the woman smoothing the material down, eagerly anticipating a visit from her secret lover. Then, in a scene years later, someone tore apart the dress for scraps. Even later, the bits of fabric were twisted and crafted into a rag doll, cherished for many years by the little girl who lovingly slept with it until she became too old for dolls.

The flashes of memory faded away. Taking a deep breath, she slowly returned to the present.

It's just a bit of fabric. She often had to remind herself of that. The memories embedded in inanimate objects tended to make them seem alive to her. But they weren't. They were just conduits for energy. And for some reason, she had the ability to sense this energy. This was a gift she'd had her whole life, and what had initially drawn her to art. Each piece had a story, an experience, rooted within it. Older art pieces could be positively overwhelming.

Of course, her so-called gift wasn't limited solely to art. There were times when it didn't seem like much of a gift at all—like when she discovered something she wasn't supposed to know. Case in point: when she'd touched her last boyfriend's cell phone and learned he'd recently used it to make an assignation with his ex-girlfriend. God, what a string of losers she'd dated recently.

The front door opened with a loud chime and Brynn snatched her hand away. Not like anyone would ever know what she'd been doing, but for some unexplainable reason, she always feared her gift would be discovered. Life was difficult enough without being branded a freak or a psycho.

She lifted her gaze to find a tall, well-built man standing in the doorway. Her breath caught as her eyes traveled from his skintight black shirt, highlighting every curve of his muscular chest, to the dark, shaggy hair framing his olive-toned face. A shiver ran through her. He embodied Dark and Dangerous, with the leather jacket to match.

And *crap*, she was ogling him like a slab of meat in a lion's den.

She wiped her suddenly damp palms against her slacks before moving forward to greet him. "Hi, welcome to Meyers Gallery. I'm Brynn."

He stared at her outstretched hand for so long that she fidgeted. Maybe he'd noticed her wiping her palms and had gotten grossed out. Great.

She started to pull her hand back, but he stopped her by at last reaching out to clasp his hand over hers. A tingle of awareness flashed across her palm, so sharp she had to struggle to hold back a startled gasp.

"I know," he said.

"What?" Brynn took a second to remember what they were talking about. Once she did, she flushed anew. This hunk of a man was making her lose her train of thought. "You mean you know my name? Have we spoken on the phone before, then? Are you here about one of the new art pieces?"

"No," he said, without releasing her hand.

His grasp was warm, heating Brynn from the inside out. The sensation was so disconcerting she needed another long second to process his response. "No? Well then, how can I help you?"

The man smiled, but something resembling regret flashed through his bluish-green eyes. Lord, they were amazing.

"Sorry," he said, the sound curling around his lips like a lover's caress.

Her gaze drifted to his full, luscious mouth, and she

couldn't look away. If she didn't get him out of here soon, she was afraid she might jump his bones. Never before had she felt so viscerally attracted to a man, and it was unnerving, to say the least. This was the sort of distraction she didn't want or need.

"You're sorry? About what?" She tried to tug her hand back, but the man's grip held firm.

"About this."

His left arm came at her so fast she only saw a flash of it, right before his fist connected with the side of her face. There was a burst of pain. Then, she went blissfully numb.

CHAPTER TWO

He'd made it all the way uptown with an unconscious woman in his arms and hadn't been spotted once. Not bad. Then again, he did have a few assets at his disposal. Like not having to use the ground.

Keegan carried the woman's limp figure into the Upper East Side penthouse apartment the Council had lent him and his brothers. The place was a far cry from the tiny shack he lived in back at home. The office alone was bigger, not to mention the four sizable bedrooms. And the amazing view of the city skyline from the wall of windows in the living room was nothing to scoff at. Too bad the magnitude of the situation didn't allow him to enjoy the view.

Taeg and Dagan, however, seemed to have no qualms about living it up. Sprawled out on the huge leather sectional in the living room, beers in hand, they watched some sports game on the large plasma television. The two of them didn't even look up when he entered the room.

"Glad to see you two douchebags can relax when this

whole world is on the verge of being destroyed," Keegan said.

"No problem," Dagan said, before turning his attention back to the screen.

Smartass.

Taeg shrugged and kicked his feet off the coffee table, swiveling his head in Keegan's direction. He was wearing a T-shirt emblazoned with the words WHY DO TODAY WHAT YOU CAN PUT OFF UNTIL TOMORROW?

Keegan stifled a snort. "Nice shirt."

Taeg rose and started toward him. "My favorite thing about Earth so far is the shirts. Followed closely by the supercool lingo. Did you know 'Fuck off' is practically a greeting in this city?" He stopped a few feet away and examined the figure of the unconscious woman lying in Keegan's arms. "Wow. She's a real looker. What did you do to her, anyway?"

Keegan would've thought that was obvious. A dark purple bruise in the shape of his fist marred her otherwise flawless cheek. He swallowed past the flare of emotion that tightened his throat. "Knocked her out. How else was I going to get her back here?"

"I could have gotten her to come with us willingly, if you'd let me go with you," Taeg said. "But no, you wanted to go off and be Master of the Universe all by yourself."

"She was my responsibility."

"Yeah, and we all know how much you love responsibility."

Keegan ignored the unreasonable stab of irritation his brother's words provoked. He was only annoyed because Taeg was an ass. No other reason. Of all his half brothers, Taeg especially knew how to push his buttons. The only way to win this battle was to ignore him.

"She's a job, and nothing more," he told Taeg. "And don't

forget what we might have to do to her."

"I haven't forgotten." Taeg smiled, though there was no humor in it this time. He obviously dreaded this as much as Keegan did. Taeg wasn't a monster. Not like their father.

Keegan's irritation melted away. His brothers didn't want to be here any more than he did. It wasn't their fault, what they were born into.

"Where's Ronin?" he asked.

"I'm here." Ronin appeared in the doorway leading from the kitchen. He was the second youngest of his half brothers, older than Dagan but younger than Taeg. "So you got her, huh?"

"Yup."

"Did she seem to know anything about Mammon or her ancestry?"

"I haven't questioned her yet. But there wasn't a trace of demon activity surrounding her. I figured I'd get her out of there first and ask questions later."

"Good idea." Ronin waited a beat before saying, "So…are you going to hold her all day, or what?"

Shit.

Embarrassment flooded through Keegan. He hadn't even considered letting go of the woman. Holding her in his arms eroded his ability to think straight, like the blood kept trying to rush out of his brain and into other parts of his anatomy.

I really need to get laid soon.

That was it. Nothing more.

Keegan turned and strode into the room they'd specifically prepared for her. For Brynn. As he carefully laid her on the bed, he couldn't help but think how well that name suited her. It was just as interesting and unusual as she was.

With her figure encased in tight wool slacks and a fitted black sweater, the outline of her slim form was clearly visible. Small, firm breasts. Flat stomach. When she'd looked up at him back at her art gallery, her eyes had been a soft, calming green.

She was beyond enticing.

The sound of a throat clearing roused Keegan from his slow survey. He looked behind him to see Ronin and Taeg crowding the doorway.

Ronin nodded toward Brynn. "Looks like you hit her pretty hard."

"Didn't mean to." What a dick thing to do, hitting her like that. But he'd had no choice. Not really. There was no knowing how close Mammon was to finding her, or if he hadn't gotten to her already. Either way, he'd needed to get her out of there fast. "I'll heal her."

"That's not necessary," Ronin interjected. "Not when I can do it with a simple touch."

Ronin started toward Brynn, but Keegan surprised himself by letting out a low growl. "I said I'll do it."

Shock registered on Ronin's face, and he held up his hands, backing off. Not that Keegan blamed him. Where did he get off being angry at the thought of his brother touching Brynn?

He must be losing his mind.

"Let him do it." Taeg's smooth voice dispelled the tension in the room. "You know how Keegan likes to suffer for his sins."

"Fuck you," Keegan said, taking a seat on the bed next to Brynn. He withdrew his iron pocketknife, flicked it open, and cut a shallow groove in his palm. After pressing his hand to her cheek, he drew it away. His blood seeped into her pores, healing her blood vessels. The swelling went down, and within a few seconds she was good as new.

He wiped the remnants of his blood off her cheek, trying not to think about how soft and cool her skin felt beneath his hand. She was just a woman, and a human one at that.

Well, mostly, anyway.

"So what now?" Ronin asked him.

"Now, we wait for her to wake up, and we question her. Then we'll decide what to do with her."

Taeg gave a soul-weary sigh. "Sounds great. I'm gonna go drink some more." He did an about-face and disappeared.

Unable to help himself, Keegan turned back to the woman. So soft and feminine.

The sound of Ronin moving behind him barely registered. "You did more than just walk tonight, huh?"

"What's that?"

Without another word, Ronin poked his fingers through the jagged slits in Keegan's jacket and shirt, making contact with the bare flesh of his back.

Keegan fought back a flush. "Oh. Almost forgot about that." Which was unusual for him, something his intuitive little brother had no doubt picked up on.

"I had a feeling," Ronin replied dryly. "Might want to change before she wakes up."

"Yeah, good idea." If she didn't settle for outright panic and screaming when she awoke, she was bound to have questions for him. He didn't need to add any more to that list. Standing, he followed Ronin out of the room and clicked the door shut, then slid the lock on the outside into place.

৪৩৫৫

Brynn opened her eyes to taupe satin wallpaper, dark wood

furniture, and the faint smell of fresh, clean linen. She turned her head to the side, confirming that she was lying on a bed. A soft, comfortable bed with silky chocolate-colored sheets and a faux fur bedspread folded across the bottom. Where the hell was she?

Wait. What happened?

It all came back in one blinding rush. The gallery, the too-hot-to-be-real man. His fist shooting toward her face.

Oh, crap.

Brynn jerked up off the bed. Her first instinct was to panic, but she forced herself to calm down. She'd been through something like this before…and she'd learned from that horrible incident that she was stronger than she looked. That was something the creep who'd dared to take her was about to find out…

She lifted two fingers to touch the spot where the man had hit her but, amazingly, didn't find even a hint of pain. What the hell? He *had* hit her, that much she knew. So why didn't she feel it?

She couldn't believe that the man had hidden behind his gorgeous exterior and managed to totally catch her off guard. Had knocked her out. And apparently brought her here. To his…to his…palace?

"That *asshole.*"

The amazing skyline view from the tall windows on one side of the room, as well as the lush décor of the massive space, told her the word *palace* wasn't too far off. She was obviously in an exclusive luxury apartment, one on the Upper East Side if she didn't mistake the view.

What kind of criminal brought his victim to a place like this? He was probably a rapist. Or a serial murderer. Well, it didn't matter. Whatever his reasons, he might have caught her off guard once, but it wouldn't happen again. And she wasn't scared of him. She wouldn't *allow* herself to be. Not with what she could do.

"Once I get my hands on you, you'll regret it," she muttered. No doubt he'd regret it.

The hollow sound of her heels clacking on the wood floor vibrated in her ear as she stalked over to the door on the far side of the room. She tried the knob. Locked. Great. Just great.

The walls seemed to close in on her, the surrounding space shrinking until she once again felt like she was inside the trunk of that car, fighting off her nausea and wondering what *he* was going to do to her. She forced herself to shake the feeling off and then pounded on the door. "Is anyone there? Hey, where are you? Let me out."

When there was no immediate response, she pounded louder. "Come on. Hello? Let me out!"

Brynn was about to lift her fist for a fresh bout of knocking when the doorknob turned with a *click*. She scampered back as the door swung open.

The hunk from the gallery stood on the other side, *sans* leather jacket. He wore an impassive expression on his face.

Her fingers clenched into fists at the sight of the man who'd imprisoned her. He was about to pay. *"You."*

He opened his mouth. "Let me explain—"

Without further thought, she rushed him, pummeling her fists into his chest. He didn't flinch, didn't even budge. He was like a freaking steel beam. But that was okay. She'd get him, anyway.

She lifted her hand to his throat and dug into his bare skin. Giving herself over to her senses, she willed the flow of energy through her body, just as she'd done so many times before. Her arm grew hot with the familiar sensation of energy drawing through her fingers, working its way inside her with an electric sizzle.

But instead of collapsing as she expected, the man merely lifted one perfect brow. "Ow."

That was it. That was all he said.

"Ow?" Brynn repeated, going numb with shock. She'd felt it! She'd felt the familiar draw of energy. But instead of falling to the ground in an unconscious puddle, he just said, *Ow?*

Ow?

"Impossible," she gasped.

He tilted his head to one side. "What exactly are you trying to do?"

This couldn't be happening. That particular ability had never failed her before.

She brought both hands to the bare skin of his muscular arm, right below the sleeve of his shirt, doing her best to ignore the spicy, masculine scent emanating from his body and the heat of his rigid flesh beneath her palms. Seriously, the man must be running a fever. He was scorching hot.

Squeezing her eyes shut, she once again concentrated on summoning her energy. Again, she felt it flow, but he stood still in front of her. He didn't even flinch.

She staggered back. "Oh, crap."

It didn't work on him.

For the first time in a very long time, a strange sensation stirred in the pit of Brynn's stomach, churning her insides to a rolling boil.

Pure, unadulterated *fear*.

She was stuck in a room with a psychopath who'd knocked

her out and kidnapped her, and she had no way to defend herself. No way to fight back.

Oh, God, she was totally screwed.

❦

Brynn stumbled away from Keegan, appearing scared for the first time since he'd entered the room. An uncomfortable twinge tightened his gut. He didn't want her to be scared of him. Which was ridiculous. After all, why should he care? She *was* the heir, that much he knew from the intel given to him by the Council. If there had been any doubt of that, she had confirmed her identity when she'd laid her hands on him and a lightning bolt of energy had shot through her fingers. No mere human would have that sort of ability.

He held his hands in the air, moved forward far enough to kick the door shut, then leaned against it, trying to look as non-menacing as possible. "Listen, I'm not going to hurt you. I just want to talk to you, okay? My name is Keegan."

She backed up until she was on the far side of the room, by the large set of windows. She seemed to notice she was wringing her hands and dropped them to her sides. "What do you want with me? If—if it's money, I don't have that much, but I'll give you whatever I have—"

"I don't want your money, Brynn," he interrupted, keeping his tone soft and calm. "Right now, I only want to talk to you."

"You're not going to—?"

"I'm not going to hurt you." Keegan tried not to wince at that lie. He might very well have to hurt her. But if he did, it wouldn't be because he wanted to.

She nodded, but she seemed to doubt the sincerity of his

tone because her gaze darted about the room as if checking for possible weapons. It settled for a moment on the bulky lamp by the bed. The lamp probably *was* heavy enough to bash in a human's head. But she'd be unpleasantly surprised if she tried using it on him.

"If you're not going to hurt me, why did you kidnap me?"

Keegan sighed and closed his eyes. The question he'd dreaded. He probably should have allowed Taeg to simply charm her into telling them what they needed to know. She wouldn't have been afraid that way. And he wouldn't be stuck coming up with a story she would believe. But as stupid as it might be, the least he owed her was her free will. He didn't want to take that from her. No, he knew all too well what that felt like.

Finally, he settled on a perverted version of the truth. "It's sort of a long story. Why don't you sit down and I'll tell you?"

Brynn cast a pointed glance around the room and then at the bed, which was the only piece of furniture she could sit on. "I don't think so," she said in an icy tone.

Keegan chuckled at her bravado. She was tougher than she looked. "Sorry, I guess not." Slowly, so as not to alarm her, he drew away from the door. "What do you know about your ancestry?"

She appeared startled, as if that were the last question she'd been expecting. And who could blame her? "My — my what?"

"Your ancestry. Where you come from. Who your ancestors are."

"I...not much. My parents weren't exactly into the whole family-tree thing. I can only go as far back as my grandparents."

Keegan scoffed. "I figured. You humans are so focused on yourselves that you forget about the past."

"Us…*humans*?"

Shit. He needed to watch what he said.

He cleared his throat. "I meant humankind in general."

Confusion gradually replaced the fear on her face. "Listen, uh…Keegan, right? I'm not really sure what you're getting at here, but—"

"Did you know that your ancestry can be traced back to the ancient Egyptians?"

"What? No." A hint of interest colored her tone. "Really, that far back? I mean, that's kind of cool, but I still don't know what it has to do with you kidnapping me. And how the hell do you know that, anyway?"

All right, here it went. Hopefully she'd buy it. "Brynn, one of your ancestors was an Egyptian priest who lived about three thousand years ago. He created something, a book. When he died, he was buried with it. And now there's someone who'll stop at nothing to find it."

All true so far. But here's where he had to start stretching the truth. "The man who's searching for the book believes you can lead him to it. He's not a good…person. If he gets his hands on you, there's no telling what he'll do."

Her confusion morphed into doubt. "But…but that's ridiculous. I don't even know anything about my *great*-grandparents, much less some obscure relative who lived three thousand years ago."

"Nonetheless, it's true." He kept his tone calm and flat. That, more than anything, seemed to sway her into believing him.

"Who keeps track of their ancestry that far back? How could he even think I might lead him to the book?"

"He's insane." Which was true. You didn't get much crazier

than Mammon. Keegan knew that all too well.

She crossed her arms over her chest, brows furrowed. "Yeah, well, that still doesn't tell me how you got involved."

"I..." *Fuck.* He took a breath. Time for some quick thinking. He settled on the first half truth that popped into his head. "I work for a secret branch of the government."

What would the Council members think to hear themselves described that way? They were far more powerful than just one government—than just one world, even.

"We're trying to stop him," he added, "and part of that means protecting you."

Unless it becomes too dangerous. Then we'll have to kill you.

"A secret government organization, huh?" Brynn's tone was ripe with suspicion, and who could blame her? "Why did you bring me here? Am I supposed to believe this is some sort of safe house?"

"In a manner of speaking."

She arched a brow. "Where's your government ident-ification, then?"

Man, but she was cheeky. And the devil help him, he liked it.

Yeah, well, don't get too caught up in singing her praises. You still don't know whether or not she's playing a game.

"We're an unofficial branch. We don't get identification." Then, before she could question further, he asked, "Brynn, have you been contacted or followed by anyone unusual the past few days?"

"Other than you?" She snorted with a slight shake of her head. "No."

Keegan straightened and pushed off the door. "I need you to be straight with me. You're not helping anyone, are you?"

"Who would I be helping?" When he took a step toward

her, she lifted her hands in front of her. "Stay back."

He stopped, curiosity getting the better of him. "What exactly is it that you can do with your hands?" He was willing to bet it was more than just mere emission of electricity.

She glanced down, appearing startled, as if she just realized she'd lifted them. "Hmm? Oh, nothing. It doesn't seem to be working, anyway," she murmured, so low that a human wouldn't have been able to hear it.

Another stirring of sympathy churned in his gut. This couldn't be easy for her, having to deal with her loss of powers on top of being kidnapped. "Do you want to try it again?"

"What?" She let out an uncertain chuckle. "You expect me to fall for that? I'm not getting anywhere near you."

"You have nowhere to go," he pointed out. "I could overpower you at any moment if I wanted to. In fact, I could have hurt you while you were unconscious, if that were my true intent."

She bit down on her lip, the simple vulnerability of her action making him feel like a total tool.

"I can sit on the bed, if you like," he offered.

After a moment's pause, she gave him a jerky nod. "Okay."

Keeping his movements even, he sat on the bed with his hands in full view at his sides.

Brynn inched forward. "Lift up your shirt."

Keegan sucked in his breath at the unexpected arousal her words caused. It wasn't as if she'd asked him to get undressed. She just wanted to make better contact with his skin. But his cock didn't seem to know that.

Down, boy.

If it kept reacting that way, there'd be no doubt in her mind what he was thinking, and she'd run across the room screaming. He tugged his shirt up to his chest, his movements slow and his breathing steady.

She crept forward, like a curious deer fearing a trap.

"I won't hurt you," he said again.

Finally, she stood only a few feet in front of him. With an indrawn breath, she placed her hands on his chest. His eyes closed of their own accord. Her hands were slightly cool to the touch, but softer than anything he'd felt before; a breath of freshness in the otherwise stale, cruel world that made up his entire existence. Once again, the strange sensation of electric current zinged off her fingertips. It tingled to the point of being uncomfortable, but nothing more than that.

"Nothing," she breathed, seemingly abandoning her fear as she knelt down in front of him and squeezed her palms tighter against his chest.

He opened his eyes to peer down at Brynn, who was clearly so focused on trying to do whatever it was she could normally do that she didn't realize she was kneeling between his splayed legs. The position put her head level with his stomach, so close her strawberries-and-cream essence practically assaulted his senses.

"Is it me? Or is it you?" She lifted her eyes to his for the first time since touching him, and her breath audibly caught in her throat. "So warm. Why are you so warm?"

Keegan's pulse raced. He couldn't help himself. With her looking at him that way, her green eyes clouded over, he didn't stand a chance.

"I just am," he whispered, all the while trying to remind himself who—and what—she was.

He wanted to kiss her, to feel those lips on his. To taste her pink little tongue. He longed to surrender to the desire that tightened every muscle in his body, to the instinctive need to *know* her. Yes, it was wrong, but he had a hard time caring right now.

Mission be damned.

He inched toward her face. Her eyes widened, but she didn't move away. If he could have one taste, he could forget about it. Get it out of his system. Go on with the mission.

Just one taste…

"Am I interrupting something?" said a voice from the doorway.

Brynn flew up and shuffled away, toward the window, as Keegan aimed his guilt-filled gaze in the direction of the door.

Taeg leaned against the doorjamb. Apparently, he'd managed to open the door without Keegan noticing. And by the look on his face, Taeg hadn't missed what had almost happened with him and Brynn.

Well, that was just great.

CHAPTER THREE

Brynn retreated to her spot by the large window as another man leaned casually against the doorframe. He resembled Keegan, but he was a little narrower and had a slight cleft in his chin. His carelessly tousled dark brown hair was quite a bit shorter than Keegan's shaggy cut.

"Who are you?" she demanded.

Keegan stood and smoothed his shirt down. "He's my brother."

Brother? Well, that explained the similar build, the resemblance, and the general hotness. Was everyone in his family just as gorgeous as he was?

Then it hit her. A mortified flush crept to her cheeks. *Oh, God.*

What on earth had she been doing, kneeling on the floor in front of him like that? If she wasn't mistaken, he'd been about to kiss her. And she'd been about to let him.

Jesus. The guy was her kidnapper. He might be trying to feed her some line of bullshit about being a government agent, but she wasn't buying. And despite that, she'd still allowed him to sway her with his good looks and his hotter-than-molten-steel body. And oh, what a body it was. His rock-hard muscles had pulsed underneath her palms. She wiped her hands on her slacks.

She'd heard of Stockholm Syndrome before, but she'd known this guy for a total of ten minutes, tops.

Lord, I'm such a slut.

"I was just telling Brynn about her ancestry." Keegan ran a hand through his hair as he addressed his brother. "About the man who's trying to find her."

"Yeah, sure you were," his brother responded, his tone saturated with sarcasm.

Rising up to her full height, Brynn assumed a challenging pose and addressed the brother. "Let me guess—you expect me to believe you're a government agent, too, right?"

"Agent?" He choked out a laugh, glanced at Keegan, and then laughed again. "Yeah, sure, I'm a regular James Bond."

"Taeg," Keegan said in a warning tone.

"I'm Taeg," he said, ignoring Keegan as he moved toward Brynn with an outstretched hand.

She stared down at his hand, hesitating.

"I won't bite." Though the wolfish smile on his face said maybe he'd like to. "Promise."

Oh, what did she have to lose?

She took his hand. "I'm Brynn. Wish I could say it was nice to meet you. But I'm not feeling too nice right now."

Taeg snickered as he let go of her hand. "I get it. Believe me."

Wait a second. He now stood right here in front of her. All she needed to do was reach out and touch him…

Without taking another second to contemplate it, Brynn placed her palms on his chest and concentrated on her powers.

"Ouch!"

He jumped back. But that was it.

"Unbelievable." Her touch had once leveled a man twice Taeg's size, and to him and Keegan it was just a minor annoyance. What was going on here?

Taeg gave her an appraising look, tilting his head to the side much as Keegan had earlier. "What were you trying to do?"

Heat rushed to her cheeks. "Nothing."

"She tried the same thing with me earlier," Keegan said from his spot by the doorway. "With a similar effect."

"Hmm…" Taeg put a hand to his chin. "You've got some powers, huh?"

"Wha—what?"

Why the hell would that even cross his mind? It wasn't like anyone ever believed what she could do, so why would a total stranger make that assumption? Sure, he'd obviously felt *something* when she'd touched him, but wouldn't a normal person assume it was just static in the air or something of that nature?

"Powers." Taeg grinned. "Want to see what I can do?"

Keegan stirred. "Taeg, stop—"

Before Keegan could cross the room, Taeg grabbed her, his hands searing hot where they touched her arms over her light sweater.

"Hey, what are you doing?" Brynn glared into his eyes. The blue depths of his irises seemed to swirl around his pupils.

She couldn't look away. Didn't want to. Nothing existed but those swirling, blue-green eyes.

"Relax," he said, his voice soft as honey.

Amazingly, a liquid sensation washed over her, slowing the rush of blood in her veins and the rapid pumping of her heart. Her body went boneless, until Taeg practically held her up by the arms. Deep down she knew she should be afraid that she was no longer in control of her own body, but she wasn't. Instead she felt calm…tranquil.

Keegan approached and grabbed his brother's arm, as if about to push him away. "I said *stop*."

Taeg's eyes turned to Keegan, and Brynn fought back a whimper. She wanted his eyes back on her.

What had he done to her?

"Let me do this," Taeg snapped at Keegan. "We have to know."

Keegan paused, an angry scowl on his face. *"Fuck."* He whirled and paced about the room.

Taeg returned his attention to her, and she exhaled in relief.

"It's all right," he drawled, a rakish smirk on his face. "Tell me, do you know anyone by the name of Mammon?"

Mammon? Who? "No."

"Has anyone unusual approached you the past few weeks, or has anything weird happened to you?"

Other than this? She shook her head. "No."

"What can you do with your hands?"

"I…" Why the hell did she feel so compelled to answer? She never shared her secret. But she couldn't stop herself. "I can make people pass out. Almost like I'm draining their energy. At least, I *used* to be able to do that."

Taeg actually looked impressed. "Pretty cool. What else can you do?"

"I…" Perspiration built at Brynn's temples from her effort

to keep her mouth shut, but she was powerless. She couldn't stay quiet. "I can read energy off objects, get their memories."

Taeg whistled, glancing over at Keegan. "You hear that? Our little friend is turning out to be pretty interesting. Over three millennia, and she's still gifted."

His words caused a tidal wave of confusion to wash over Brynn. What did he mean, still gifted?

Keegan stopped pacing long enough to spit out, "Hurry up and finish it."

Taeg chuckled and turned to Brynn. "Do you know how you got your abilities?"

"No." She licked her lips, which suddenly felt too dry. "How are you doing this?"

Taeg smiled at her. Right now, his face was the most captivating thing she'd ever seen. The angular cheekbones, the almost imperceptible cleft in his chin. The shadowy stubble just starting to grow on his jaw. His voice was smooth as butter when he said, "Don't you want to kiss me?"

Now that he mentioned it, she really did. How had she ever lived without kissing those impossibly full lips before?

"Yes," she whispered, moistening her trembling lips. She leaned forward, but before she reached Taeg, Keegan rushed him. Jostling her to the side, he grabbed his brother by the throat and slammed him against the wall.

Now that Taeg no longer supported her, her limbs felt like goo. She stumbled and fell to the ground. The crazy compulsion to kiss Taeg faded until she wondered if she'd ever really felt it.

"What do you think you're doing?" Anger radiated from Keegan in violent waves, making Brynn's stomach knot. From this position, he resembled a feral animal, one with no qualms about killing its prey.

Taeg choked out a laugh as he reached up to pry Keegan's hand from around his neck. "I was just screwing around," he rasped, clearly amused, even though it looked like Keegan was throttling the life out of him.

Keegan said something else, but it wasn't in English. Instead he spoke a deep, guttural language Brynn had never heard. But she didn't have time to contemplate that, because she could only focus on one thing.

Taeg had done something to her. When he'd touched her, looked at her, she'd done whatever he had asked, whatever he'd suggested. Even now, the reminder of how full and kissable his lips had seemed made her heart pound and her body temperature heat.

Holy crap—Taeg had powers, too!

She wasn't alone anymore.

Brynn rose to her feet, forcing herself to brush aside that one rogue thought. Because right now there were far more pressing matters to discuss. She raised her voice so she could be heard over the two men, who even now yelled at each other in a foreign tongue. "Okay, who *are* you guys?"

৪৩৫৩

Keegan glanced at Brynn, who stood facing him and Taeg like some angry warrior queen. Her fists clenched into tight balls at her side, and her chest heaved in a way that accentuated what lay beneath her top. The fact that Taeg probably hadn't missed that, either, pissed him off to no end.

He turned to his brother and spoke once again in their native tongue. "You were supposed to find out what she knows—not make her question us even more. What is wrong with you?"

"I told you I was just fucking around," Taeg responded in the same language. "Now stop being a dick and get your hand off my throat."

"Have you forgotten who she is?" Keegan punctuated his words with a shake of his wrist. "You really think it would be a good idea to get involved with her?"

"I could ask you the same thing."

Keegan froze, flustered by the sudden uncomfortable feeling that his brother had just set him up with that whole little display.

"I can't understand you two," Brynn said from across the room. "What language are you speaking?"

Keegan ignored her. He unclenched his fist and released Taeg, his anger disappearing as quickly as it had arrived. His brother had only been trying to make a point—and he'd made it well. Brynn was clearly off limits.

"I don't know what you're talking about," he lied to Taeg. "She was trying to use her power on me when you walked in earlier, and I let her, so she'd know it didn't work on me. There was nothing else going on."

Taeg threw him a disbelieving look as he massaged his throat. "Whatever helps you sleep at night, bro. Just remember—she's the key to the fucking apocalypse. Not just here on Earth, but maybe every planet there is. If we can't find the book before Mammon does, she's gotta get dead. And fast."

Keegan gritted his teeth and resisted the urge to pounce on Taeg once more. Damn it. He had to calm down. He turned to Brynn, who stared at the both of them in confusion, no doubt wondering what they were saying. "I *know* that, man. I barely know her. And if I have to, I *will* kill her."

"Good," Taeg said. "Just remember that. Because you may very well have to. And if it comes down to it and you puss out, know that *I* will."

Every muscle in Keegan's body tightened at the clear warning in Taeg's words. With a menacing growl, Keegan whirled to face him. "Are you threatening me, *little* brother?"

"You've never let me down before." Taeg raised his hands in a conciliatory gesture. "But you're my brother. It's *my* job to keep you in line if you're being a shit. Just make sure you follow through with what you need to do, and there'll be no problem."

That was it. Taeg had pushed him too far. He always pushed him too far. How dare he even suggest Keegan wouldn't live up to his responsibility? He wasn't their father.

He straightened his back, putting him a good inch or two taller than Taeg. "What exactly are you implying?"

Taeg looked at him dead-on, a challenge in his eyes. "I think you know already, bro."

Keegan gritted his teeth, seconds away from lunging, when Ronin's even voice sounded out from the doorway. "What's going on in here? I heard the yelling and banging from down the hall."

A sense of peace and calm washed through Keegan, the mark of Ronin's presence. Most of the time, that particular ability came in handy, but every once in a while, he just needed a good fight.

"Let me guess," Brynn said from across the room. "Another brother, right?"

Keegan glanced at Brynn, who was staring at Ronin with an expression of disbelief. He switched back to English. "This is our younger brother Ronin."

"Of course he is." Brynn let out an incredulous chuckle. "Did they specially breed you guys in a lab or something?"

He exchanged a confused look with Ronin. What did that mean?

Brynn must have caught the glance, because she explained. "Since you're all so hot, I mean." Then, as if just realizing her words, she flushed a bright red, which only served to make her that much more alluring.

Keegan fought back a reluctant chuckle.

Taeg wasn't quite as reserved. He gave Brynn an impish grin. "You're pretty hot, too."

Keegan's amusement vanished in a flash. Another low growl rose in his throat, aching to tear out. He cleared it instead. Something about her made him territorial, but he couldn't afford to indulge in his true nature. Not with this woman, and especially not with his brother on his ass.

Brynn laughed and shuffled her feet uncomfortably, as if fighting an instinctive urge to back away. "Are there any more of you?"

Ronin smiled at her. "Our youngest brother, Dagan. He's out for the moment, though."

Out? Keegan switched back to their native tongue. "Where did he go?"

"Bar down the street," Ronin replied.

"He went to a bar? *Now*?"

"Think about it, man," Taeg said to him. "You know he's a softie. He doesn't want to get to know her if we're going to have to end up killing her."

Ronin gave a curt nod in agreement, and Keegan felt a moment of guilt that he hadn't considered that. Dagan was a lover of women. An unrepentant playboy, yes, but he would never physically hurt a woman. Of course this would be hard on him. Well, it was for the best that Dagan wasn't here, because if he had been, he'd probably be trying to get into Brynn's pants, too.

"Can you guys please speak English?" Brynn asked, placing extra emphasis on the last word.

"Sorry." Keegan turned back to her. Despite all she'd been through today, she was still standing. Still fighting. He could only hope he wouldn't have to extinguish that light in her eyes.

Unfortunately, it wasn't up to him. For that reason alone he had to tread carefully.

Brynn edged over to the bed and sat, her gaze wide and unfocused. "So that's why you guys are keeping me here? You have abilities like me, don't you?"

Taeg gave Keegan a glance and let out a casual shrug. "Yeah. Sure, that's it."

"You're part of a secret organization for people with powers," she continued in amazement.

Well, if that made her feel better about this whole thing, Keegan wasn't about to disabuse her of her notion. Especially since her fear had evaporated as she uttered that statement.

"That's right," he said to her.

"Like a gang of superheroes," she added.

She thought they were superheroes? Taeg's and Ronin's gazes shot to Keegan. They looked as startled by her assumption as he was.

How wrong she was.

But on the other hand, now that she mentioned it, it seemed like a perfectly good cover.

He turned back to Brynn, fighting to keep his face expressionless. "Yes, that's what it is."

She tilted her head and studied him, her eyes filled with a tinge of uncertainty that twisted deep in his gut. Devil help him, he didn't want to hear the sadness in her voice, didn't want her to be afraid.

"How am I supposed to trust you?"

Keegan directed his gaze toward Ronin and crooked his head.

Taking the hint, Ronin crossed the room and crouched in front of Brynn. "I know this must be hard for you. But we're trying to protect you. We need for you to trust us."

Even from where he stood, waves of calming energy radiated off Ronin. Brynn obviously felt them, too, because her shoulders relaxed and the tension smoothed out of her face. "Okay."

"See, bro," Taeg said, so that only he could hear, "things go better when we work together."

Keegan nodded in acknowledgment. Taeg was right. Smug and annoying most of the time, but right.

Taeg clasped his shoulder and squeezed before leaving the room.

"Have you eaten dinner?" Ronin asked Brynn as he rose from his spot.

"I was taken before I could. And by taken, I mean Keegan knocked me out." She glowered at Keegan, and he broke eye contact so she wouldn't see the guilt on his face.

Ronin touched Brynn's arm. "I'll make something for us to eat." He glared at Keegan as he made his way toward the door. "Dinner in an hour. I'll need some help."

Keegan waited until Ronin had left before speaking. "I'm sorry for hitting you. I didn't think you'd come with me if I explained all this to you, and we needed to get out of there fast.

We don't know how far Mammon has come in locating you."

"Okay." Brynn thoughtfully rubbed her chin. "Why don't I hurt, by the way? Is that one of your gifts? You *are* gifted, too, right?"

Damn, he didn't want to talk about this right now. Or ever. "Yes."

She appeared to consider that for a second. "What else can you do?"

Oh, no. He wasn't about to discuss his other abilities with her…especially not the ones he had no real control over. "Why don't we talk about this another time? I've got some things to settle before dinner."

Without giving her a chance to respond, Keegan turned and stalked toward the door.

"Will you at least leave the door unlocked?" she called behind him. "You know I'm not going anywhere."

He didn't dare turn around. Those green eyes of hers were far too distracting. If he looked into them, he was afraid he might go weak. He already felt way more for her than he should. "Not this time."

Keegan closed the door and bolted it. The sound of something soft hitting the door punctuated Brynn's shout of frustration. He chuckled. Apparently she didn't like to be locked up. But then he sobered. After all, who did?

Ronin paced the length of the living room while Taeg leaned against one of the large windows, staring out of it.

"What do you think?" Keegan asked.

"She's telling the truth," Taeg said. "She doesn't know anything about what she is, or about Mammon. The girl's as innocent as they come."

Even though Keegan had already arrived at the same

conclusion, it was still a relief to hear it coming from Taeg's mouth.

Ronin stopped pacing and turned to face Keegan. "Now what?"

Taeg closed his eyes and sighed. Keegan opened his mouth to reply, but Taeg beat him to it. "Now we kill her."

Unexpected fury coursed through Keegan's veins, boiling his blood. "No," he said, at the same time that Ronin said, "What?"

Taeg raked a hand through his short hair. "Do you think I want to kill her? She's sweet, not to mention hot. But she's too dangerous to live. We're talking about the end of the worlds as we know them, man."

"No." Keegan said it again, because it was worth repeating. "We're not going to kill her just like that. Not when there's a chance we can stop this without having to shed her blood."

"I agree with Keegan on this one," Ronin chimed in. "We don't kill unless there's no other option. We're not Mammon."

Taeg sighed, keeping his gaze steady on Keegan. "You're just saying no because you've got a thing for her."

"What?" Ronin said. "Is that true, Keegan?"

"No." The word came out shakier than he'd intended, and Keegan had to clear his throat before repeating, "No. You both know that I'll do my duty above all else, but I don't want to take an innocent's life unless it becomes a necessity."

Ronin pressed his lips into a thin line and turned back to Taeg. "She's mostly just a woman. An innocent woman."

Taeg ran a hand through his hair again, a simple gesture that belied his frustration. "Dagan would agree with me, and you know it. That's why he's at the bar getting shitfaced right now, instead of here with us."

"We're *not* doing it," Keegan said. "Not yet, and not if we don't have to."

After a long moment's silence, Taeg sighed. "Okay, fine. We'll hold off for now. Have dinner with her. Treat her like a guest who can't leave. If she has any questions about us, we'll go with that stupid superheroes story."

Ronin nodded. "Agreed." Without another word, he turned and headed toward the kitchen.

"Superheroes," Taeg muttered. "Fucking ridiculous."

"Should we tell her that we're demons instead?"

"Only half." Taeg's response was automatically defensive, born from years of trying to justify what they were.

"She'd believe the other half even less," Keegan reflected dryly.

Taeg grumbled in wordless acknowledgment. "I need a beer." He turned to follow Ronin, but then stopped and faced Keegan dead-on. "Take my advice, bro. Stay away from her. She's dangerous. And I don't just mean in a *key to the apocalypse* sort of way."

Much as it irked Keegan, he had to agree with Taeg. Brynn was dangerous. And it appeared he was weaker than he'd ever thought, because even now all he could think about was how inviting her lips had looked when she'd asked him what else he could do.

The problem was, even though he knew better, he really wanted to show her.

CHAPTER FOUR

Was she dreaming? Was this entire day some deluded figment of her imagination?

The events of the past few hours were too crazy to believe. First, she'd been kidnapped from her gallery and forced to relive the fears of her past; the memory of that childhood incident had returned so forcefully and vividly that she'd practically choked on the stifling heat of the air in the trunk of the car.

Then she'd found out her kidnappers were gifted like her and that they might actually be good guys. Brynn never would have even considered buying that story if Taeg hadn't shown her what he could do.

Even though she'd arrived on less than promising terms, something inside her longed to place her trust in Keegan and his brothers. Maybe it was because they'd had every opportunity to harm her but instead had treated her well. After all, why would they have bothered explaining anything to her if they intended to hurt her?

Or maybe it was the amazing discovery that they had abilities, too. She'd never been so vain as to think she was unique in the world, but honestly she never thought she'd meet other people with abilities. Not even her own father had admitted what he could do, and he was her flesh and blood.

She had finally found other people like herself. What would it be like, to be able to confide in others about her powers? To learn more about their own? To not be so alone anymore?

Brynn let out a ragged sigh. She'd just found out her abilities were due to her ancestry. At last she had an explanation for what she could do. Even more, perhaps she would be able to learn the limits of her powers—to determine whether she could do more. She should be excited at the prospect, but she wasn't. Not when she was locked in this room like a prisoner. There was no worse feeling than being trapped…even if this luxurious space was a far cry from where she'd been imprisoned that one horrible time.

Shuffling into the bathroom connected to the bedroom, she examined the area. Even for a bathroom, it was vast. Every movement sparked an echo that bounced off the cream-colored walls. She picked up a silver-plated hairbrush lying on the countertop. Maybe it could give her a glimpse into the lives of the men who were holding her.

Closing her eyes, she concentrated on the heavy feel of the brush, on the ridges of the metal beneath her fingertips. It heated in her palm as the memories drifted to her in waves. She caught glimpses of the brush passing from one set of fingers to another in preparation for storage. Other than that? Nothing.

Like everything else she'd touched in this room, the brush

was new, and no true memories had been associated with it yet.

Crap.

She released the brush and it fell to the marble countertop with a loud *clang*. She walked into the bedroom and slumped onto the bed. It would have been nice to learn a little more about the brothers, but the objects in this room weren't telling their stories. The men's odd language made it obvious they weren't from around here. But if they were foreign, their American accents were perfect.

For the millionth time, Brynn's mind wandered to Keegan. He was similar to his brothers in so many ways—certainly no more strikingly handsome than they were—but something about him called to her, made her hormones go into overdrive. For God's sake, she'd almost kissed him earlier.

If only she could trust that he really was just trying to protect her. But certain things about his story didn't make sense. Something was off. They knew about her abilities, for one. And about this Mammon guy, who was supposedly tracking her just because she happened to be the ancestor of some long-dead Egyptian priest. Who the hell did that, anyway?

Brynn sighed, feeling a knot of tension curl up between her temples. She was probably being a total idiot for not acting more freaked out. After all, someone who wanted to protect you didn't generally knock you into unconsciousness and then keep you imprisoned, no matter how nice the prison. That much she knew from her past. But Keegan didn't feel dangerous—at least not in a psycho-killer sort of way…and so far he was night-and-day different from the psychopath who'd once taken her.

This was all so confusing.

The door to her room unlocked with a *click*, jarring her from her jumbled thoughts. Brynn rose as Keegan opened the door. He leaned against the doorjamb. "How are you doing?"

She fought to calm the sudden racing of her heart as she drank in the sight of him by the doorway. How could he affect her so intensely? "I'm fine, but I've got a lot of unanswered questions. And I don't like being locked away."

The strength of her voice surprised her, but then, she'd come a long way from the frightened little girl who didn't know her own powers…even if they didn't seem to be working the way they should. She was still strong. She *would* be brave.

He nodded, an expression of understanding on his face. "I'm sorry about that, but it's for your protection."

"Don't I get to decide how I should be protected?" She crossed her arms, trying her hardest to look pissed off instead of conflicted.

His brows knitted, and he pressed his lips together. "Not this time."

Brynn swallowed her exasperated sigh and tried for reason. "Listen, if what you said earlier about protecting me is true, then you're being a caveman. You seem to think you can just club me over the head and drag me away, no questions asked, but it doesn't work like that anymore."

He chuckled and spoke under his breath. "Believe me, if I were a caveman, we wouldn't be talking right now."

She opened her mouth to retort, but then closed it as the innuendo behind his words struck her with all the force of a speeding bullet.

He couldn't have meant it like that.

Keegan reddened, likely realizing what he'd implied, and cleared his throat. "I meant if I were a caveman, I wouldn't have bothered explaining anything to you."

"Oh." She shifted her weight from one foot to the other.

"We'll talk some more over dinner. Come on."

He didn't have to tell her twice.

Brynn strode forward, trying not to show her discomfort when Keegan didn't give her enough space to walk by without touching him. Her heart thumped as she slid past him. *From fear and not excitement,* she told herself, though even she couldn't be sure if she was lying. The heat of his arm seared her shoulder.

Pausing, she turned to face him. "Are you feeling okay?"

"Yes." He wrinkled his brow. "Why do you ask?"

"You feel so warm," she said. "Your brothers did, too, come to think of it."

Keegan stared at her for a moment before throwing her a playful smirk. "Didn't you say we were hot earlier?"

"I…" Her cheeks heated. He was teasing her.

Keegan lost his flirtatious smile and shrugged. "We all run a little hot. Got it from our father."

"That's weird."

"Probably the least weird thing about any of us." He pushed away from the door. Then he motioned to another door directly across from hers. "That's my room."

Before Brynn could reflect on the fact that his room was mere steps from hers, Keegan said, "Come on, I'll show you the rest of the place."

He started forward several feet ahead of her, giving her the space she so desperately needed, and led her through a long hallway decorated with marble flooring and elegant wall sconces. They passed two more doors.

"Taeg's room, and Ronin and Dagan are sharing this one," Keegan said as they walked by. He pointed to the final door in the hallway. "That's an office."

"This place is huge. Whose is it?"

"So, obvious that it's not ours, huh?"

"Well…" Brynn paused before admitting, "I tried reading just about every object in that room, and they all seemed to be new. No real memories attached to them. If it's yours, then you just moved in."

He nodded in acknowledgment. "We've got it on loan, actually. Belongs to that government agency I told you about."

"The secret branch of the government? You were serious about that?"

His lips twisted into a brief half smile. "Yes."

Not sure whether or not to believe him, Brynn whistled. "No wonder taxes are out of control, if this is what Uncle Sam is buying."

They reached the end of the hallway, and he pointed to another short corridor. "The foyer is over there, and this is the living room."

"Whoa." Brynn crept behind him.

The living room was massive, with floor-to-ceiling windows lining one entire wall.

She slid forward until she stood in front of them and took in the view. "This is absolutely amazing."

The window glass reflected the image of Keegan moving behind her. Her heart rate quickened.

"Yes," Keegan murmured, his hot breath fanning the back of her hair. "It is a breathtaking view."

The hint of huskiness in his tone confused the hell out of her. Despite the fact that this situation made her skin prickle with fear, the spicy, unique scent emanating from him caused her womb to grow achy and moist. It was crazy, how she responded to him. *The guy kidnapped you, remember?* But her body couldn't seem to make sense of it...of *him*.

"There you are."

The sound of Taeg's voice made Brynn jump. By the time she turned to face him, Keegan had already scooted away, his expression shuttered.

Taeg smiled, though it didn't quite reach his eyes. "Dinner's ready."

She slunk behind Taeg and Keegan as they headed into a small dining room next to the oversized kitchen. Their tense silence made her feel guilty, like she'd done something wrong. The table was set for four, with an Italian feast: lasagna, Italian sausage, peppers, and baked ziti. Even a few more dishes she couldn't identify. It looked like enough food to feed a dozen men.

Brynn stared at it for a moment, then addressed Ronin, who seemed the likeliest culprit. "You can cook?"

"No, but I'm excellent at ordering in," he admitted. "Sit down, please."

She waited until Keegan and Taeg were seated before speaking again. "Okay, now I want some answers."

Keegan exchanged a glance with his brothers. "What's the question?"

"Well, first off, if you expect me to believe all this, how did you first find out that I was... gifted?"

He took a deep breath. "The government keeps a tab on everyone with powers. We don't know how they do it."

"Okay. Then how did you find out about this guy Mammon, and that he's after me?"

"We were told about it," Taeg jumped in. "You know, by this covert branch of government superheroes we work for."

Brynn stared at Taeg for a long moment, and then blinked.

"I can't tell if you're fucking with me or not." The tone of his voice indicated he was, but the four of them appeared so serious.

Keegan spoke to him in their language, and Taeg answered in kind. Even while she internally acknowledged that Keegan's guttural speech was some weird sort of turn-on for her, it annoyed her she couldn't understand the men.

"English, please? And where are you from, anyway? I don't recognize that language."

Keegan toyed with the silverware next to his dinner plate. "A remote province of Serbia."

"Really?" Why did she feel like she was getting half truths at best? "Your English is excellent. You don't even have an accent."

Keegan directed his gaze down with a small cough. "We're well-studied."

There was a moment of marked silence, punctuated by the sound of Taeg's fingers tapping on the tabletop. Brynn studied her clasped hands as she contemplated Keegan's words. "So, if what you've told me is true, then this person named Mammon is after me because I'm related to an Egyptian priest who lived over three thousand years ago, right?"

Keegan nodded. "Yes."

"And he believes I can lead him to the priest's tomb, and to the book that was buried with him?"

Taeg snorted.

Keegan pierced him with a dirty look before saying, "That's what he believes, yes."

"And you plan on...what? Protecting me until he's caught?"

Taeg and Ronin examined their empty plates while Keegan

responded. "Yes."

"Well, how long do you think that will take?" she pressed. "And you don't expect to keep me locked up here the whole time, do you? I mean, I have a life. A job. I can't just stop showing up to my own gallery."

"You're the owner," Keegan said. "Couldn't you close it down for a few weeks or get someone else to run it? You could tell them you had some pressing business to attend to."

Well, her assistant, Amanda, realistically *could* take over for a week or two. Brynn didn't have anything major going on. Still...it didn't add up. Special gifts or no, why would the government go to all this trouble just to save her from a crazy man? Why, when they could just surround her with around-the-clock security to shadow her every move?

The truth hit her full-on. She flew to her feet, and her chair scraped loudly across the wooden floor. "You want that book, too, don't you? And you somehow think I'll be able to lead you to it."

Taeg fired a startled glance at Keegan, who sighed and rested his chin on his knuckles as if he were thinking about what to say. "We do want it, but we don't hold anything more than an optimistic hope that you'd somehow be able to help us find it."

Brynn bit her lip. On a fundamental level, she'd known there was more to the story than what he'd told her. But she was surprised he'd admitted it. She sat back down and scooted in her seat, taking her time to reply. "What's so important about it? And don't lie and tell me nothing."

Taeg garbled something in their language, followed by Ronin. Keegan made a staccato reply.

"English, remember?" she said, keeping her voice purposely

sweet.

Keegan returned his attention to her, appearing hesitant for the first time since she'd met him. But after a brief pause, he said, "The book your ancestor created is referred to by many as the *Book of the Dead*."

Taeg groaned. "Come on, man."

"She deserves some truth," Ronin said to him. "We're asking her to trust us. Let Keegan tell her why."

Brynn ignored the two of them, keeping her gaze directed at Keegan. "The *Book of the Dead*? You mean the Egyptian funeral rites?"

He shook his head. "No, not those, but a true book of the dead. A book containing a magical spell with the ability to bring back those who have died. To resurrect them. Whoever used it would be stronger than any human—indestructible, but at a price. Those brought back to life would require sustenance in the form of flesh."

She stared at him, waiting for the punch line. When it didn't come, she chuckled. "You're telling me that this book is supposed to create *zombies*?"

"Zombies?" Keegan looked pensive for a moment, then nodded. "Yes, zombies. In a manner of speaking, yes."

Oh, sure, why not? 'Cause zombies were actually possible. Her chuckle became a full-blown laugh. "And this guy Mammon actually believes that's true? Wow, he really *is* crazy."

Keegan took a deep breath. "What if he isn't *that* crazy?"

Nobody else laughed. Instead they stared at her as if she were the crazy one. She sobered. "What do you mean?"

He leaned forward, completely earnest now. "Brynn, what if it's true?"

CHAPTER FIVE

Ronin couldn't sleep. Dagan was still out, doing the devil knew what. He'd probably met some woman at the bar and ended up going home with her. Things were too quiet without the steady tempo of his heavy breathing. Funny how quickly he had become accustomed to sharing a room.

"Damn it." He gave up trying and hopped out of bed. Padding out into the hallway, he contemplated walking toward Keegan's and Brynn's rooms but decided against it. If Keegan was acting stupid, he didn't really want to know right now.

He knocked once on Taeg's door before opening it. His big brother lay on his bed, watching something on the large LCD screen mounted to the wall. He glanced at Ronin, then picked up the remote and turned the television off.

"How many times have I told you to knock first, bro? I could have been in here watching porn, for all you know. How'd you like to walk in on that?"

"Wouldn't be the first time this week," Ronin muttered. "Besides, I did knock. If you didn't blast your television so loud, you would have heard it."

Taeg sat up. "What's going on?"

Ronin closed the door and leaned up against it, swallowing hard. "You were right. Keeg does have feelings for her."

"I know." Taeg sighed and combed a hand through his hair. "So what are we supposed to do about it?"

"I don't think there's anything we can do. Besides, no matter what he feels for her, he's all about doing the right thing—obeying the Council's orders."

"Yeah, after all the shit Dad did, who can blame him?" Taeg scowled. "He's the oldest, the one who was under Dad's thumb the longest. Sins of the father, and all that crap."

Ronin nodded. "He'll do what he has to do."

"I know," Taeg said. "Still, we should keep an eye on him. That girl is nothing if not tempting. And you and I both know Keegan doesn't get laid nearly enough."

"Anything less than once a week isn't enough, as far as you're concerned," Ronin said.

Taeg chuckled. "I can't help it if I'm irresistible. You might get lucky more often, too, if you didn't scowl all the damn time."

Ronin shook his head, biting back a laugh. At least Taeg wasn't as bad as Dagan.

"Now get the fuck out." Taeg lay back down and picked up the remote. "*Good Will Humping* is about to come on."

⁖☍⁗

Keegan stood outside Brynn's door, staring at it like some lovesick schoolboy.

What was wrong with him? She was just a woman. A

human woman. But his body didn't seem to care who she was or what he might have to do to her. It liked her anyway.

He'd given up lying to himself about not being attracted to her. Oh, he was. And the more he learned about her, the more he liked her. Earlier tonight, after he'd dropped the bombshell about the *Book of the Dead*, she hadn't believed him. Judging by the way she gaped at them, she thought they were a bunch of psychos. But she didn't freak. She listened when he explained to her that supernatural forces existed, and then she said she needed time to think about it, before picking up her fork and finishing her meal in silence.

Brynn was strong. Stronger than he'd imagined any human woman could be. But would she take it in stride when he told her about her ancestry, or when she learned that demon blood flowed through her veins?

The practical part of his brain wondered why he should bother telling her. After all, it didn't change anything—either they'd find the book before Mammon did and discover a way to destroy it, in which case Brynn would be free to return to her normal life, or they wouldn't. And then he'd have to kill her.

But he refused to take the coward's way out. He'd tell her as much as he could without damaging her sanity. He owed her that much, at least. He might be many things, but he wasn't a monster.

He wasn't his father.

Sighing, he pressed his forehead against Brynn's door. She must be long asleep by now. Sleeping peacefully, he hoped, despite the circumstances. But what if…

What if he opened the door and walked to her bed, lifted the covers, and crawled in beside her? She might scream. Or welcome him.

He closed his eyes as he imagined touching his lips to hers, sure they'd taste of strawberries. That little tongue of hers would meet his. Perhaps she'd boldly open her legs to take him in. Rake her nails down his back as he thrust home.

Keegan groaned at the thought. His cock rose to impossibly hard heights, tenting the fabric of his pajama bottoms as if pointing the way to Brynn's bed. To his salvation.

Or to his doom.

It wasn't *that* late at night. If he were smart, he'd get dressed, wander down to the corner bar, and pick up the first willing woman who looked his way. He'd be pumping away inside her within the span of an hour and would alleviate the ache that had only seemed to build ever since he first laid eyes on Brynn. But somehow, that idea was almost as unappealing as bedding a belakor demon.

No, he was better off using his hand. The devil knew he was already well acquainted with it. With a heavy sigh, he walked back into his room. No point in fighting it—he already knew exactly who he'd think of while he jacked off.

ജ‍ോ‍ഗ

Brynn was on fire. Warm hands seared her flesh as they dragged her sweater over her breasts and then, in the span of a heartbeat, slid her slacks down and off. Ragged breaths of hot air heated her neck a moment before smooth, full lips pressed a kiss there. A flaming tongue licked a trail up her throat before flicking across her lips. A moment later, a mouth claimed hers, their tongues tangling over and over.

She couldn't open her eyes. Or maybe she just couldn't see.

"Keegan?" she panted.

"Yes," he murmured. With a quick tug, he tore away her bra as if it were made of no more than tissue paper. Then his lips closed over one breast, teeth dragging across the taut bud with a roughness that tore a cry from her lips. He moved to the other, tongue rolling over her nipple.

Brynn moaned softly. "No, we can't."

"Shh," was all he said. He shifted, and another tear sounded as her underwear fell away. Before she could suck in a breath, he'd placed his hands on her knees and tugged them apart. His slick tongue seared her core.

"Oh...yes," she cried. Her fingers tangled in his hair as he used his lips and tongue to propel her to the edge of ecstasy in the span of less than a minute. Her breath hitched and she bit her lip to stifle any further encouragement. She shouldn't want this so much...but then she'd never before been caressed by a man who actually knew what she could do. Who accepted her for who she truly was.

Keegan rose with a husky laugh. "Are you ready for me?"

Niggling concerns invaded her dreamy haze. She didn't even know this man, for Heaven's sake. "But—"

With one long, hard stroke, he thrust deep inside.

Her back arched and the soles of her feet dug into the mattress. "Oh my God!"

The sound of her own heavy cry jarred her awake. She sat up, chest heaving.

Disoriented, she glanced around. Enough light streamed in from the large windows for her to see that no one else was in the room. She peered down—her clothes were in one piece and on her body where she'd left them. The sheet lay in a tangled mess at her feet.

"What was that?" she whispered, still panting. She'd just had the most intense, mind-blowing orgasm of her life, and it had all been a dream? A *dream*?

She threw herself backward onto the pillows, trying to calm the erratic beating of her heart. The dream had just exploded on her and her heart felt like it was about to burst in her chest. In retrospect, she should have immediately realized it was nothing more than an illusion. She'd barely uttered a word in protest, and she'd known Keegan for less than twenty-four hours. She would never be that slutty in real life.

Would she?

"Oh, crap," she moaned, thumping a fist on the bed. She was in trouble. Here she was, dreaming about a man who might very well be a total nutcase. After all, he actually believed there was a book that contained a spell to create zombies. It was laughable. Totally absurd.

Or was it?

Most people would never believe in someone who could drain energy with a simple touch. Or someone who could control others with hypnotic eyes.

Maybe, just maybe, this *Book of the Dead* really did exist.

Argh, this was all so confusing. It would be easier if she could trust that the men were here to protect her, rather than imprison her. But the locked door definitely wasn't a good sign. Were they being truthful with her, or was there something else going on here? Something far more frightening than a madman searching for a magical book?

On top of all that, she had nothing other than the clothes on her back, and that was just damned annoying.

Brynn kicked at the sheets until they dislodged from around her ankles. "That's it."

Tomorrow morning she was going to demand that they

either let her go home to get more clothes, or accompany her there. After all, Keegan had insisted she wasn't a prisoner here. If they weren't willing to do something as simple as that, it didn't matter that her powers didn't seem to work on them. She'd find a way out of there, regardless.

CHAPTER SIX

Mammon reclined on the four-poster, king-size bed in his luxury Egyptian hotel suite, a warm woman laying facedown beside him. He crossed his arms under his head as he contemplated the book. It seemed to be the only thing he thought of these days.

What a discovery that was, to learn the fabled *Book of the Dead* did, in fact, exist, the culmination of his many years of research. It was utterly exhilarating.

When he found it, he would bring to life creatures so indestructible they'd tear apart man and demon alike. And every one of them would answer to him. Finally, he would have the wealth and power he deserved.

First, he would take over Earth. He liked this world, with its abundance of vices. He would linger here as long as he could. Once he'd exhausted these resources, he'd move on to another world. And then another.

Nothing and no one would have the power to stop him. Not even the damned Council. After decades of having to obey their commands, of being forced to witness the things they'd done under the guise of the greater good, he would finally have them bowing to him. Oh, and bow they would. Right before he broke them. He would be an infinitely better ruler of all dimensions than the Council was.

As for Keegan, Taeg, Ronin, and Dagan, well, they had their part to play in this, too. And they would. All he needed was the book. That, and the heir.

But it was simply a matter of time until he discovered the heir.

Loud rapping sounded outside the door leading into his room.

"Enter." Mammon didn't bother covering his unclothed form. He didn't give a fuck who saw him naked, and the woman lying next to him was too unconscious to protest her own nudity.

The door opened and Leviathos entered. Not for the first time, Mammon was struck by Leviathos's resemblance to a boy he'd once known. Belpheg had been the most powerful being Mammon had ever encountered; even as a young adolescent, his ability to manipulate energy had been uncharted, something Mammon had learned when he'd rescued the child from the edge of his village while the Council was in the process of decimating the boy's entire clan. How he wished he hadn't lost track of the boy after he'd saved him from annihilation. His abilities would be helpful to Mammon now. But there was no lamenting the past. Besides, once he had his army of the undead, he would need assistance from no one.

"I hope I'm not interrupting," Leviathos simpered.

With Leviathos's good looks and suave demeanor, it was sometimes difficult to believe his second-in-command was, at heart, a total fool. If Mammon had sensed anything resembling

Belpheg in Leviathos when he'd first taken him in, he'd quickly been disillusioned of that notion. But if Leviathos could be counted on for one thing, it was for his resentment of others' good fortunes. Jealousy was what made him such a good lackey now—and the reason Mammon would have to kill him as soon as he came into power. Leviathos's grasping ways would never allow him to remain a minion the whole of his life. Fool he might be, but Leviathos posed a danger to him if Mammon allowed him to live.

"What is it?" he asked Leviathos.

"I've brought the daily report as you requested, Lord," Leviathos said, using the title Mammon had commanded of all his minions. "Our Egyptian scholar is still tracing the priest's genealogy."

"Still?" A tide of rage surged within him. He rose and stalked toward Leviathos, taking perverse pleasure in the way he winced and inched backward. "The search has taken too long as it is."

"W-we are getting closer, m-my Lord," Leviathos stammered. "The scholar has been working around the clock, but this world is full of billions of humans. It isn't an easy task."

"Then tell him to work harder," Mammon snarled, poking his finger into Leviathos's chest. "In fact, I suggest you aid in the search yourself. If we fail to uncover the heir, it will be on your head."

Leviathos nodded and turned to leave the room.

Mammon waited until he was almost to the door before asking, "How goes the search for the book?"

Leviathos paused, and then turned. A flicker of fear crossed his face. "We have an army of men searching every inch of the Valley. It cannot be much longer now before it is found."

He had better hope so. If the Council discovered the book before he did…

Life on the run held no appeal for him, but he faced a lifetime of it if he failed in this mission. That wasn't about to happen. He would die first.

"You know what I would do to you if you ever tried to double-cross me, don't you?" he asked in a silky voice.

Leviathos flinched but met him with a steady gaze. "I would never do that, Lord."

Liar. But he would never get the opportunity. Leviathos's days were numbered.

Turning, Mammon motioned to the woman in his bed. He didn't know her name. He didn't care. She was simply an object to slake his lust. Given that she'd been unconscious the better part of his session with her, she was likely a drug addict. That, or Leviathos had slipped her something before bringing her to him.

"Take her out of here," he said. "But keep her handy. I may have use for her again."

Leviathos walked to the woman and hoisted her into his arms. Her head rolled to the side at an unnatural angle, and he examined her closely. "The woman is dead, my Lord."

"Dead?" Well, he couldn't feel remorse for that. Women were weak. Far weaker than men. They could be counted on for nothing more than momentary physical satisfaction. That was a lesson his own father had taught him at a fairly young age. "What a pity. She was a tolerably good fuck."

"Should I dispose of the body?"

After a moment's thought, Mammon gave a careless shrug. "Hold on to her. She'll keep for a few more hours."

⍟

Much as he'd done just a few hours before, Keegan rested his forehead on the door leading into Brynn's room. He'd barely slept last night, his mind consumed with thoughts of her. And if she'd had any idea of the sorts of dreams he'd had, she would have blushed clear into next week. He was pretty sure more than a few of the things he'd dreamt about were illegal in some states.

Clearing his throat, he unlocked the door and pushed it open. Brynn was already up, her bed made. She sat on it, running a silver brush through her hair. Damned if she didn't turn bright red when she saw him.

"Good morning." Keegan fidgeted, fighting off the uncomfortable feeling that she knew what he'd dreamt about. That was impossible.

Brynn averted her gaze, and she set the hairbrush down beside her. "Wish I could say the same."

"What's wrong?" The question came out far more clipped than he'd intended it to.

"What's wrong?" She let out a bitter laugh and met his eyes with a haunted look. "I'm a prisoner here, that's what's wrong."

They were back to this? "I thought we already covered that it's for your own good—"

"Yeah, you've told me before. You're not holding me prisoner—you're *protecting* me." A flash of temper sparked in her eyes. "Well, whatever. All I know is you won't let me leave. How am I supposed to feel safe and secure in a situation like this?"

"I'm trying to protect you," he answered gruffly. "Not

make you feel safe."

"How can you expect me to calmly sit here when you haven't given me any evidence of what you claim? All I have is your word."

She had every right to be angry. He would be, too. But he sure as hell wasn't going to let her go. "My word will have to be enough for now, Brynn. I won't risk letting you loose and having something happen to you."

Her lips twisted into a frown. "So, what? I'm just supposed to pretend I'm happy with this whole scenario? I mean, I don't even have any clothes to change into."

Shit. She was right. He hadn't considered that.

"Look." She tugged at her hair, her eyes darkening with exasperation. "I just...I don't do well behind locked doors. And you can't blame me for being a little concerned. You expect me to believe what you're telling me, but you haven't given me any proof that you're the good guys."

Good guys. Yeah, right.

"I'm not asking for much," she said, her pleading making him feel even guiltier. "Just let me go home and get some clothes. If what you're saying is true, then I'll come back here with you of my own accord, not as a prisoner."

"I can't let you leave," he told her. "Even if you promise to come back. It's too dangerous. What if...what if I go buy you some new clothes?"

Devil, had he just volunteered to go *shopping* for her?

Brynn stepped toward him, a plaintive expression on her face as she touched his arm. He forced himself not to fidget at the spark of awareness. For all he knew, she didn't feel the same way.

"Keegan, I appreciate that. But please, let me go home and

get some of my own clothes. You can come with me. Think of it as a show of faith. You do this, and I'll come back with you, okay?"

He gritted his teeth, knowing what his brothers would say if he agreed to this. To put it mildly, they wouldn't be pleased. He opened his mouth to refuse but the words wouldn't come. For all he knew, he would have to kill her soon. She deserved to have *some* sort of concession from him.

Screw it. She wasn't asking for much, and with the four of them there, they could protect her. "Fine. Okay. Just give me a few minutes. I'll be right back."

Brynn sighed, her shoulders relaxing with relief. "Thank you."

With a brusque nod, Keegan stepped into the hallway and closed the door. He hesitated for a moment before walking away, leaving the door unlocked.

He found Ronin and Taeg in the kitchen. Ronin sat at the counter, surfing his laptop, while Taeg scarfed down a huge bowl of cereal at the table with an open beer next to him.

"You're a fucking drunk," Keegan muttered.

Taeg shrugged, taking no offense. "I think better when I'm not sober."

"Hey, man," Ronin said without looking up, "I'm researching Egyptian tombs."

"Yeah," Taeg added, "we can't just sit around on our asses waiting for the Council to find the book."

Ronin nodded. "It's a needle in a haystack, but we might as well start searching for where this Egyptian priest was buri—"

That was all well and good, but somehow trying to find a possible location amidst all of Egypt didn't seem as imperative as making sure that a woman who was facing the possibility of death enjoyed her last days as much as possible.

"Get dressed," Keegan interrupted. "And wake Dagan up, too."

That got their attention.

"Where are we going?" Ronin asked.

"We're gonna take Brynn to her home so she can pick up some clothes."

Taeg sputtered, choking on his cereal. "Are—are you out of your mind?"

CHAPTER SEVEN

"I love this deli. They have the best croissants," Brynn said to Keegan as she inhaled the mouthwatering scent of baked goods. Her fear and doubt had begun to melt away as soon as she hit the sidewalk, especially since he'd let her use his phone to call her assistant, Amanda. She'd made up an excuse for why she'd left in such a rush and wouldn't be back for a while. Amanda seemed suspicious, but Brynn didn't want to involve her in any of this. Not if there really was a madman stalking her. In the end, she'd told Amanda she'd be keeping the gallery shut down until further notice. Not the best situation for her pocketbook, but thanks to her parents' inheritance, she could afford to keep things afloat. For a little while, at least.

Keegan's willingness to let her call someone backed up his claim that he wasn't keeping her prisoner. Hell, the man had even volunteered to go shopping for her, and she hadn't missed the look of distaste on his face when he'd said it.

His brothers walked several feet behind her, though none of them appeared particularly happy to be taking this trip and

Taeg kept mumbling to himself. Earlier, she thought she'd heard him grumble to Keegan, "Why don't we take her to Disney World next? The Taj Mahal?"

"Shut it," Keegan had snapped.

Dagan joined them, and he was just as good-looking as his brothers. Not that she hadn't already expected it. She'd met him back at the apartment when he staggered into the living room, clearly hung over. He'd barely said two words to her, though his words had sent a shiver down her spine. His voice was the most amazing she'd ever heard, the kind that could coax a woman into doing pretty much anything. Right now, he stayed as far away from her as possible. She didn't know what she'd done to make him dislike her, but it was clear that he did.

Whatever. She had bigger problems. Like the fact she couldn't even look at Keegan without the memories of last night's dreams flooding into her mind, leaving her aching for things she shouldn't desire…especially from a man who'd knocked her out and then locked her in his apartment. But then, he was taking her back home now, wasn't he? If that wasn't a gesture of good intent, she didn't know what was.

"Thanks for bringing me back to my place," she said.

"You're welcome." The beauty of Keegan's smile blinded her for one heart-stopping moment. Lord, he was gorgeous.

Focus on something else. Anything else. Oh, like maybe the fact that he kidnapped you.

Yet she found she couldn't bring that topic up again…not when there seemed to be the beginnings of an uneasy sort of truce between the two of them.

"I would think the government could afford a private driver rather than having us take the subway," she half joked instead.

"I usually just fly—" He hesitated, his brows drawn together.

"Never mind." He slid a hand across his hair, an awkward silence hanging between them.

Eager to dispel it, she jumped on the first thought that came to mind. "You never told me what it is that you can do. Is it the same thing as Taeg?"

"Charm others?" Keegan laughed. "No."

"So, what is it?" she pressed when he didn't go on.

"I…I'd rather talk about you right now. How long have you known about your powers?"

Ah, so he was uncomfortable with what he could do. Well, she knew all too well what that was like, so she let it slide. For now.

"I've been reading memories off objects for as long as I can remember. I think my father could do something like that, too, though he never admitted it. To be honest, I never thought I would find others with abilities."

"You sound relieved," he said.

"It's hard being around normal people when you aren't." She shrugged. "I guess you know all about that."

"I suppose so." Keegan chuckled, and then hesitated for a fraction of a second. "So there's no one waiting for you at home, then?"

"No." Definitely not. "It's hard to date when you can read a man's memories. Even a simple brush of his shirt might coax me to learn more, and that's not the sort of compulsion I can always fight. A lot of times I see stuff I'd rather not know."

Case in point, her first serious boyfriend, an investment banker named Mark. She'd been so in love with him, and had thought he felt the same way…until she'd met him out for dinner after work one day. The moment he'd pulled her in for a kiss, the sleeve of his shirt had touched her palm, setting off a tidal wave of memories. Suffice it to say, he hadn't spent the afternoon in client meetings as he'd claimed. Not unless a naked gymnastics session at a hotel with a curvy blonde counted as a client meeting.

He gave her a curious look. "What sort of stuff?"

"Oh, you know, stuff they've done." She laughed to cover her embarrassment and the residual hint of pain she felt whenever she thought of Mark's betrayal. "Usually, I find out a lot more than I'd like to know about their love lives. It tends to be a turnoff."

Keegan nodded and arched a brow. "I can understand that. What about your ability to drain other people's energy?"

The memory of the day she'd discovered that particular power came back to her in one big rush, threatening to choke her with its heaviness. Sweeping the panic aside, she locked the memory back into her mental vault. She wasn't ready to talk about it. Might never be.

"You know, it's weird," she said instead, turning her gaze to him. "What I can do—the energy draining thing—it's worked on everyone I've tried it on." It had certainly worked well enough on Mark that day. He'd dropped like a stone, leaving her only slightly mollified as she walked away from him and out the door of the restaurant. "Everyone except you and your brother, that is. I wonder why?"

Keegan hesitated, rubbing the back of his neck. "I—"

"Don't mean to interrupt your little heart-to-heart up there," Taeg shouted, his voice sarcastic, "but isn't this where you live, Brynn?"

She glanced at the building next to her. *Whoa.* They'd almost passed her apartment building. Taeg, Dagan, and Ronin had stopped right in front of it, close to twenty feet behind them.

"Oh, yes it is." Heat burned her cheeks. Being in Keegan's presence was far too distracting...and she was beginning to realize that might turn out to be very dangerous indeed.

⸻

Keegan was screwed, and the icy glares his brothers lobbed at him as they climbed the stairs to Brynn's apartment only reaffirmed that conclusion. He liked Brynn. Liked her to the point that he wondered how he'd be able to off her if the Council ordered him to.

Damn it. How had he allowed himself to get into such a bind? He thought he was above this. But a few vulnerable looks from her, and all he wanted to do was please her. Brynn's demon ancestry was clearly on full display here. Only a woman with succubus in her blood could bring a grown man to his knees like this.

He ran a hand through his hair, willing himself to calm down. In all honesty, that wasn't fair. Brynn didn't know what she was, and any mystical powers of seduction had likely diluted, along with the bloodline, in the 3,000 years since that Egyptian priest had mated with the succubus. Anything he felt for her was on him, a hundred percent.

He couldn't forget their true mission. Wouldn't. She was just a job, and a very important one at that. If he had to destroy her to save the world, he would.

"Here we are." Brynn's nervous smile quickly dimmed. "Oh crap, I don't have the key. It's in my purse back at the gallery."

Keegan exchanged a glance with Taeg, who muttered, "Be

right back," before walking down the hallway and turning the corner.

She turned to him with an apologetic look. "I guess we have to go back to the gallery first."

"No we don't," Dagan responded flatly.

Brynn tilted her head in Dagan's direction. "What? Why?"

A second later, her front door clicked. When it opened, Taeg stood on the other side. He adopted a roguish grin. "Come on in."

She gasped. "How did you do that?"

"Magic," he quipped. And in a way it was. Taeg's particular brand of fae magic.

Brynn stepped into her apartment. "No, really, how did you do that?"

Taeg sobered. "You don't want to know."

She opened her mouth as if to protest, but she must have decided to let the matter drop because she simply exhaled and turned away. Keegan didn't fool himself into believing the matter was over, though. She'd eventually ask again, and she'd keep asking until she got an answer that left her satisfied. That much he was sure of, from the short time he'd known her.

"I'm going to go change my clothes. I'll be right back." Brynn disappeared through a door and swung it shut.

Keegan glanced around the tidy living room. It was tiny but very bright, with blond wood floors and daisies arranged in a glass vase on the coffee table. From what he already knew of Brynn, it suited her.

A hard, unexpected shove sent him staggering toward the wall. Taeg pounced on him, grabbing him in a chokehold. "What the devil is *wrong* with you, bro?"

Dagan stepped behind Taeg. "I'm with Taeg on this one,

man. I'm doing everything I can to avoid getting attached to the chick, and here you are, eye-fucking each other already?"

"Fuck off," Keegan said.

"Right back at you, bro," Taeg snarled.

"Settle down, everyone." Ronin stepped forward with his hands up. "Let's think this through."

Ronin's soothing energy spread through Keegan, and he fought it back with a low growl. He didn't want to calm down. Right now, he was itching for a fight.

Taeg must have felt the same way because he shouted, "Tone that shit down, Ronin," keeping his eyes on Keegan the entire time.

Keegan pried Taeg's hands off his throat, pushing him away with a hard shove. "Don't forget who's in charge here, *little* brother."

"You'd never let me, *big* brother," Taeg shot back. "And right now, you're being a *huge* asshole."

"That's it," Keegan bit out, lunging at Taeg. His fist connected with Taeg's jaw.

Taeg's head whipped back. He rolled his neck before looking back at Keegan with a devilish chuckle. "All right, let's go."

He flew at Keegan, slamming his fist into the side of Keegan's face. Keegan swung Taeg around, about to retaliate, when Ronin's voice boomed, "Stop it *now*!"

The barely restrained fury in Ronin's voice stopped them, all the more effective because he rarely lost his temper.

Keegan's rage faded as quickly as it had come. Taeg's, too, apparently, since he mumbled out a quick "Sorry."

"They were just letting off some steam," Dagan said to Ronin with a casual shrug.

"Yeah, well, any other time you two can pummel each other to the ground and I won't give a rat's ass," Ronin said through gritted teeth. "But right now we've got bigger things to worry about."

"I know." Keegan started pacing. "Damn, I know that."

Once he'd calmed down enough to speak rationally, he turned to face his brothers. "I won't deny that I find her attractive or that I feel bad for her. But I'll do what I must." When they continued to look dubious, he said, "I will. I have to. There is no alternative. If it's one life or the destruction of billions, then I'll do what has to be done."

After a tense silence, Ronin nodded. "We all will."

The heavy air in the room dissipated.

"You really do need to get laid, bro," Taeg said.

Dagan chuckled, but his expression became pensive. "You know, I met these adventurous twins the other night—"

He broke off as the door to Brynn's room opened. She stuck no more than her head out. Devil, was she only half dressed? It sure looked like it from this angle.

"Is everything okay in there?" she asked. "I thought I heard something bang against the wall."

"Fine," he said, while his brothers mumbled similar responses.

"Okay. I'll be right out." She shut the door and Keegan let out a deep exhale. He could stand around here all day, getting into pointless fistfights with his brothers...or he could come up with a plan.

Keegan turned back to Taeg. "Hey, what about that incubus friend of yours who moved to this world a few years back, the one who worked under Mammon for a while?"

"Cresso? He was in London last time I heard from him."

"Can you track him down, maybe see if he can get wind of what's going on in Egypt?"

Taeg nodded. "No problem, man. He detests Mammon. I'm sure he'll be happy to help."

"You and Ronin are right," Keegan said. "We need to do something to find the book, even if we have to dig up all the damn graves in Egypt ourselves. We—"

"Shh," Ronin interrupted him. He slanted his head to the side. "Do you feel that?"

Keegan stilled and concentrated. If Ronin sensed something, that meant something was there.

Yes, there it was. Like a pulse of energy. Something malevolent.

"Shit." Keegan's eyes darted toward Ronin as they both realized what it was. "Demons coming—"

The front door exploded, and a small army of demons marched inside, some humanoid like them and the rest glamoured into human form. But the energy that emanated off them gave them away. Demons always recognized other demons that way.

The invading demons stared uncertainly at one another before one of them turned to Dagan and said, "Who the fuck are you?"

"One, two…" Taeg counted the demons out on his fingers before shooting Keegan a deep look. "Ten of them, bro. You know that fight you've been itching for?"

"Yeah." Keegan bared his teeth at the nearest demon. Ten to four? He probably wouldn't have minded those odds if Brynn wasn't in the same apartment.

As if she'd sensed his thoughts, the door to her room opened. "What—?"

She cut off with a gasp, shock and confusion etched all over her face.

"Get back in your room," he ordered. "Lock the door."

He didn't have time to make sure she heeded his command before one of them jumped him. The demon's fist smashed into the left side of his face. His head jerked to the side, the loud *crack* in his jaw accompanied by a burst of pain and the metallic tang of blood. He ignored it, using the momentum to duck when the demon swung again. The demon lost his balance and stumbled forward. Keegan shoved him at the same time he swung his left fist. It caught the demon square on his ear. He hit the ground hard and didn't get back up.

"You want some?" Dagan yelled somewhere behind him. "Take that!"

Keegan turned just in time to see his brother's obvious relish as he knocked another demon to the ground with a brutal blow to the head. A quick glance confirmed his brothers had wholeheartedly thrown themselves into the fray. Guess they all needed to let off some steam. He turned his attention to the next demon.

Blocking jabs and throwing punches consumed the next few minutes. The demons got a few lucky ones in, too, and one asshole broke Keegan's nose with a kick to the face and dropped him to the ground. These guys were trained to fight, and this was taking too damn long. What if more of them showed up?

Shit. Times like these, he wished he had more control over his other abilities, the ones he'd inherited from his mother's side of the family. But no—they were too sporadic, too uncontrollable. Too fucking dangerous.

"Watch out," Taeg yelled.

He whirled. A long, wicked dagger headed for him. Blocking the hit just in time, he disarmed the demon and slit his throat.

Finally, there was no one left to fight. His war haze cleared enough for him to see Taeg, Ronin, and Dagan standing over the bodies, shallow wounds covering their faces and torsos.

Keegan nudged one of the demons with his foot, rolling him onto his back. His glamour had slipped in his deep state of unconsciousness. Red horns sprouted from his green, pockmarked face. Two mouths existed where one should be. Maliki demon. Flesh-eater.

"Ugly asshole," he commented to no one in particular.

"Oh, shit," Dagan said.

Keegan turned his gaze toward him. "What's wrong?"

Dagan's eyes darted over the bodies of the fallen demons. "Only nine of them here. One escaped."

"Not good." Keegan let out a curse as worry and fear settled in his stomach like a lead weight. Not good at all.

"This was obviously Mammon's work," Taeg said.

Ronin touched his fingers to a gash on his arm, which immediately knitted itself together. He gave Keegan a meaningful glance. "You know what that means, right?"

Keegan nodded at him. Oh, he knew. His tone flat, he voiced what they had all clearly deduced.

"It means Mammon knows about Brynn."

CHAPTER EIGHT

Brynn leaned against the locked door of her bedroom with her ear pressed to the cold, hard wood. Thumps, yells, and crashes had punctuated the huge brawl in her living room. There had been so many of them—more than Keegan and his brothers. That much had been clear.

Her heart hammered against her ribs as she searched her room for potential weapons. But of course, she didn't own any. With her gift, she'd never thought she might need one. Now she didn't know if her abilities even worked anymore.

The fire escape. She could take that. But what if more men waited downstairs for her?

Oh, this sucked. Big time.

Fear and uncertainty filled her. What should she do? The primitive urge to scurry away warred with her desire to stay and make a stand. If anything, she was pissed as hell that a strange group of men had invaded *her* personal space—her sanctuary. But she was no match against a small army, not if her powers weren't working.

After what seemed like an eternity, the sounds of battle had died down, settling into a murmur of voices. *Please, please, let that be Keegan and his brothers.*

She'd strained, trying to hear. Finally she heard the unmistakable sound of Keegan's voice saying, "We've gotta move. Now."

"Oh, thank God." Taking a deep breath, she unlocked her door and swung it open. A loud creak interrupted the silence, and she poked her head out. Keegan and his brothers stood in the living room, battered but largely unhurt as they examined the figures of the men lying on the floor.

Superheroes. That was what she'd called them yesterday, and obviously she hadn't been far off. Her own little band of superheroes. Respect and admiration for them swelled up inside her. These guys kicked major ass.

"What was that?" Her voice cracked from the remnants of her fear. "Was it Mammon?"

Keegan swiveled his head toward her, his nose bloody and crooked. His face lit with alarm. "Stay in there."

Wait a second…*his face.*

"Your nose, it's healing." She stumbled toward him, surveying him and then his brothers. Taeg's and Dagan's wounds weren't disappearing, but Ronin… "You, too, your wounds are healing. How is—how is that possible?"

"Brynn, go back into the room," Keegan ordered.

Keegan and Ronin could *heal* themselves? Amazing. No wonder they were so badass.

The large gash down the center of Keegan's nose closed itself. Other than a few stray droplets of blood, his nose seemed untouched. She took another step toward him, but her foot collided with a hard object. She'd run into one of the downed men. She lifted her gaze back to Keegan.

Wait!

Doing a double take, she stumbled backward to get a closer look at the figure of the man at her feet. No, he wasn't a man. *Not a man!*

His characteristics were definitely male and his body mostly human, save the gray pallor of his skin. But his face—it was all wrong. Five eyes instead of two. Rhinoceros-like horn instead of a nose. Ridged spikes covered his forehead. His nauseating stench burned her nostrils, like a horrid mixture of wet dog and burning asphalt.

Warm hands gripped her arms, and someone shook her. "Brynn. *Brynn.*"

She instinctively fought back before looking up to see Keegan's face. His lips moved and he was clearly trying to reassure her, but she couldn't hear him over the loud, shrill sound of an alarm.

He shook her harder. "Brynn, stop screaming!"

She realized with a start that he was right. Shutting her mouth abruptly, she moved her gaze back to the thing on the floor. She couldn't help it.

"Look at me," Keegan said, his voice harsh.

She focused on his eyes, his lips, his nose—his fully healed nose. When she found her voice again, she sputtered, "What the fuck is that thing?"

Another figure on the floor moaned and stirred. Taeg strode over and kicked him, and he stopped moving. But even from here, it was obvious he wasn't human.

"What are they?" she whispered.

Keegan closed his eyes and took a deep breath. When he reopened them, they blazed with the intensity of some unspoken emotion. Almost like he felt sorry for her. But when he spoke, all he said was, "Demons."

"Demons?" She laughed. Then laughed some more, wrenching out of his grasp. In some distant part of her brain, she recognized she bordered on hysteria. "Demons?"

Keegan just stared at her.

"Are you kidding me? *Demons*?"

"You freely accept people with special abilities," Ronin said as he moved next to Keegan and pinned her with his gaze. "Is it too much of a stretch to believe that demons might also exist?"

"Yeah, but…" What were they going to tell her next, that aliens were real, too? "But I *have* special abilities."

Dagan coughed. "You also have dem—"

"Dagan," Keegan snarled, followed by a string of foreign words. Dagan yelled back in the same language. Keegan shook his head and pointed to the front door, punctuating his movement with a few staccato words. Even though she didn't understand Dagan's response, it didn't take a genius to figure out that it was some sort of curse. Dagan shot Keegan the finger before whirling around and stomping out the front door.

She concentrated on reading Keegan's expression. "You actually expect me to believe those were demons?"

He nodded. "Yes."

His flat, no-nonsense response sparked an inkling of a suspicion she didn't even dare acknowledge. She took several deep, calming breaths. "How? How do you know all this? How can you tell me with such certainty that these are demons?"

He exchanged a serious, telling glance with Ronin before answering her. "Because, Brynn…I am one."

ക്കരു

Back at their borrowed apartment, Keegan paced the length of the living room while Taeg stood by the windows. Dagan and Ronin sat on the leather sectional, though relaxation looked like the last thing on their minds. Tension filled the air, thick and oppressive to the point that it overwhelmed.

"Shit," Keegan said. "Where is Mammon getting his info?"

"Good question," Taeg grumbled as he stared out the expansive windows. "He discovered Brynn's identity right after we did, and we've got the whole damned Council on our side. If I didn't know any better, I'd wonder whether he has an informer on the inside."

"He doesn't know where she is now," Dagan pointed out. "At least we have that."

Ronin shook his head. "With intel that good, it's only a matter of time before he figures it out."

Double shit.

Keegan punched the wall nearest him, not caring that it gave way beneath his fist.

Ronin was right—if they stayed here, Mammon would eventually find Brynn. If that happened, Keegan feared what would occur. Not just to Brynn, but to this entire world.

"Okay." He withdrew his hand from the rubble and watched the scrapes heal. "Until we've recovered the book, the best thing we can do is move. Ronin, find somewhere else for us to stay in another city. We'll move every couple of days."

"Got it." Ronin rose and left the room.

"Taeg, Dagan, you two go to Egypt. Try to find out everything you can about possible locations where the book might be buried. Also, see if you can get Cresso to talk to the local demon population, maybe catch wind of something."

"What about you?" Taeg asked.

"Ronin and I will guard Brynn. Splitting up is the best way to spend our time right now."

"Divide and conquer, and all that rot," Taeg quipped halfheartedly. He turned to Dagan. "I'll flash over to London, round up Cresso. Once you know when your plane is coming in, give me a call. I can meet you at the airport."

"Done," Dagan said.

Taeg grunted and turned to Keegan. "Listen, bro. Be careful, okay?"

Keegan gave him a terse nod. "Yeah."

The air shimmered almost imperceptibly in front of Taeg, creating the invisible fae path only he could travel. He stepped into it and disappeared, leaving Keegan alone with Dagan.

"You think Brynn will be okay?" Dagan asked.

"Don't know," Keegan answered truthfully.

After he'd confessed his ancestry to her, she'd clammed up. She'd simply stopped communicating, though she had enough presence of mind to allow him to usher her downstairs and into a taxicab. They'd ridden in silence the whole way back to the apartment, and once they arrived she'd gone straight to her room, where she'd stayed for the past half hour.

Would her mind handle the stress of what she'd just learned? She had to accept the truth, or her thread of sanity might snap. After all, she was mostly human.

"I'll go check on her," he said.

Dagan nodded and turned to leave, but then he paused. "I'm worried about you, dude."

"I'm fine," Keegan answered automatically.

"Just…don't get in over your head, okay?"

Keegan gritted his teeth and fought the urge to snap at Dagan. He was just being a caring brother, after all. If Dagan didn't care, he would be little better than a monster.

"Don't worry about me. I'm in control."

Dagan hesitated, opening his mouth as if he wanted to say more. But in the end, he nodded and left.

Keegan started down the hall toward Brynn's room. No point in putting off the inevitable. He had to make sure she was okay. But he couldn't help but wonder if she would welcome him, or if she'd have a million questions about what he was and what he could do. Maybe she'd shrink away in fear, cower in front of him the way others did before his father. She might see him as a monster.

If she did, would he be able to deal with it?

ᏉᎧᏨ

Brynn sat on the bed and stared out the window, not really seeing anything. To think that yesterday, her biggest worry had been figuring out why Keegan kidnapped her. That seemed like a cakewalk compared to today's problems.

Demons. Keegan actually expected her to believe he and his brothers were demons.

Even if she did believe in demons—which she wasn't willing to admit just yet—she'd never believe Keegan was one. Those things lying on the floor of her apartment? *They* looked like demons, with their grotesque faces and off-colored flesh. But not Keegan. Not his brothers.

On top of that, he didn't seem evil. She'd seen some real evil in her life, and yeah, she supposed he might be pretending, but no one was that good an actor. No one.

She jumped at the knock on her door. Before she had time to answer—or even decide if she wanted to—Keegan walked in, his movements deliberate and his hands visible at his sides. He paused near the door and left it open, clearly doing everything he could not to frighten her further.

"Brynn, we need to talk."

"About what?" She chuckled humorlessly. "About the demons littering my apartment floor? About your claim that you're one, too? Or that maybe I've gone insane?"

Keegan leaned against the wall. "You're not crazy."

"Right."

"Listen, I know how hard this must be for you."

"No," she interrupted, her tone flat, "you don't."

"Okay. No, I don't. But as crazy as it might seem, this is your reality. You have to deal with it. Your life depends on it."

She shook her head in the vain hope that it would clear her thoughts. "What do you want me to say? Before today, I never knew if I believed in Heaven, and now you're expecting me to believe in Hell? In demons?"

"No."

Keegan strode toward her and dropped to one knee in front of her, and she fought the instinct to scoot back. She forced herself to study his face, so very human in appearance. Two eyes, a normal-looking nose. He wasn't a demon. He couldn't be.

"No, Brynn. Everything you believe about demons is wrong. A perversion of tidbits of information humans have gleaned throughout the years. Demons aren't evil creatures from Hell."

Brynn blinked at him. "They aren't?"

"There is no Hell. At least not as far as I know."

She furrowed her brows. "Well then, what are they?"

"Demons are…well, they're a different race. To be specific, they're a race of beings from a world that exists in another point of space."

Huh? "Um…what?"

"Another dimension, Brynn," he said gently.

"You actually expect me to believe you're from another dimension?"

Keegan's gaze bored into hers, his bluish-green eyes burning with an intensity that spoke to the depth of his emotions. "It's called Infernum. I was born there, and it's where I live. I was sent to Earth to stop Mammon."

Brynn laughed. She had to. If she didn't, she would cry. Or scream. "You were sent to Earth? So, how are you supposed to have gotten here? Through a tornado?"

"What?"

"You know, like Dorothy? *Wizard of Oz*?"

Straight-faced, he said, "I've never met this wizard."

"Never mind," she muttered.

Keegan raised a brow and tilted his head to the side. "There's a portal to the Otherworlds. It's guarded by the Elden Council, composed of elders from each of the worlds. The Council allows inter-dimensional travel under given circumstances. It's how Mammon arrived here on Earth. Me and my brothers, too."

How could she respond to what he said? It was so insane.

"Okay, let's say that I buy this. It goes against every belief I've ever had, but I can't deny what I saw back in my apartment, and those things were definitely *not* human. But"—she inhaled deeply—"you expect me to believe you are one, too?"

"Yes," he responded, his gaze even. "I do."

"No. No, you don't look like they did. You look like a normal person."

Keegan chuckled. "There are all types of demons, just as there are all types of humans. Some, like me, appear human. Others less so."

"I don't believe it."

"Brynn," he said, placing his hands on her knees, "I can prove it."

Her heart stopped for a fraction of a second before resuming its staccato beat in her chest. "How?"

Keegan breathed in and closed his eyes. When he reopened them, their usual bluish-green had been replaced by a deep, fiery red, the color swirling in his eyes like a whirlwind of flames.

"Holy shit," she cried. She scrambled backward on the bed, away from Keegan, and covered her mouth with her hands.

He shut his eyes, and when they flickered open, they were back to normal. He rose and walked around the side of the bed toward her. "Brynn."

"No." She brought her hands up in front of her. "No, wait."

Keegan froze, expressionless. His tone was gruff when he said, "Don't fear me."

"Oh, God." She rubbed her hands over her face. How quickly her life had morphed into a Stephen King novel. "I can't believe this is happening."

"Brynn—"

"Just let me think for a moment." A firestorm of thoughts blazed through her mind before she settled on one thing. "If most of what we know about demons is false, does that mean you aren't evil?"

Keegan fidgeted, his fingers rubbing absently over the fabric of his dark jeans. How sick was it that even now, she noticed his long, artistic fingers, their flawless masculinity?

"Our culture doesn't view morality on the same terms as yours," he said. "My world is much darker, more morally ambiguous. But I will say that there are those who are evil and those who aren't. Same as your world."

He had a point. She'd found that out firsthand at the age of eleven, the day she learned about her other power. Humans could be pretty sick, too. Actually, now that she thought about it, maybe those sickos weren't human. Maybe they were demons. That was something she'd never before had to consider. How many of them were there on Earth?

She gulped. "My power—how I can drain energy? It doesn't work on you."

Keegan nodded. "Because of what I am. I don't believe your ability works on demons."

Well, that answered her question. Talk about a cosmic *Fuck you.* "So wait. Now that I know there are really scary things like demons out there, you're telling me that the one thing that's kept me safe all these years doesn't even work on them?"

He sighed and rubbed his hand over the back of his neck. "I'm sorry that your sense of security was destroyed. Really, I am. But it was false to begin with. You aren't invincible. There are things out there that can hurt you, that aren't affected by your abilities."

The truth of his words seeped into her very core. "I can't believe this."

"I know it's hard to believe, but it's true."

She gave him a shaky nod. Carefully, she studied him. He appeared so very human, with his lean, muscular physique, the heavy pectorals outlined under his T-shirt, his sculpted face and jaw. Even his eyes seemed normal.

Maybe she didn't want to know, but she had to ask: "Is this what you really look like?"

"Except for the eyes. Those are glamoured."

"Glamoured? You mean…magic?"

Keegan chuckled and sat on the bed next to her. "There's magic in all worlds. Even yours." He slowly reached forward and took her hands in his, giving them a pointed look. "Is that so difficult to believe, given what you can do?"

She gently pulled her hands out of his. Everything Keegan had told her made sense, in some crazy way. But there were still some things that didn't add up. "So this guy who's supposedly after me, this Mammon—"

"Is a demon," Keegan finished. "What I said about him coming after you is true. He discovered that the *Book of the Dead* exists, that it really can resurrect the dead."

Her mouth fell open. "It really can do that?"

"Not only that, but you are the key to the resurrection."

The key?

"But, how? How could I possibly do that?"

"When your ancestor made the book, he created it so that only one of his bloodline could work the spell."

Only one of his bloodline. Ah. "That's me."

"That's you," Keegan confirmed with a short nod. "In fact, from what the Council can tell, you're the only one left."

"I don't understand. Why does Mammon want to create an army of *zombies*? That's just insane."

Keegan laughed, although the sound was humorless. "If he has control of the book, he can command them. They'd be stronger than humans, stronger than even demons. And they'd follow his bidding."

Brynn shook her head. "I still don't understand."

"Mammon is an avaritia. A greed demon. He desires wealth and power above all, though he might try to convince himself and others that he's doing all this for a good reason. He's starting with this world, but he won't rest until every human being is subjugated...or eaten. Then he'll move on to other worlds until, ultimately, they've all been destroyed."

"This is totally crazy," she murmured.

"But true, nonetheless."

"How did you get stuck with the duty of going after him?"

"Me and my brothers work for the Elden Council as *Detainors*. Inter-dimensional bounty hunters of sorts. It is our job to hunt down and bring violators from Infernum to the Council for punishment. And for now, to protect you."

God, this was all so fantastical. If only...if only she could trust him.

Wait. There was something she could do.

"Do you have anything old with you, anything from your home world?"

After a long moment, Keegan nodded. He reached under the collar of his shirt and withdrew a thin leather cord that hung around his neck. On it was a talisman made of some sort of metal. "I've had this ever since I can remember. I think it was a gift from my mother." He drew it over his head and handed it to her. "She died when I was a baby."

She traced the shape with her finger. "A dragon?"

He nodded.

"It's beautiful." She closed her hand around it, shut her eyes, and gave herself over to her senses.

A barrage of images and emotions flooded over her,

beginning with a woman standing before a wooden crib. Overwhelming love and acceptance flowed from her as she removed the same necklace, and with a teary smile, pressed it into the bedding where an infant slept.

The scene faded, replaced by the image of a little boy, his fear unmistakable as a handsome but frightening man loomed over him, his fists raining down with punishing force. *"I'll teach you yet, boy. You're my son. Don't you ever forget it!"*

Another scene replaced the last. The little boy had grown older, and the same man arrived after a long absence, along with a terrified nursemaid who carried a bundle in her arms. The man coldly summoned him forward as he bade the woman to unwrap the bundle. *"Meet your new brother, boy. His name is Taeg."*

Yet another scene formed. The frightened boy had grown into a young man. He watched in helpless fury as the same man beat another brother to a bloody pulp. With sudden, blinding determination, he resolved that—even if it were over his dead body—this would never, ever happen to Ronin again.

Brynn let go with a cry, snapping back to present day. Remnants of emotions borrowed from Keegan intermingled with her own. She dimly realized he'd taken her into his arms and now supported her. Throwing her arms around his neck, she gasped as the emotions tore through her. His masculine scent comforted her, making her feel safe and warm.

After some time, Keegan pulled her back. "Are you okay?"

Brynn nodded and spoke around the heavy lump in her throat. "That horrible man I saw was your father, wasn't he?"

He lowered his gaze, his mouth tight. "And a truly evil demon."

"Tell me about him."

He didn't speak for some time before he let out a deep exhale. "Growing up, I knew my father's word was law. He always wanted us to be like him, but we weren't. We tried to be, for a time, but it was pointless. To him, every other person was nothing more than a tool to be used for his personal gain. We couldn't be that way. We couldn't *not* care, and we couldn't use and abuse others the way he did."

"So he beat you," she said softly.

Keegan shrugged. "Whenever we did something that he didn't approve of—which was often—he punished us all."

"But he was hardest on you," Brynn whispered.

"No. He was hardest on Ronin. Unlike the rest of us, who went to live with my father as infants, Ronin didn't join us until he was almost ten. He was stubborn and disobedient, so my father constantly tried to beat him into submission. I stepped in whenever I could."

"You mean you purposely antagonized him to take the heat off your brothers."

"Yes. But after a while, even that stopped working. That's when we escaped."

The depth of his emotions—as well as his despair at not being able to protect his brothers from their father—sat like a heavy weight on Brynn's chest.

"You were very brave to stand up to him."

"I should have gotten in between them, should've made sure he never touched my brothers. The night we escaped, it was only because he'd almost killed Ronin and Dagan. No matter how I try to justify it, the truth is that I was a coward. I failed them."

Brynn placed her fingers under his chin and turned his gaze

toward her. "You're crazy. You didn't fail them—you protected them, when you were little more than a child yourself."

He scoffed at her words, clearly not believing them.

"Ask any one of your brothers and I'm sure they'll tell you the same." She'd bet his brothers would be horrified to hear him say that he failed them.

Keegan dropped his gaze and swallowed hard. When he looked at her again, his eyes blazed with emotion. "My whole life, I've resolved that no matter what, I wouldn't be anything like him."

"You're not. You could never be," Brynn whispered fiercely. She might not have known him long, but after sharing some of his memories, she might understand him better than almost anyone else. Despite his upbringing, or maybe because of it, he was inherently good.

Keegan shook his head. "You don't know that. You don't know what I am capable of, or the things I've seen and done, or the things I've sworn to do."

The bleak look in his eyes broke her heart. What would it be like to grow up in such a dark, hellish dimension with no mother and an evil, abusive bastard for a father?

Another tide of emotions swept over her, but this time they were sharper, sweeter. They were her feelings for Keegan, and sympathy comprised just one part of them.

"Keegan," she said.

He opened his eyes. Whatever he saw there must have surprised him, because he sucked in a breath. His gaze grew hot and hungry, the pupils of his eyes darkening as they lost their focus.

Brynn touched his lips. They were firm yet soft, his breath making fiery little puffs against her flesh. "You really do run hot, don't you?"

He let out a husky laugh. "Demon heat. We clock in at over one hundred degrees."

More evidence that while he might appear human, he wasn't. But her body didn't care what he was. It wanted him so badly she feared she might melt into a puddle of desire. She needed to feel him. To touch him. To taste his lips on hers.

She leaned toward him. "Keegan—"

"Brynn." With half-lidded eyes, Keegan slowly closed the space between them. But a mere second before their lips touched, he lurched backward.

"What's wrong?"

He rose and strode across the room, faced the windows, and thumped one with his fist. "Damn it."

She blinked as the sharp desire she felt for him faded to a dull ache. "What is it?"

"We've got too much going on right now. Another layer of complexity would…it would be foolish." He sighed and pressed his forehead against the glass.

Brynn's body filled with heat when she realized she'd been soundly shot down. Was he just using their situation as a convenient excuse to let her down easily? Or could he in fact desire her, the way she did him?

Keegan turned and silently walked toward the door.

"Wait," she said.

He paused, his back still to her.

"I forgot to ask earlier. Back at the apartment, I saw you and Ronin heal. Then, a few minutes later, Taeg and Dagan were fully healed. Can all demons do that?"

Keegan turned around, seeming reluctant to do so. "The demon race is, as a whole, stronger and quicker to heal than the human race. But many of us have unique abilities. While Taeg and Dagan heal quickly on their own, Ronin and I can heal both ourselves and others."

"So you each have different abilities?"

"It's not so surprising, given we have different mothers."

"Your ability to heal comes from your mother?"

"Yes."

She opened her mouth to ask another question, but he beat her to it. "Right now there's something else you need to know."

The way he said that made her mouth go dry and her heart skip a beat. She tried not to let her trepidation show in her voice. "What is it?"

Keegan fidgeted, then flat-out said the words that would change her life forever.

"Brynn, you're part demon, too."

CHAPTER NINE

"You were what?"

"Overpowered, my Lord," the frightened demon sniveled, his nervous gaze darting from here to there as if he searched out an escape route. "There were several of them, and very powerful. There was nothing we could do."

"You could have killed them," Mammon roared, slamming his fist onto the exquisite wooden coffee table gracing the sitting area of his luxurious Four Seasons suite. The force of his blow punched a hole straight through it. He absently wrenched his hand through the mess of splinters.

"I'm sorry. We tried," the demon whined. He looked plaintively at Leviathos, as if he would save him from Mammon's wrath. As if he *could*.

"Damnation." Mammon rose to stare out the large window. Not even the expansive view of the Nile could calm his temper now. "You say the demons were protecting her?"

"Yes," he said. "They called for her to retreat into another room before we attacked."

Well, this changed things. Apparently, the Council members weren't quite as foolish as he'd thought. They'd somehow managed to locate the girl before he had. Yet he couldn't allow them to win. Their twisted reign must come to an end.

"I'm very disappointed, Leviathos," he said.

"We did everything we could to locate her, Lord," Leviathos said, a hint of defiance in his otherwise conciliatory tone. "It was the scholar. He didn't act quickly enough."

Mammon gritted his teeth. Snarkiness aside, Leviathos was right. The damn scholar had been far too slow. Yes, he would pay for this. "Have him tortured for two weeks and then kill him. No…better yet, save him for me. I'll do the honors myself."

Leviathos let out an almost imperceptible shiver. "Yes, Mamm—Lord."

Mammon turned to pace the room. "This complicates things. Now we must discover who has taken her, and where."

He would have to visit her dreams and coax her into telling him. A laborious process, to be sure, but now that he knew her name and was assured she was the heir, it was doable.

"Did they do or say anything to give you an indication of their identities?" Mammon asked the frightened demon. "Did they call each other by names?"

"No, my Lord." The demon shook his head emphatically. "But there were four of them, and one of them called another *bro*."

Mammon froze in midstride with his back to the demon.

"Bro?" Leviathos repeated in alarm.

Mammon whirled to face the demon and prowled

toward him. The menace in his expression must have been unmistakable, because the demon rose from the couch, cowering in front of him, his expression terrified.

"What did these men look like?" Mammon asked.

The demon squeaked at the steely, foreboding tone in his voice. "They all looked si-similar, my Lord. Tall with dark hair." He dared a glance at Mammon, lowering his hands from his face. "Somewhat like you, in fact."

"What?" Mammon roared.

Barely realizing what he was doing, Mammon wrapped his hand around the demon's throat. The demon's eyes widened, and he managed to utter one sharp squeal before Mammon twisted and yanked. His body fell to the ground as his head detached from the rest of him.

Mammon eyed the head for one moment before dispassionately tossing it over his shoulder. He turned to Leviathos, who had risen and was currently regarding him with a look of abject horror.

Mammon growled, his mind consumed with only one thought.

"Keegan… "

৪৩৪৪

For the second night in a row, Keegan wandered the halls instead of going to sleep. Strange, he hadn't initially cared one way or another about this borrowed apartment. But now that they'd be leaving it tomorrow, he realized he would miss it.

Brynn infiltrated his mind the way she had ever since he'd first seen her. But this time, it was with a growing sense of desolation.

They were running out of time.

Mammon had already discovered her identity. How much longer before he found the book? If he got to it before they did, their options would be drastically limited.

Maybe there would be no choice at all.

Things might have been simpler if he hadn't given Brynn his necklace, and if he hadn't allowed her to read its memories. Something inside him couldn't help but wonder if giving her access to his memories had been a crucial mistake. Her obvious distrust had morphed into compassion, and then into horror for what he'd experienced as a child. Who knew what she would have thought if she had learned his other secret, his mother's legacy? Would that have been too much for her? Or would she have handled it just as gracefully as she'd handled everything else so far?

She truly believed he was a good man, and she trusted him now. And if he'd correctly read the lust etched onto her face, she desired him. How could he betray her?

Keegan paused outside her room, his forehead to the door, as if by that simple act he could forge an unbreakable connection with her. For the first time since he'd broken free of his father, he wished he were somewhere else, living someone else's life.

He didn't want to bear this responsibility. Didn't want to have to make a choice between this vibrant, engaging woman and the rest of this world. Maybe all of the worlds.

He hadn't expected Brynn to be such a shining beacon of hope and life, and he hadn't expected to connect with her so deeply. If he was charged with ending her existence, if he went through with it, would he really be any better than his monster of a father?

His heart told him no. But what were his options?

One life or many?

There was no winning choice here.

Keegan lifted his palm to the door. It was cold and hard beneath his hand. The way he should be. But apparently, he wasn't wired that way, no matter how hard he tried.

He couldn't fail. The Council depended on him. His brothers depended on him.

This was his duty.

With a deep sigh, Keegan pushed away, stepped into his own room, and shut the door. With any luck, he would sleep a dreamless sleep tonight. But as he settled into bed and closed his eyes, something told him that was as likely as Mammon deciding to abandon his nefarious plot.

୫୦୧୪

His fists flew at her with abandon.

"I'll train you yet, boy."

"No," Brynn tried to choke out. "No, I'm not…"

But he didn't listen and continued to hit her, blow after punishing blow.

The scene faded, and the pain with it. Now she walked within a dark, moist cave. Glimmers of moonlight shone in from cracks in the ceiling, illuminating portions of it. Somewhere deeper inside, water trickled, landing on the ground with marked little *plop*s.

Fear permeated the air, palpable in its intensity. This place terrified her.

A shout from farther inside the cave pricked her flesh. Heart pounding, she followed the low noise, winding through a narrow passage. It opened up to a larger space, moonlight streaming in. Brynn bit back a cry at what she saw.

A woman was chained to the wall. She had an ethereal appearance, with long blond hair flowing in heavy waves to her waist. Her gown was so white it almost gleamed in the soft light, and in front of her stood a man. He was tall and slender with full dark hair cut short. Even though his back was to her, Brynn recognized him as Keegan's father.

"Please don't," the woman begged him, tears rolling down her cheeks.

He laughed. One hand carelessly snatched at her dress, rending it in two.

"No," Brynn cried, her voice a perfect echo of the woman's own panicked scream. Neither of them heard her. The woman continued to stare at Keegan's father, fear and horror on her face. When he began to unbutton his pants, Brynn screwed her eyes shut.

"Brynn, are you okay?" said a deep voice.

She opened her eyes, and she was back in her apartment. In her own bed.

Keegan sat on the mattress beside her, a question in his eyes.

She took a deep breath, then let it out slowly. "Bad dream."

Keegan smiled. "You're still dreaming."

"I know," she whispered. Part of her recognized how intrinsically odd it was to be having such vivid dreams, but compared to everything else that had happened these past few days, she could deal with a strange dream or two.

"How are you doing with everything?"

"You mean how am I dealing with finding out my ancestor

mated with a succubus? That I've got demon in my bloodline? That this is how I got my abilities?" Brynn snorted. "Yeah, no big deal."

He touched her face and caressed her cheek, a wicked expression crossing his eyes. "You're tough. You'll deal."

She nodded, and he turned to her window, covered only by a sheer, billowing curtain. "It's almost daylight outside. Not much time to waste."

"For what?" she asked.

Keegan shot her a cocky grin. "For this."

His hand moved to the back of her neck and he pulled her to him, taking her mouth in a demanding kiss. She moaned and plastered her body to his, deepening their kiss. He lowered her back onto the bed, snatching away her sheet. His searing tongue traced a path from her throat to her collarbone. There, he paused to pull down the thin strap of her silky nightgown, his breath causing a shiver on her sensitive flesh as he bared one breast.

"Yes," Brynn moaned.

Keegan chuckled before lightly blowing on her nipple. It puckered from the heat of his breath. Then, an agonizing heartbeat later, his lips closed over it, rolling the sensitive bud around in his mouth and tugging on it.

"Keegan," she breathed, tracing her hands from the heavy, corded muscles of his back down to his rock-hard backside. She wanted to feel the heat of his flesh under her fingertips. Her fingers crawled underneath the fabric of his pajama bottoms, while his hands slid her nightgown up to her thighs.

"Do you like this?" he asked, his voice husky.

Brynn gasped as his fingers expertly found that sensitive spot between her thighs and one finger dipped inside.

"You know I do," she panted.

"Hmm," he replied in satisfaction. He kissed his way down her stomach, thrusting his finger deeper this time, as his head journeyed downward.

Brynn moaned and closed her eyes, reveling in the exquisite sensation of his fingers playing over her. Moving inside her.

"Ooh, that… Don't stop," she whispered.

He chuckled, and it sounded a little different this time.

"I'm definitely liking this dream," he said. His voice had changed, more gravelly now. A little deeper. The atmosphere had suddenly shifted, going from playful to menacing.

Brynn's eyes flew open, and she screamed. It wasn't Keegan's face smiling at her anymore.

It was his father's.

"Brynn," he rumbled, a sinister look coming to his face, "I need you—"

She awoke with a jolt. Sweat glistened all over her body and her heart galloped in her chest, as if it longed to race away from the horror of that dream. She scanned the entire room, making sure there was no one else there. But sure enough, she was alone. Unlike her dream, she wasn't in her apartment, but rather in her room at Keegan's borrowed condo.

"It was just a dream," she whispered. "Just a dream."

Lord knew she'd had pretty vivid ones the past two nights.

But it didn't *feel* like a dream.

She lay back down, willing her heartbeat to slow a fraction. She closed her eyes in the vain hope she might somehow fall asleep again, but when she did, all she saw was Keegan's father. And the unholy glaze in his eyes as he'd ogled her, taking in her bared breasts with satisfaction.

How quickly it had morphed from a hot, wet fantasy into a nightmare. She could practically feel the heat of Mammon's gaze on her naked flesh. The sinister cruelty of his smile. Just thinking about it made her skin crawl. When he'd said, "I need you," she'd gotten the sense he wasn't talking about sexual satisfaction. Ridiculous, she knew. Her mind was only manifesting him due to the stress of the past few days. But still…it was more than a little disturbing.

Well, she knew one thing. If she never had one of those dreams again, she would die a happy girl.

CHAPTER TEN

It took Taeg well over a day, and visits to more than ten local demon bars, before he managed to track down Cresso's London address. Other than a few visits Cresso had paid to Infernum, they hadn't kept in touch since he'd moved to Earth. It wasn't like there was cell-phone service on Infernum or anything.

After all these years, Taeg still wondered how the hell Cresso had managed to get clearance from the Council to move. Guess some demons just had all the luck.

He didn't bother walking the short distance from the bar to the address the bartender had given him. What good was being half fae if you didn't make use of the fae paths?

Taeg concentrated on the address and a shimmering path opened up in front of him. Only certain types of fae—or, in his case, half fae—could see or travel the paths. Even then, they couldn't traverse to other worlds—just to different points in the one they were on.

The current caught him, pulling him forward as if he were

weightless. The best way he could describe it to his brothers was that it was like water-skiing over a rainbow. Totally exhilarating.

In the span of an instant, Taeg stood in front of Cresso's apartment. He gave a sharp rap on the door. After several minutes, he knocked again. Finally, the door opened, but instead of Cresso, a beautiful woman with flowing black hair stood on the other side. She wore only lingerie, and she eyed him in a way he couldn't help but respond to. The energy emanating from her identified her as some type of demon, but even through her glamour, it was obvious she was one of the good-looking ones.

"Well, *hello* there," he said in an appreciative voice. She was hot enough, and he'd gone without for long enough that he couldn't help himself, even though he knew that if she was with Cresso she was a succubus, and therefore off limits. Unless he wanted to die an awful, soul-sucking death, that was. Sex demons like incubi and succubi could only mate with each other without killing their partners, and that was some fucked-up shit if he'd ever heard it. Kind of like nature's way of thumbing its nose at the species.

She smirked and opened the door wider, cocking her head in blatant invitation. "Hey, yourself. Why don't you come in, handsome?"

Even while his brain told him he needed to focus on finding Cresso, his cock fought and won the battle to respond. Damn thing had a mind of its own. "Don't mind if I do."

Taeg strode in and turned to face her as she closed the door. Behind him, another door opened. He whirled to see a second demon, this one blond, exiting a room. Unlike her companion, she wore nothing other than a set of lacy panties. She saw him and slid the door shut before stalking toward him.

"What do we have here?" she asked, her voice a sexy rumble in her throat. The hungry once-over she gave him put him in mind of a predator spotting its prey. Her gaze lingered on the words stamped across his T-shirt: ORGASM DONOR. Lips curving into a slow smile, she glanced back up at him. "I'll take three."

"I saw him first," whined the black-haired demon.

"We can share," the blonde retorted, shooting him a wicked little smile. "We always do."

Oh, shit. These two were definitely putting off succubi vibes, which made them dangerous as hell. If he didn't focus on the objective, he could be in serious trouble here. "Wait, I'm actually looking for—"

"Ladies, ladies, what have I told you about playing with my visitors?"

Taeg turned toward the sound of Cresso's voice. He stood outside the door the blonde had come out of, with another barely clad woman on his arm. His hair was messed up and he wore only a pair of slacks, the fly still undone. It was more than obvious what he'd just been doing.

The blonde gave Cresso an exaggerated pout. "Sorry, baby. He just looked so delectable. We couldn't resist."

"Cresso, man, it's good to see your ugly mug again," Taeg said to his old friend.

"You, too." Cresso beamed at him. "It's been too many years. How the hell did you find me?"

"Asked around. You don't keep a low profile, you know." Taeg strolled forward to clasp Cresso's hand.

"Never have." Cresso chuckled, then addressed the women. "Give us a moment if you will, loves."

"Okay," they replied in unison, then turned to shuffle back

into Cresso's bedroom. The blonde grabbed Taeg's ass as she walked by him. Saucy wench.

Taeg shuddered and watched them go. He waited until they'd shut the door to turn back to Cresso with a sharp whistle. "Three of them, man? You always were a fucking pervert, but still. Come on."

Cresso laughed. "My appetite only seems to increase with age. Want a beer?" He headed toward the kitchen without waiting for a reply, buttoning his slacks as he walked.

Taeg followed him in. "Yeah, well, if you don't mind my asking"—he pointed his thumb toward the direction of the women—"they're—"

"Succubi," Cresso said. He tossed him a beer. "Of course they are. I just saved your ass back there."

Taeg fought an embarrassed flush as he pulled out a chair, taking a seat at the small kitchen table. "I would have stopped them."

Eventually.

"Yeah. Right." Cresso sat at the table and took a swig of his beer. "You know, I'm working on a little theory, trying to find a way for succubi and incubi to mate outside the species without killing their partners. But I'm not quite there and I'm guessing you didn't come all the way to Earth because you wanted to fuck a succubus. So, why are you here?"

"Mammon," Taeg said simply.

"Hmm, my old mentor?" Cresso's nose wrinkled in evident disgust, but then, the incubus knew just how monumentally fucked up Mammon was, since he'd had the misfortune of working for him before Cresso got transferred to Earth. "What's that bastard done now?"

"Oh, he only plans to take over all of Earth. For starters.

And he's actually found a way to do it."

Cresso let out a disbelieving laugh. "How?"

Taeg filled Cresso in on the *Book of the Dead* and the events of the past several days, including Brynn and her role in the whole thing.

"Shit. This is not good, man," Cresso said. "And he already knows that this Brynn is the heir?"

"Yes." Taeg stared grimly at his beer. "If we don't find the book before Mammon does, the Council will order us to kill her to stop Mammon from succeeding in his plan. And I really don't want to do that."

Cresso nodded in understanding. "I agree it's no fun to have to take an innocent life."

"Not just that." Taeg chugged the rest of his beer, then turned to Cresso. "Keegan has feelings for her."

Cresso winced. "Ooh. Tough break. Well, you know I'm always in for a good fight."

Yeah, Taeg knew it. Not only was Cresso a loyal guy, but he hated Mammon almost as much as Taeg did.

"So, what do you need me to do?"

"Head to Egypt. From what we hear, Mammon has gotten quite a few demons on his side. He's promised them a demon hierarchy once he's taken over the world, and they're foolish enough to believe it. See if you can talk to a few of them to find out where they're searching for the book. I can't do it, for obvious reasons."

"Nor your brothers. Mammon is bound to have told his minions to be on the lookout for the four of you." Cresso nodded his agreement. "I'll make flight reservations to leave within the day. Unlike *some* of us, I can't just disappear in one place and reappear in another."

"Yeah, I'm just special that way," Taeg replied, his voice deadpan.

Cresso was silent for a long moment before shaking his head. "I'll never get over how perfectly normal you and your brothers are, given the circumstances."

"Yeah well" — Taeg shrugged — "we don't get to choose who we're born to."

CHAPTER ELEVEN

By the time their plane landed in New Orleans, Brynn was tired and on edge. Her nightmares last night, on top of everything else she'd learned in the past few days, weighed on her shoulders until she wondered how much more she could possibly take. Add to that her growing attraction to Keegan, and there was no way she could have rested on the plane. Not with him sitting right next to her, so close she could've reached out and licked him, had she dared.

Her body didn't seem to care that Keegan was a demon, or that they were on the run. It didn't care about anything other than how good he smelled and how deliciously small and safe she felt next to him. She couldn't help but wonder if he had felt the same way. Once they'd landed, he practically dove off the plane in his haste to get out.

Then again, maybe he'd never been on a plane before.

"I can't believe this," Keegan muttered to Ronin, who was navigating the rented car through the crushing traffic toward their French Quarter hotel. "I tell you to find us another place to go, and you bring us here."

"No better place to hide than among a crowd of drunken revelers. Besides, the Council keeps a hotel suite on permanent reservation in this city."

Though Ronin's reply was breezy, he acted as anxious and tense as she felt right then. Even though he drove confidently, his erratic weaving made Brynn suspect he'd never driven before. But more likely it was due to the tenuousness of their position. They couldn't run from Mammon forever. Damn her ancestor and his weakness for that succubus. It was because of them that Brynn was here right now.

On the way to the hotel, Keegan explained more to Brynn about her ancestry. She'd been too overwhelmed last night to ask about it in detail, but the Council he worked for seemed to know quite a bit about the Egyptian priest who was the cause of all this mayhem.

"His name was Iyri," Keegan said. "What you should know is that demons have been crossing over to Earth for many millennia. Humans have crossed over to Infernum, too, though few have lived to tell the tale.

"Iyri was one of the very few humans who have a natural resistance to succubi, something he discovered when he was seduced by one. As you can imagine, Sitha was pretty surprised when, instead of dying, he seemed to have a limitless supply of energy she could feed from. And he was shocked to learn the beautiful young woman who'd just seduced him was, in fact, a demon."

"Yeah, that would put a damper on any relationship," Brynn murmured. He threw her a dry look. Too late, she realized she'd unintentionally insulted him.

Red-faced and feeling like total shit, she opened her

mouth to apologize, but before she could say a word, Keegan continued. "Being a man of magic as well as faith, Iyri used a spell to trap Sitha, to bind her to him. He spent the next several months studying her while she fed off him. However, it seems, somewhere along the line they fell in love."

"What did they do then?" Brynn asked.

"The problem was that Sitha was on the run from the Council—a fugitive—for some past crime. The Council learned of her whereabouts and ordered that Iyri return her to them for punishment."

"But he didn't?"

"He loved her too much to let her go. And by that time, she was already pregnant with his child. A true rarity, the child of a demon and human."

She fought back a blush. "So humans and demons *can* actually, you know, *mate*?"

"Yes. It happens more often than you might think. Though as I said, children from those matches are rare."

"What about…" This time she did blush. She couldn't help it. "I know it probably wasn't a concern back then, but what about diseases?"

Keegan turned his intense gaze on her. There was a hint of a question in his eyes. Lord, he didn't think she was talking about the two of them, did he? That wasn't what she was getting at, even if her awareness of him was so acute that her heart sped up with every move of his body.

"Demons don't carry diseases," he finally said. "Nor can they transmit them."

"Oh," she replied.

"At any rate," Keegan continued, "Iyri created the book. It contained a spell that allowed for the resurrection of the dead, in a form that was stronger than human or demon. They would be strong enough to protect Sitha from the Council. But there's always a price to pay for strength. The dead had to feed off living flesh in order to subsist."

Brynn shuddered. "That's horrible. But he did it anyway?"

"Love makes people do strange things," Keegan said. "Because he recognized the danger of this book, he crafted the spell so that only one of his bloodline could activate it. With it, he would be able to control the army of the dead."

"God, that's crazy. He loved her so much he went to any length to save her."

Keegan nodded. "Even at the expense of his own world."

"So what happened then?" she pressed.

"The Council found out about his plan and stopped him before the spell was fully completed. The dead were in the process of reanimating, but they crumbled to the ground when Iyri was killed. The Council tried to destroy the book, but Iyri had made it indestructible, so they buried it with him in a hidden, unmarked tomb. Many believe the tomb is somewhere in the Valley of the Kings, but no one knows where. Not even the current Council. The old Council members purposely didn't keep any record of it. In fact, no one was supposed to know about it at all, but one of the men responsible for digging the grave spread the tale, and it survived to modern day."

Brynn sighed. To be sure, her ancestor had committed an evil act, but he'd done it with only the best of intentions—for love. "What happened to Sitha?"

"They allowed her to live long enough to give birth to the child. Female offspring of succubi are born full succubi themselves, but male offspring take on most of the characteristics of their fathers. Since the child was a boy, he was given to a human family with no knowledge of his demon heritage."

"My great-great-grandfather, many times over."

Keegan nodded, a strand of hair dropping to cover his eyes. Right then, they blazed blue-green, but she couldn't help but recall what they had looked like unglamoured—red, intense, and expressive. Beautiful, in an alien sort of way.

"Sitha's gift, as well as Iyri's magic, was passed on in various, progressively weaker incarnations," he said. "Until you. You can drain humans of their energy and read inanimate objects, all because of Sitha and Iyri and their love for each other."

Brynn closed her eyes for a long moment, the details of her distant past penetrating her mind. "It's such a sad story."

"That's life," he said. "Shit happens."

As they pulled up to their hotel in the middle of the French Quarter, she couldn't help but think about Keegan's blunt response to the story. The events of the past few days had made it perfectly clear that he was right: shit did happen.

ഇരുഅ

Ronin stood on the expansive balcony of their two-bedroom suite. Thankfully, it faced the street, so Brynn could see the crowds of people roaming below, even if she couldn't partake of their revelry. She'd done nothing but pace their suite since they arrived yesterday, and he couldn't blame her. Her life, even all of her perceptions about life, had done a one-eighty in the past few days.

Keegan was on the phone in one of the two bedrooms, debriefing with a Council liaison. Devil only knew what was going on in there.

Hurting a woman went against everything Ronin stood for. Growing up with the knowledge of what happened to his mother, he'd vowed to never abuse a woman. So far, he'd managed to hold true to that vow, even when his father's fists had tried to sway him otherwise. But now, if the Council ordered it, he would have to stand idly by while Brynn's life was snuffed out. Or worse, if Keegan couldn't go forward with it, he'd have to do it himself. It was enough to drive a man to drink.

Where were Taeg and Dagan when you needed them?

As if on cue, his cell phone rang, the caller identification showing Taeg's number. "Yeah?"

"Well, hello there, Miss Sunshine," Taeg's voice rang out. "You manage to keep from beating in Keegan's face yet?"

"That's only a concern with the two of you," Ronin said.

"Oh, yeah." Taeg let out a dry chuckle. "I tried Keeg's cell, but he didn't answer. What's our big bro up to?"

"Council debriefing."

"Aw, fuck a duck. That shit is so annoying. Anyway, let him know I met Dagan's skinny ass at the airport. Cresso's flight is due to arrive in a couple of hours. I'll touch base again once we know more."

"Got it."

There was a short beat of silence before Taeg spoke again. "Hey, man, I got a hunch."

"Not another one of your hunches," Ronin said, rolling his eyes. "What is it?"

"Our guy Iyri was a high priest, right?"

"Right."

"And wasn't the priest's ceremonial office located in Memphis?"

"From what we've read, yes."

"So I'm betting that's where he was when he was captured," Taeg said.

"Yeah, that makes sense. You're thinking—"

"What are the odds the Council would decide to bury him right there?"

Ronin thought about it for a minute. "Knowing the Council, pretty damn good. Shit. I bet Mammon's got his demons searching in the wrong place."

"That's what I'm thinking. I'll flash over to the site of ancient Memphis while Cresso's making the rounds locally."

"Sounds good. In the meantime, I'll do some research, see if I can narrow down a location for you."

"Ten-four. Over and out," Taeg said before hanging up.

Ronin let out a chuckle. "What a dick."

But an amusing one.

He headed inside for his laptop, but no, it was locked in the room with Keegan. He was stuck waiting for him to finish.

Ronin paused in front of Brynn's room. She'd been awfully quiet the last few hours. He knocked on the closed door, and then again, a bit louder. She didn't respond.

Shit.

There was no way she could have left without him noticing. Could she?

"Brynn?" He twisted the knob and pushed open the door. His timing couldn't have been worse.

She chose that moment to walk out of the bathroom, a towel wrapped over her head. And not a stitch of clothing elsewhere. She let out a sharp scream, snatched the towel from her head, and used it to cover herself.

"Sorry," Ronin choked out, slapping his hands over his

face. It was too late to un-see what he'd seen, though, and the image of that would stick with him. Her curves were subtle, but they were most definitely there. If Keegan found out, he'd be a dead man.

"What do you want?" Brynn gasped.

His cheeks grew warm, and he opened his mouth to reply, but the hot air that blew along the back of his neck choked off his response.

Oh, shit.

Keegan's voice growled behind him, sounding more animal than man. "What the hell's going on here?"

CHAPTER TWELVE

Keegan speared Ronin with his glare, waiting for him to respond.

"Nothing," Ronin said, though it was obvious that wasn't true. "Nothing's going on."

He tried to calm the unreasonable bloodlust that rose within him at the thought of his brother seeing Brynn naked. Clearly, that had been a mistake; Ronin's crimson face betrayed his embarrassment. Still, the beast within him wanted to fall on his brother in a mass of snarling fury.

"Why didn't you knock?" Brynn asked Ronin irritably.

"Sorry." Ronin opened one eye, and once he was sure she was fully covered, the other. He glanced at Keegan, and Keegan knew Ronin's words were mostly for his benefit. "I did knock. Twice. I got a little worried when you didn't respond. Guess you didn't hear me."

"Oh," Brynn said in a soft, embarrassed voice. "What's going on?"

Keegan stopped glaring at Ronin long enough to look at

her, but then he wished he hadn't. He couldn't stop thinking about what was underneath that towel. "Nothing new."

"You spoke to the Council?" Ronin asked.

"You did?" she asked eagerly. "What did they say?"

"Nothing new," he said. Which was true. They hadn't made any headway in locating the whereabouts of the book.

"Oh, that's too bad," she said, her face falling into a little frown.

"Listen," Ronin said to Keegan, "I heard from Taeg. He's got a hunch on something."

Thank the devil. Keegan honestly didn't know how much longer he could stand just a few feet away from a barely clad Brynn. Knowing she was one tug from being naked drove him insane.

"Wait," she cried, as Ronin started closing the door. "I want to hear this, too."

"It, um, doesn't really have much to do with you," Ronin said.

She bristled at those words. "Doesn't *everything* about this mess have to do with me?"

Ronin gave him a questioning frown, and Keegan shrugged. As long as what his brother had to say didn't have anything to do with the Council's possible death order, what did he care if she listened in? As long as she was fully clothed.

"Get dressed, then meet us in the parlor," Keegan said. Fighting the urge to indulge in another once-over of her body, he turned and left.

Ronin followed him. "So, really? Nothing new from the Council?"

Keegan was beyond frustrated. "They've got their scholars searching their records, but there aren't any clues on the tomb's location. Mammon's already placed a team there, under the guise of being a wealthy investor funding a major archaeological dig, and they don't want to red-flag human leaders to a potential problem."

Ronin sighed. "Bureaucratic bullshit."

"Never ends," Keegan agreed. "By the way, stay the fuck out of Brynn's room. Got it?"

His little brother broke out in a fierce blush. "Yeah, got it."

He seemed appropriately embarrassed, so Keegan moved on. "What's Taeg's theory?"

"Oh, get this," he said, excitement spreading across his face. "What if everyone's searching for the book in the *wrong place*?"

"What do you mean?"

Ronin relayed the conversation he'd had with Taeg.

"No shit." Keegan had to admit that something about his brother's hunch seemed dead-on. If a high priest was going to make a power play against a mighty council of otherworldly beings, wouldn't he want to do it from his ceremonial headquarters?

Brynn's voice sounded behind him. "What is it?"

Keegan watched her stride into the parlor, a curious expression on her face. "Taeg thinks we might be searching for the book in the wrong place. There's a good chance the tomb it's buried in is located in Memphis."

"Memphis?" she echoed, lifting a brow in obvious disbelief.

"The ancient Egyptian city of Memphis," Ronin clarified.

A pink flush brightened her cheeks. "Oh, that one."

"If we could only find out exactly where he was when he was captured…" Ronin trailed off, his mind apparently already occupied by thoughts of the ancient city. "I'm going to go do some research."

He left the parlor.

Keegan was struck by the uncomfortable realization that this was the first time they'd been alone since he'd almost kissed her. How foolish he'd been.

Worse, he still wanted to kiss her. Very much.

Seeking to break the tension, he walked to the window and glanced out of it. Crowds of revelers swarmed the streets. It would be so easy to get lost in a crowd this size. So very easy. What would it be like, to forget about all of this turmoil for a while and just enjoy life? To allow Brynn to experience at least the illusion of freedom?

He surprised himself by turning back to Brynn. "Want to go out for a bit?"

"Really? I mean, yeah, I'd love to." She hesitated. "I hate to ask, because I really, really would like to go, but is it safe?"

"Should be safe enough in the crowd of people. The odds of Mammon finding us here are slim. It's not as if he has a GPS tracker on you. Your apartment and your gallery, on the other hand, won't be safe to return to until this mess is figured out."

"My gallery." Her face took on a pained expression that disappeared so swiftly he thought he might have imagined it. She grabbed her long black coat and followed him to the door. "Why do I need to stay inside at all, if Mammon can't track me?"

"I said the odds are slim. Not impossible. He's got demons working for him everywhere. Given the consequences if he does find you, I'd say it's better to err on the side of caution."

Brynn appeared lost in thought as they hopped in the elevator and he pressed the button for the opulent lobby. When she turned to him, a vulnerable look haunted her gaze. "Are you going to be able to find him, Keegan? Do you think you'll be able to stop him?"

The quiver in her voice just about killed him. Hoping to reassure her, he lifted his hand to caress her cheek. "Yes, Brynn, I do."

Something hot and heavy blazed in her eyes, something that made it impossible to look away. His breath caught.

The elevator opened and three interested pairs of eyes peered at them. For the first time he realized they'd edged closer together, until they stood mere inches apart. Clearing his throat, he hastily broke away.

Brynn hugged her coat to her as they stepped into the frigid cold. The smell of stale beer and piss stained the air around them. Drunken revelers wearing masks and beads careened past them, laughing riotously as they zoomed down the street carrying beer cups.

"I didn't realize it was Mardi Gras until we got here," she said.

"Mardi Gras?" He frowned, unfamiliar with the phrase. "What's that?"

With an exasperated shake of her head, she said, "How is it that you seem so normal, yet you know nothing about popular culture?"

"We learn as much as we can before visiting other worlds, but our timelines are usually pretty short."

"Sometimes you amaze me."

She explained the history behind the celebration while he watched the throngs of people walking past, some barely dressed.

"I'm afraid some of these people are going to freeze to

death," he told her.

Brynn followed his gaze to a thin woman wearing nothing more than a mask, pasties, a thong, and what looked like her weight in beads. She laughed. "Most of them have probably had so much liquor they barely even notice."

Surely, a dangerous state for beings as fragile as humans. He saw something ahead and grabbed her hand. "Come on."

"Where are we going?"

Fighting to pull her through the crowd, he led her to a booth where a man sold masks and beads. Keegan picked an elaborate purple and gold full-face mask with feathers on one side. "This one suits you."

"It's pretty." She put it on and he moved behind her to tie the strings in the back. "If I'm wearing one, you need one, too."

Keegan shrugged, then chose a black and gold jester mask that he figured was masculine enough. He squatted, waiting impatiently while Brynn tied it behind his head. Her intoxicating scent closed in on him, overwhelming even the foul stench of the streets.

Too close. She stood far too close for comfort.

As soon as she finished tying the knot, he pulled away and turned to face her.

"That looks great on you," she said.

Laughing, he paid the man at the booth. He led her away from the huge, swaying mass of people on one end of the street. When they approached another crowd pocket, he grabbed her hand, and this time he didn't let go. He told himself it made sense, given the amount of people on the street. But he didn't try to fool himself—touching her felt good. Her cool hand warmed in his, and he envisioned what it would feel like for her soft fingers to caress other parts of his body.

Cursing inwardly, he forced himself to think about something else. He scanned the crowd, searching for any signs of danger, but found nothing. "Maybe Ronin was right about hiding out here."

Her glance was curious. "Why do you say that?"

"The crowd—not to mention the masks—should provide more than enough safety."

"Ooh, does that mean I actually get to leave the hotel room?"

Keegan laughed at her eager tone, squeezing her hand. "As long as one of us accompanies you, I don't see why not."

They walked for several long minutes, taking in the craziness around them, before he paused in front of a restaurant with only a small line of people waiting to eat.

"Do you like French cuisine?" he asked her.

"Love it." She practically skipped to the end of the line.

Later, when they'd sat at a private booth and ordered their food, she asked, "So do you need to eat, just like huma—you know, just like *we* do?"

"Not quite the same. Our foods are similar, but I could get by eating once a month if I had to."

"Weird." Brynn blinked. "How about liquids?"

"Same." She opened her mouth to ask another question, but he decided to beat her to it. "Do you find it difficult to restrain your natural abilities in crowds like this?"

"Huh. I never thought about it." Her gaze tilted upward while she mulled over his question. "No, I suppose not. My powers are hidden, waiting to be called out. But for the most part, I control them, and not the other way around. I can use these, for example, without too much trouble." She lifted the fork set on the table in front of her. "What about you, with your powers?"

"Same."

Brynn studied him carefully. "What is it that you can do, anyway? You never told me."

Damn. He hadn't considered his question might lead to this. He tapped his fingers on the table as he considered how best to answer. "It's my blood that has the ability to heal, and it happens quickly."

"Can it heal just you, or others, as well?"

"It can heal others, too."

"Impressive. So how does that work? People don't have to drink it or anything, do they?"

"The blood is simply placed on the wound and it heals. Works on bruises, too."

"Bruises? Oh, so *that's* why I didn't have a sore jaw when I woke up in your apartment?"

He winced. Now that he knew her, the memory of striking her filled him with shame. Wordlessly, he nodded.

"Huh." Her face took on a considering expression. "Okay, what else can you do?"

Keegan shrugged and shifted in his seat. He briefly considered not answering at all, but knowing her, she would keep asking. "Demons are generally stronger and faster than humans, which is why we can be such a danger to them."

"Yeah, but why come here, anyway? I mean, why not stay in Infernum? Is it that bad?"

She had no idea.

"It's not exactly welcoming. It's barren and primitive in many ways. Desolate, like your deserts, and always dark, but constantly hot, even at night."

"And you work there as a...*Detainor*?"

Keegan nodded. "I hunt down treaty violators from Infernum who flee the Council."

"How did you get the job of capturing Mammon on Earth?"

He couldn't very well tell her the truth. At least not all of it. But she deserved to know something—it was her life that was in danger—so he settled for bits and pieces. "Mammon is a special case. He was a well-respected scientist back in Infernum, and he had a position as a high- level adviser to the Council."

Brynn blinked at that. "A…a demon scientist?"

"Yes." He chuckled. "Why so surprised? Our world studies science, like yours."

"I don't know. I guess I assumed from your description that it isn't very advanced."

"As it happens, Mammon is a brilliant demon. The Council used to send him on missions to other worlds, to catalog the different species and study their biology."

"You've said *worlds* several times. Just how many are there?"

"Dozens. Thousands. Who knows for sure, other than at the highest level of the Council?"

"Thousands?" She gaped at him, wide-eyed. "You've totally blown my mind."

"It's a large multiverse, Brynn."

"Why does the Council want to catalog species?"

"It's made up of males and females from a variety of worlds, and I suspect its members don't trust one another. That's why someone from Infernum was sent to catalog humans, whereas someone from Earth might have been sent to Infernum to catalog demons and angels. We—"

"Hold on, hold on." Brynn lifted both hands. "Did you just say *angels*?"

"Again, not quite the same as what you humans have imagined. They are a species of beings who can fly. They fancy themselves the royalty of Infernum, living in castles built into the sky, far from the mayhem located on the ground."

"Why call them that, then? Why angels and demons?"

"More than likely, human perceptions of angels and demons have been borrowed from prior interactions with both species, stretched and twisted over time, idealized into notions of good and evil."

He reached across the table and took her hand in his, giving it a squeeze. Even though he knew better, he couldn't help but want to comfort her. "I know this is difficult for you. I'm impressed with how you've been handling things."

"Yeah, that's me"—Brynn gave him a trembling smile—"totally unflappable."

He chuckled, letting go of her hand when the waitress arrived with their food.

"So," she said once the waitress had left, "the Council members didn't know Mammon was dangerous?"

"Oh, they knew he was capable of evil." They knew it all too well. "But to them, evil is relative. As long as he did his job— and did it well—they overlooked some of the less savory things he did."

"Which were?"

"Doesn't matter now." Hopefully she'd get the hint and drop it. He didn't want to go into this. Not now. Not ever.

"What?" she insisted. "I want to know."

Of course she would. And she deserved to, never mind how much he didn't want to speak of it. "He had a weakness for kidnapping females in the worlds he visited and raping them."

She gasped. "And the Council knew about this?"

"Yes."

"And they did nothing to stop him?"

He couldn't mask the bitterness in his tone. "As I said, to the Council, evil is relative."

"Unbelievable," Brynn muttered, fury written all over her face. "How can you stand working for people like that?"

"Things aren't always as black and white as they seem. There is one good thing that's come of all this, though—once the Council learned of Mammon's latest scheme, they couldn't pretend it wasn't happening. This time, they had to act."

"So you and your brothers were sent here to stop him."

"Exactly."

When she opened her mouth to speak again, he motioned to their food. "Let's eat."

Sighing, she nodded. They ate the rest of their lunch in companionable silence, and then started back toward their hotel with their masks back in place.

A few blocks from the hotel, Brynn asked, "What are your lives like at home?"

What could he say to that? It was dangerous, but she wouldn't want to hear that. And unfulfilling. "Me and my brothers mostly work, and we're lucky to have jobs. There isn't much in the way of occupation in Infernum."

"Really? What does everyone do, then?"

He snorted. "Every demon's occupation is to avoid getting killed, and for many of them, to find a way off the damn world."

"So, you don't have anyone waiting for you back at home? A wife? Children?"

Now her questions were becoming too personal for his comfort. "No."

Brynn quickly averted her eyes. "Oh."

They entered the lobby, and he followed her into the elevator, taking off his mask. She did the same. When her gaze didn't meet his eyes, he realized she was embarrassed.

Shit. He hadn't meant to make her feel bad about questioning him. It wasn't like she'd known she was going to hit on a sore subject.

"I would like to have a family," he grudgingly admitted. "But my world is too dangerous."

She met his gaze, not bothering to hide her surprise. "Have you ever thought about leaving?"

Had he ever thought about it? Sometimes it was *all* he thought about.

"I've requested clearance, but it's been continuously denied. One of the hazards of being a productive citizen of my world, I suppose. Those who don't benefit Infernum are generally the only ones granted visits to the other worlds, since so many of them fail to return."

"But then don't you have to track them down?"

His lips twisted into a brief smile. "Only the dangerous ones."

She didn't seem to notice when they got to their floor, not until the elevator door began to close and he stuck his hand out to stop it. He held it open for her, trying in vain to ignore the way the perfume of her essence wrapped around him. But when her arm brushed against his chest while she exited the elevator, he couldn't ignore how his skin heated and his heart thumped.

This woman was dangerous, and not just to the world.

Alarmingly out of control, he edged in front of her and

walked toward their suite, his legs not moving fast enough. Ronin would provide just the buffer he needed. And *now*. By the time Brynn caught up with him, he'd already reached the door and retrieved the key card from his pocket.

She closed her fingers around his arm. "Keegan, did I say something wrong?"

Damn it. She'd touched him. He glared at the hand that rested on his arm, then slowly brought his gaze up to her face. Something in his eyes must have frightened her, because she inhaled, her pupils large and unfocused. The air around them changed, grew heavier. Blood rushed into his ears with a low, roaring sound, overpowering all his other senses.

"Keegan?" Her voice came out breathy as she tilted her head in question.

Fuck it. He couldn't hold back anymore. He needed to know what she tasted like. Just *once*.

He grasped her hand, pulled her forward so that her back hit the door to their suite, until she fully faced him. Even over her heavy coat, he felt the rapid beat of her heart, like a frightened rabbit. Moving slowly enough to give her a chance to turn away, he bent his head toward hers.

Her lips curved into a smile, clearly welcoming him. He groaned and crushed her to him, claimed her mouth in a kiss that was hauntingly familiar, while at the same time completely new.

She moaned, flicking her tongue against his lips as she molded her body to his.

Devil, but she was intoxicating. She tasted of the most exotic essence of fruit, as if she were meant to be devoured. Right now, that was all he wanted to do—peel the layers of clothes off her body and taste every delicious inch of her bare flesh. He would wrap her legs around his waist, sink into her warm flesh, and pound away inside her until he took them both into oblivion.

No. He couldn't do this. It was wrong, like the worst sort of betrayal to her and to his brothers. To the damned Council, even.

Aw, hell.

Brynn whimpered in protest as he broke away. Muttering an oath, he hit his fist against the wall, leaving a dent.

"What's wrong?" she asked.

"We can't." He turned around to face her. "No, we can't do this."

"I don't understand." Her face, still softened with desire, took on a pleading expression. "So what if things become more complicated? They already *are* more complicated."

She was right. She didn't understand, didn't know what was at stake here. And he would never tell her. Damn Mammon. Damn the Council for putting him in this position.

There was only one way to push her away: lie to her.

He shook his head, letting out a bitter laugh. "You don't understand. I've already got enough problems having to babysit you all over the fucking place. You think this is fun for me?"

She stared at him, stunned. "I thought—"

"Yeah, you *thought*," he bit out. "For one second, maybe you should think about something besides yourself. I've got enough to deal with right now. I don't need any more complications."

Her eyes went round as saucers. "But…"

Stomping forward, he swiped the key card across the lock, then pushed the door open. "Get inside."

She obeyed, turning to look back at him. The confused, hurt

expression on her face almost destroyed him. "Keegan, I—"

Without another word, he yanked the door shut.

~oc~

Brynn stared at the door for several long minutes, blinking back the frustrated moisture that threatened to leak out of her eyes. What was that all about? He was the one who'd pulled her in for a kiss. Then he'd broken away all offended, like she'd stolen it from him or something. Was he out of his mind?

She stalked into the parlor, throwing the mask to the floor.

Where did he get off treating her like that? It wasn't like she'd begged him to kiss her. He'd been just as willing a participant as she was in the whole thing. She didn't understand him at all.

She moved out to the balcony and looked below to where crowds of people still milled about, many of them probably headed toward the next parade or to one of the numerous novelty shops. Her body was a mass of quivering nerves, fury blending with the remnants of sexual desire. What a mess her life had become.

Random spots of color caught her eye as she looked down into the crowd. All the chaos down there was beautiful, in its own strange way. Her fingers itched with the sudden urge to paint. But she hadn't packed any art supplies when she'd been at her apartment. The demons had attacked before she could decide what to bring, and afterward…well, she hadn't thought much of anything other than the monsters lying in her living room.

She could really use her paints now. It was the one thing she could always count on to calm her down. Biting her lip,

Brynn glanced back inside the suite. Keegan had stormed off somewhere to do God knows what, and Ronin was apparently still holed away in his room researching. Her gaze moved down to the mask lying on the floor. She wouldn't foolishly put herself in a dangerous position just because she was angry, but Keegan had said they should be safe enough on the streets wearing their masks.

She'd find some supplies, maybe even be back before they noticed she was missing…

He would kill her if he found out. But right now, she didn't care. Taking a deep breath, she went inside and grabbed the mask, then snatched a spare key card and some money from the coffee table. After a quick peek outside the door to make sure Keegan wasn't still there, she put on her mask and left.

CHAPTER THIRTEEN

"You're such a dick, Keegan."

He'd been called a great many names in his life, but none as bad as what he was calling himself right now. He leaned against the side of the hotel building. What a tool he was. He'd been a total ass to Brynn. And what had she done, other than allow him to kiss her?

"Fucking douchebag," he muttered.

The guy in front of him heard, and must have thought Keegan was talking to him because he whirled around, an indignant look on his face. From the way he stumbled and almost fell, it was obvious he'd drank way too much. But not enough that he didn't see the deadly glimmer in Keegan's eye and backed down.

"Sorry," the guy mumbled before rushing away.

How could he treat Brynn like that, all because of his own attraction to her? Because of his own weakness? When she had touched his arm, questions written all over her face, he'd been unable to stop himself. He'd *had* to kiss her, and damn the consequences.

It was all his fault.

He banged his head against the building. If he was going to blame others for his own shortcomings, he was no better than his father.

He refused to be like him. Would never be like that.

Keegan pushed away from the wall and strode back into the lobby. He rode the elevator, wondering how he would apologize to her. He'd be lucky if he could spit the words out without her taking a swing at his head. And if she did, he wouldn't blame her. In fact, he'd probably let her.

He entered their suite and walked to Brynn's door, rapping lightly. "Brynn?"

When there was no answer, he knocked again, repeating her name.

Again, no answer.

He hovered at the door, uncertain if he should open it. What if he caught her in a state of undress the way Ronin had earlier? He didn't want to intrude on her privacy. But at the same time, he had to make sure she was okay and tell her he was sorry.

Keegan slowly swung the door open and poked his head inside. "Brynn?"

Her bathroom door was wide open, and the light off. He went inside and peeked around. Anxiety gripped him when he realized she wasn't there. After jogging to his and Ronin's room, he opened the door. His brother sat at the small desk, tapping away at his laptop.

Ronin didn't bother looking up. "What's up?"

"Where's Brynn?"

"What?" Ronin jerked his head up. "I thought she was with

you."

"Oh, shit." He turned and ran to the parlor, then the balcony.

Ronin followed, not far behind. "I don't understand. You two went out a few hours ago."

He turned to face his brother and admitted his failure. "I dropped her off here and left about half an hour ago."

"Without telling me?" Ronin grabbed the collar of Keegan's jacket. "What is wrong with you?"

"Fuck off." Keegan pushed him away.

Ronin staggered backward but came at him again, shoving him against the wall. Keegan fought back, snarling, before his brother tore away from him. "Stop. Let's stop. This isn't helping anything."

Keegan's chest heaved as the bloodlust dissipated. Ronin was right. Each moment they stood here fighting each other like dumb assholes was another moment when Brynn could be getting farther away.

"Could she have been taken?"

Ronin thought about it for a moment before shaking his head. "No. At least, not here. I would have known."

"Okay. So she's out there somewhere. We'll go look for her. She's probably wearing a mask," he said, and described it.

"Got it. Do you think she's in the hotel somewhere, or could she have left the building?"

The most dangerous thing for her to do would have been to leave the building. Somehow, Keegan had a feeling that was exactly what she'd done. "Let's look outside."

They raced downstairs, neither of them bothering to mention the obvious fact that finding her among this crowd would be nearly impossible. He wasn't going to think about it.

They had to find her, for their sakes. For *her* sake.

When they reached the outside, Keegan motioned to the right. "You go that way. I'll head over here."

"Done." Ronin rushed off.

Keegan raced down the street, searching every alley and corner along the way. He found a few women wearing Brynn's mask, and when he'd ripped them away, one screamed, another stared at him dumbfounded, and two giggled and tried to kiss him. An hour later, evening neared, and he'd had no luck finding her.

With a heavy heart, Keegan walked back toward the hotel. What was he going to do? What if she'd been taken? It would mean disastrous things, not only for the world but for Brynn.

He was two blocks away when he saw a woman up ahead, moving in the same direction as he. She carried a shopping bag in her hand, a mask tied around her head, and her clothes and hair matched Brynn's. He raced to her and whirled her around.

She jumped, a fearful look in her eyes, until she recognized him. "Keegan," she breathed, looking relieved.

Damn, he thought he'd lost her. He'd thought…

He hugged her to him, burying her head in his chest.

"Argh, you're suffocating me," Brynn choked out.

"Sorry." He pulled away, closing his eyes for a moment. "I was worried about you."

"I'm sorry. I just—"

Relief suddenly gave way to fury. He grabbed her shoulders and shook her. "What the hell is wrong with you?"

"I—"

"Do you know how dangerous this was?"

A passerby saw them and stopped. "Ma'am, are you okay? Do you need help?"

"Fuck off," he said, shooting the man an icy glare.

The man appeared frightened, but he stood his ground. "Ma'am?"

Brynn turned to give him a shaky nod. "I'm fine, thanks."

"Suit yourself." The man shrugged and stalked off.

"Come on." Keegan took her arm and half dragged her toward the hotel. Standing inside the elevator, he punched the button for their floor, taking deep, full breaths to calm his rage.

"I… I'm sorry," she said.

"Take off that fucking mask."

Fingers trembling, she obeyed.

When the elevator opened on their floor, he led her to their suite and ushered her inside. "Go to your room. I have to call Ronin and let him know I found you."

Keegan was half surprised when she didn't argue or bristle at his tone, just walked into her room and closed the door. He took out his cell phone and called his brother. A low beep came from the room he shared with Ronin. Following the sound, he found his brother's cell phone lying next to his laptop.

"Shit," Keegan said, hanging up the phone. Ronin must have forgotten all about it in their haste to find Brynn.

He gave himself a few minutes to calm down before he went to Brynn's room and opened the door without knocking. She sat on the bed, her coat thrown haphazardly to the floor in front of her.

He couldn't hide the note of accusation in his voice. "Don't you realize what could have happened if Mammon's minions had found you?"

Fire burned in her eyes. Her voice quivered. "I was upset, and I needed to paint. It's the only thing that calms me. So I went to get some supplies."

She motioned toward her shopping bag.

Keegan sighed and closed his eyes, racked with guilt. He was such an ass. He'd never bothered to ask her if she needed anything to help her relax—hadn't even thought about it.

"Why did you act like that earlier?" she asked.

"Doesn't matter," he replied, ruthlessly tossing those guilty feelings aside. No matter how shitty he'd behaved, she shouldn't have left the room. She should have known better. And *he* should have known better than to leave like that. "You are not to leave this hotel without Ronin or me, understood?"

"Listen," she said, standing. She walked toward him, stopping just a few feet away. "I know you're trying to protect me and all, but you need to chill. You said it was safe enough out there."

Protect her? That was a laugh. Little did she know, she wasn't his ward. She was his prisoner.

"Even if there weren't demons out looking for you," he said, "the streets are filled with drunk, crazy assholes."

"I had my mask on, for God's sake. Besides, have you forgotten what I can do to humans? In fact, one drunken idiot did try to feel me up, and all I had to do was touch him with one finger and he fell to the ground."

His hands clenched into involuntary fists. "Someone tried to touch you?"

"And I *protected* myself," Brynn said. "Like I've done all of my life."

His fury built to a crescendo. But not at her, at the nameless guy who'd tried to grab her. He wanted to head downstairs so he could find the man, but it wasn't like he knew who it was— he'd have to kill every guy on the street.

"Brynn, you are not to go out alone."

She stared at him, chest heaving as her gaze shimmered with unspoken fury.

"Why did you act that way earlier?" she asked.

He refused to back down, and he wouldn't give her what she wanted, wouldn't bare his soul. She was the one who would answer to him. That was the way it had to be.

Keegan ground his teeth together as he pushed off the wall and walked to her, knowing full well that his height would intimidate her. But he used it anyway. She had to understand that she couldn't just waltz out of here whenever the mood struck her. "You stay in the suite. Do. You. Understand?"

"Don't talk to me like that."

She hurled her fist toward his face. At the last moment, he caught it and swung her around, her back knocking against the wall. He stood in front of her in an instant, imprisoning her with his body. Taking her wrists in his hands, he pinned them above her head.

This time he didn't feel so guilty about the fear in her eyes. Not when they unmistakably intertwined with excitement.

"Don't push me," he warned, his face inches from hers.

She gulped, and after a moment, her eyes hardened with challenge. "I'll do whatever I pleas—"

Before she could finish, he captured her lips in a punishing kiss, thrusting his tongue inside her sweet-as-honey mouth, swallowing her gasp as he kissed the air right out of her lungs. She moaned, and his already hard cock twitched. Keeping her arms restrained, his tongue moving with hers, he poured all of his emotions into that one kiss.

Something rammed into his groin.

"Son of a bitch!" He broke away, dropping both hands to

protect the sensitive spot. Brynn stayed plastered to the wall, her chest heaving. He looked at her in disbelief. "You…*kneed* me."

"It's no more than you deserved." Her eyes blazed as she glared at him. "What did you expect? First you kiss me, then you insult me, and then you jump me all over again. And you think I'm going to take it without any argument? What is your malfunction?"

"I…" Straightening, he backed up a few inches when she poked her finger in his chest.

"Did you mean what you said earlier? Am I really just an inconvenience to you?"

"No." What a vision she made. Anger flushed her cheeks and darkened her normally calm green eyes to the color of the sea during a raging storm. He didn't know whether to be wary or turned on, but right now he was a little of both. "You aren't an inconvenience."

"Then what?" she persisted, her brow crinkling. "Why did you push me away?"

"Because…"

"Finish it. *Why*?"

"Because I shouldn't want you, that's why," he admitted, unable to stop himself from saying the words, despite the fact that he fucking knew better. "But I can't help it. I do."

Her eyes narrowed in on him and he drew back, raking a hand through his hair as he pondered where they would go from here. From the way she stared at him, he half expected her to try and punch him again. No doubt he deserved it.

"Oh, Keegan…" she said instead, her voice soft and somber. "I—"

Before he could say anything further, she jumped him,

expertly closing her mouth over his. He stumbled backward a few steps at her unexpected weight before wrapping his arms around her and returning her kiss. Knowing the whole time it was wrong, but unable to stop.

She lifted first one leg, then the other, to wrap around his hips. Her movement brought his cock right in line with her core, and he rubbed up against her. Even then, it wasn't enough. He needed her closer, until he was inside of her. He wanted it with a burning intensity that overwhelmed all sense of reason.

"I told you not to push me," he reminded her hoarsely, breaking away.

Her luscious lips curved into a wicked smile. "But I *want* to push you."

That much was clear. With a muttered curse, he stumbled a few steps to the low dresser and sat her on top of it. Her new position aligned her perfectly to his body, as if she were tailor-made for him.

"Be careful what you wish for." Bending down, he claimed her lips in another deep, searing kiss.

❊❉

Brynn was on fire. Keegan's tongue thrust against hers, matching the pulsing rhythm of his arousal rubbing between her thighs. It was almost too much. She arched her back as her hands traveled under the light fabric of his shirt. She tugged his jacket off and tossed it to the side, gasping when he did the same to her sweater.

He gazed at her black, lacy bra for a long moment before groaning and cupping each of her breasts with his hands. Then, with a simple flick of his hand, the bra came off and fell on the floor alongside her sweater.

"Damn, you're beautiful," he said, stroking his thumbs along her nipples. "Just as I'd dreamed."

Her cheeks warmed. "You dreamed about me?"

He chuckled, obviously amused, as he lowered his head to take one breast into his mouth. She arched with a low cry, pressing his head to her body. Then he moved to lavish the same attention on the other, tugging and rolling his tongue across the nipple.

She needed to feel him—not just the corded muscles of his back, which even now rippled under her touch, but his length pressing so determinedly against the front of his jeans. Keegan let out a harsh groan as she unbuttoned his fly. The hardened heat of his arousal felt like steel against the fabric of his jeans. What would he feel like under her fingertips?

Nothing would stop her from finding out.

"Brynn," he gasped.

She unzipped his jeans, then took his silky length into her hands. He was big and hard and oh-so-hot against her palms. Closing a fist around him, she slid her palm up, then down, reveling in the feel of his flesh. He tore his mouth from her breasts and buried his face in her neck, breathing in ragged bursts of air. "That feels so good."

He rewarded her with another kiss, keeping time with the shaky movements of her hand. But he broke away with a husky laugh and gazed down at her, an almost sad expression crossing his face. "If there were a Hell, I'd be going to it for sure."

Gently, he tugged her hands away from his arousal, and in response, she made a mewling protest that she could hardly believe came from her. She whimpered when he licked her belly button, and at the same time, his deft fingers unbuttoned her jeans and tugged off her boots. Faster than she could blink, he'd slipped her jeans down and off her.

"Wow, you're fast."

He chuckled, his breath caressing the bare skin of her belly. "Sometimes you have to live in the moment."

Her giggle turned into a soft cry as he knelt down and tore off her lacy underwear, just as easily as he'd done in her dreams. Tossing her legs over his shoulders, he cupped her ass and lifted her off the dresser. His tongue found her slick core and unceremoniously dipped inside.

"Oh, God!" Her shaky arms supported her body while he pleasured her with his mouth and tongue. In seconds, her whole body shook uncontrollably as she panted, on the verge of orgasm. "Please...don't stop."

She moaned her disappointment when he broke away and rose. She was *almost* there. But then he kissed her, slow and erotic, and soon she was squirming once more.

He looked at her with marked satisfaction. "Just as I'd thought."

She blinked. "What?"

"You *do* taste like strawberries and cream." His lips found hers as he thrust a finger inside her wet core. She struggled for breath, pushing her hips upward. He withdrew it, then held her hips down with one hand. The other hand moved between her legs. Before she could brace herself, he'd thrust two thick, long fingers all the way inside. She cried out, arching her back. Her body convulsed in a mind-shattering orgasm that only increased in intensity as he continued to move his fingers in and out. He didn't stop until the last of her spasms had died away.

"Brynn…" he groaned against her lips.

Pulling away, she dropped her gaze to where his erection jutted out of his half-undone jeans. She circled her hand around it. "Please. I need you."

"I need you, too. More than you know."

Crushing her into his arms, he breathed into her neck for a long moment before lifting her off the dresser and carrying her to the bed.

A loud knock cracked through the air a split second before they reached the bed. Ronin's voice was barely audible through the wooden door of the suite. "Keeg, are you in there? I forgot my cell phone. My key. Fuck. Keegan?"

The door rattled again, sounding perilously on the verge of being broken in.

Keegan cursed. Dropping her on the bed, he broke away hastily, his expression equal parts lust, guilt, and regret.

Feeling uncertain, Brynn watched in silence as he quickly zipped himself back up.

"Keegan?" she whispered.

"Get dressed," was all he said, before turning and striding out of the room.

The door rattled after he closed it, like he was doing something to it.

She found her clothes and pulled them on. When she stood in front of the door, Keegan's and Ronin's muffled voices filtered through the wood, though they were too low for her to pick up any actual words. Holding her breath, she carefully turned the knob. It stuck. Stifling a curse, she tried to pull it open, but nothing.

That asshole! Somehow he'd jammed the lock as he'd left. Once again, she was imprisoned.

Brynn willed herself to calm down as she slid to the floor, her back against the door.

It's okay. It's for your own protection. You're not a prisoner.

The problem was, she wasn't so sure she believed it anymore.

CHAPTER FOURTEEN

He couldn't sleep.

Ronin finally gave up trying and rose off the bed, staring across the room to where his big brother lay on the second double bed. He had a funny feeling Keegan couldn't sleep, either, but was pretending otherwise.

"Keeg?" he said, testing his theory.

His brother's chest continued to rise and fall evenly. Not even a twitch.

Yeah, he was definitely faking it. That fucker.

He needed a drink.

Ronin padded out to the parlor. After filling a glass to the brim with straight whiskey, he opened the door to the balcony and stepped outside. Even now, crowds of half-naked drunk people stumbled throughout the streets.

"Idiots." He chuckled. Damn, how he envied them. No cares in the world. No idea just how precarious the fate of their world was right now. They were so blissfully ignorant.

Not once had he ever had that luxury.

Ronin took a big gulp of his whiskey, feeling it burn down his throat and wishing it would drown his worries. But he knew it wouldn't. He knew what Keegan and Brynn had been up to earlier. Was his brother stupid enough to think he'd buy the line of bullshit he'd tried to feed him about how he was "talking" to Brynn? Yeah, right. *Talking.* That he'd even tried to get him to believe that spoke to Keegan's desperation.

Keegan was in immediate danger of going over the edge, if he hadn't done so already. And Ronin couldn't do a damn thing to stop him. Worse was the realization that if Brynn wasn't the heir, he wouldn't want to stop him. Keegan deserved some happiness in his life. Too bad the woman who seemed most likely to give it to him was the one woman they might have to destroy. And if Keegan somehow lost his mind and tried to challenge the Council, they would kill him.

Why can't life ever be easy?

Now he had to decide whether or not to report what had happened to Taeg. If Taeg knew, he'd probably flash over and terminate Brynn himself. Not because he was an asshole—which admittedly, he was—but because he loved Keegan too damn much to let him risk his own life.

ဆ

Brynn was back inside her New York apartment. Some distant part of her brain recognized this wasn't possible. She was dreaming. It felt real, though.

A breeze blew in through the open window, fluttering her sheer curtain so that it resembled a butterfly taking flight on gossamer wings. She pulled the curtain all the way to the side. Instead of her familiar nighttime street view, she saw a never-ending backdrop of desert. Nothing but desert.

"Egypt."

"Is that what you see?" said a gravelly voice.

Brynn's heart pummeled her ribcage. She forced herself to swallow hard before glancing behind her. It was Keegan's father. Again. He stood beside the door to her room, an intrigued expression on his deceptively benign face. She recalled her earlier dream of the woman in the cave and fury rose within her, followed in equal parts by fear. This man was the personification of evil…and for some reason she couldn't explain, the image of him haunted her sleep.

"Get out of my dream." She turned back to the desert scene, making sure her dismissal of him was clear. Instead of obeying, he stood next to her and surveyed the view, the fabric of his slacks sliding against her nightgown. She stifled a shudder of disgust, reminding herself that it was only a dream. She could make herself wake up whenever she wanted. Couldn't she?

At least this time, they were both fully clothed.

"What part of Egypt is this?" he asked in a casual tone.

Answering him seemed idiotic, considering he was part of her imagination, but somehow she felt compelled to. Maybe if she engaged him, whatever dark recess of her mind had conjured him up would be appeased. "I've never been to Egypt before, so I can only guess it's Memphis."

Keegan's father stilled. "Memphis?"

Brynn shrugged. "I imagine. Since I heard the name, it's been rooting around in my subconscious."

"Indeed."

Brynn surveyed him closely, studying the similarities and the differences he had with Keegan. "What are *you* doing here?"

"Same thing, I imagine." He gave her an oily smirk. "Rooting around in your subconscious."

That made sense. She still hadn't processed the whole deal in her mind. Keegan's memories had shown her just how evil his father was. How had such a heinous demon, an abuser and a rapist, managed to create four decent sons? Mind-boggling.

He surveyed her room. "No Keegan here tonight, I see."

She'd noticed that, too. "No. Not tonight."

"Hmm...I would have thought you'd be dreaming of where you are right now."

"The hotel?" she scoffed. "No, no unresolved feelings about that."

"But it's such a nice location."

"Yes," Brynn agreed. "I always did like this city."

He didn't speak for a long moment. "I would so love to see your view from your hotel."

She stared at him. This was easily one of the weirdest dreams she'd ever had. "You *have* seen my view. You're my subconscious, remember?"

"Yes." He chuckled. "Still...paint a picture for me, will you?"

"Whatever." With a careless wave, Brynn pictured the hotel suite. In a flash, her apartment disappeared and they stood outside on the hotel balcony, staring down at a small crowd of people littering the streets.

"Ah, Royal Street," he breathed. "I always did like New Orleans."

"I already said that," Brynn noted, and shook her head. Now she was starting to repeat herself. Weird-ass dream.

He turned back to her. "Thank you, dear."

"For what?"

Keegan's father grabbed her hand and bent down as if to kiss it, but she snatched it back before he could. Her skin crawled as if a thousand ants crept over it, provoking an unreasonable stab of fear. She choked in a breath and her fright morphed into anger. This was *her* dream, and she controlled it.

"I don't care if you're a figment of my imagination. Don't *touch* me, asshole."

"I do so like a fighter." Laughing softly, he straightened and peered over the railing. "One more thing, Brynn."

"What?" she snapped.

His lips curved upward. "Good-bye. For now."

Before she could respond, he reached out and gave her a hard shove that sent her flying over the balcony railing. She somersaulted in the air, then hung there for a moment, unable to do anything more than stare at him in shock. Gravity kicked in, and she zoomed toward the ground.

Could you die in a dream? Was that even possible?

She let out a sharp scream as the ground grew closer… *Shit!*

She jolted awake. Gasping, she sat up in her bed and tried to calm the galloping of her heart. If the stress of everything that had happened over the past few days didn't kill her, then these crazy dreams might.

₧┬┮

Early morning light trickled into the room, casting shadows along the wall. The streets were probably at their emptiest. If he was going to leave, now was the perfect time.

Keegan heard sheets rustling behind him as Ronin shifted in his bed, but he didn't bother to look. His brother wouldn't be waking any time soon, not unless he woke him. He'd just gone to bed a few hours ago.

At least one of them had managed to get a few hours' sleep. As for him, well, he'd lain in his bed all night, doing little more than dozing off here and there. The few moments of sleep he had gotten had been haunted by nightmares of his father and the horrifying ways Mammon had tortured him and his brothers. For years after they had initially escaped, Keegan had feared their father would hunt them down and take his revenge. Eventually he'd come to accept the notion that they were finally free of him...but he was wrong. They would never be free, would never be able to outrun the past. The best they could do was try to counteract the horror of their youths with all the good they did now, catching fugitives for the Council. And that was why it was so important to complete this mission.

The chains of responsibility weighed down heavily on him. His obligation was to the Council. To his brothers. How many times had he impressed upon them the need to do what was right, to do the opposite of what their father would have done? And now here he was, putting everything in jeopardy. All because of his dick.

No. That wasn't true. It wasn't his dick that was a danger to him.

Brynn had gotten under his skin. Somehow he'd let her worm her way under there, with her green eyes and laughing face, and her undying optimism and belief that others were inherently good.

Ronin'd had that particular trait once, before his father had beaten it out of him.

He harbored no doubt that Ronin hadn't believed a word of what he'd said yesterday. The silent censure in his eyes was proof enough. But he hadn't challenged him, like Taeg or even Dagan would have. No, he'd kept quiet, to mull things over in typical Ronin style.

Shit. What was he going to do?

He wasn't good enough for Brynn. That was obvious. Here she was, trusting him implicitly, and all he could do was feed her half truths, at best.

She wasn't meant for him. But, by the devil, she had fit him perfectly yesterday, tasted divine. Keegan closed his eyes, savoring the memory of how right for him she'd felt.

One thing was certain: he couldn't just sit here, awaiting an order that might mean the difference between Brynn's life or death. He had to do something.

Keegan moved to Ronin's bed and bent to shake his shoulder. He awoke with a start, sitting up with a questioning look in his eyes. "What's wrong?"

"Nothing. You keep an eye on Brynn. I'll be back by tonight."

Ronin rubbed the sleep from his eyes. "Where are you going?"

"To meet with the Council in person."

Alarm crossed his brother's face. "Keeg, no."

Keegan didn't bother to listen. What was the point? He'd already made up his mind.

He turned and left the room, fighting the urge to unlock Brynn's door and look in on her before he left. For all he knew, it might be the last time he'd see her. Because once the Council heard what he had to say…

They might very well choose to end him.

CHAPTER FIFTEEN

Taeg flashed over to Cresso's tiny studio apartment in the middle of Cairo, where he had taken up residence ever since arriving in Egypt just a short while ago. Since Cresso expected him, and he didn't want to risk blowing his cover by being seen with him, he didn't bother knocking. Instead, he landed on the other side of the front door. "Anybody home?"

"In the kitchen," Cresso called.

Taeg walked the three steps it took to get from the front door through the barren living room and into the shoebox-size kitchen, decorated in depressing shades of beige. A mini stove and set of double cabinets lined the far wall. Cresso was seated at a tiny round table that had collapsible legs.

"There's my favorite faerie," he quipped, throwing Taeg a mischievous grin.

"Fuck you," Taeg said without heat. Cresso knew how much he hated that.

With a chuckle, Cresso motioned toward the only other chair. "Got us some Chinese takeout."

"This place is a shithole, man." Taeg took a seat and picked up one of the white cartons, taking a peek inside. "Ooh, lo mein."

"Gotta play the part," Cresso said with a shrug. "Can't be staying in a four-star hotel if I'm supposed to be a down-on-his-luck demon looking for some quality work."

"Suit yourself, man. I've got eight-hundred-thread-count sheets on my four-star hotel bed, thank you very much. So, have you found anything out yet?"

"Spoke to one guy so far. He said they've still got demons working night and day to comb through the Valley."

"Yeah, I figured. There was no activity going on in Memphis when I went there yesterday." Taeg practically inhaled a huge bite of lo mein, then pointed his fork at the carton. "This is some good stuff."

"Leave it to you to still have an appetite." Cresso let out a dry chuckle. "So what do we do next?"

Great question. And he knew just the answer. "Got any beer?"

"Help yourself." Cresso gestured toward the tiny refrigerator.

Taeg grabbed two beers before responding. "We need to get ourselves a team to start digging up Memphis, I guess. We'll have to do it on the down-low so Mammon doesn't catch wind. Ronin's been working on narrowing down the location for us."

"What about the Council? Will they help with some men?"

"The Council?" Taeg snorted. "They've been supremely unhelpful to this point. It's almost like they're trying to disclaim any responsibility for what happens."

"Well, that's fucked." Cresso shook his head. "Sounds like them, though—a bunch of bureaucratic assholes."

"You would know, since you work for them."

"Adviser—not employee," Cresso pointed out. "Besides, you work for them, too."

"Oh, yeah," Taeg said, his voice deadpan.

They ate in silence for a few minutes before Cresso asked, "What's Dagan up to?"

"I told him to go out and relax, take a load off. This whole deal has got him moody as a chick."

Cresso sneered, shaking his head. "You and your brothers baby him way too much. Just because he's the youngest doesn't mean he shouldn't have any responsibility. He's a grown-ass man."

Taeg shrugged. "So?"

"*So*, he could really be useful if you let him. In fact, he'd probably kill to feel like he was useful. Instead you encourage him to screw around like he doesn't have a care in the world."

"Whatever, man. I don't encourage him, but at the same time I'm not stopping him, either. Let him have some fun. At least one of us gets to."

Cresso snatched one of the beers. "Suit yourself."

Taeg didn't bother to reply, because Cresso didn't understand. Dagan was upset about what they would likely have to do to Brynn, and who could blame him? If one of the four of them could escape his worries for a while, why not let him?

Let Dagan have his fun. Taeg would do what had to be done in order to save this world. No matter how unsavory the prospect.

80G8

"What do you expect us to do about it?" the monotone voice

of the Council member asked.

Keegan stared at the Councilman's eyes, trying hard not to let his fury show. The Council used some sort of cloaking spell when it met with petitioners and the eyes were all he could see. Even though he knew there were quite a number of them seated around the large semicircular table located on a raised platform, the entire area appeared pitch black, save the one Councilman's large, almond-shaped eyes. His voice was the only one Keegan could make out, too. The rest, when they spoke, sounded like incomprehensible whispers. He had never quite figured out what species that one Councilman was, but he certainly wasn't demon or human.

"What do I expect you to do?" Keegan finally responded. "Provide enough people to make a quick dig for the book would be a good start."

There was a chorus of whispers all around him. The Councilman's gaze shifted from here to there before finally returning to him. "We cannot spare large numbers. The fewer who know about this, the better."

Keegan shook his head in disbelief. "With all due respect to the Council, I don't understand you. You give us no help, knowing Mammon has recruited an army of hundreds here on Earth, yet somehow you expect us to stop him."

The Councilman's voice was cold as ice when he responded. "Need I remind you that you asked for this opportunity to stop Mammon? In fact, as I recall, you insisted."

"You know why," Keegan said, no longer caring that he showed the full extent of his fury. "And when my brothers and I agreed, we certainly didn't realize that it would be just the four of us."

More whispers echoed, and the Councilman whispered

back, until finally he turned to Keegan. "We will do our best to accommodate your request. We will be in contact within the next few days."

Great. Fucking great. They were brushing him off.

Keegan gritted his teeth. "What about the heir?"

The Councilman's eyes blinked at him. "What of her?"

Keegan breathed in and out several times. Losing his cool would accomplish nothing. "As I've already told you, she is an innocent."

"Many are."

"Allow her passage into another dimension," he urged, restraining the angry growl that threatened to spill forth. "She will be safe there, since Mammon can no longer use the portal without facing immediate imprisonment."

"That would require the agreement of Earth's Grand Council member, and we cannot—"

The Councilman was cut off by angry whispers. His eyes swung wildly from one spot to another.

Keegan's mouth dropped open as he realized the truth behind the Councilman's unintentional revelation. They had to be kidding him. "She doesn't know, does she? Earth is in serious danger of having all of its humans wiped out, and you're not even going to tell its leader?"

"You risk much, saying this," the Councilman hissed.

The whispers continued all around him, and Keegan realized the immediate peril behind his situation.

Fuck me.

The Council couldn't help him. Its members couldn't even agree among themselves.

There was a lot more going on behind the scenes than he'd ever imagined. Things he couldn't even comprehend. If the

Council was keeping things from its own members…

He was in serious trouble. Time to do some major backpedaling.

"I've reconsidered my position," he said in a smooth tone that belied the furious pounding of his heart. Thank the devil they couldn't hear it. He hoped. "I can have my brothers dig while I guard the heir."

The Councilman conferred with the other members for a moment. "Agreed. And if Mammon should find the book before you…"

Keegan stood still, waiting for the rest. Somehow, he knew he wouldn't like it.

Finally, the Councilman turned back to him. "If he finds the book first, there will be no need to contact us for further instruction. You are to immediately destroy the heir, then report back to us."

The words hit him like a blow to the chest. Keegan breathed in deeply. It wasn't like he hadn't expected this, especially after his lousy attempt at saving face. Still, it hurt. He'd failed Brynn. One more mark on his long list of failures.

"Understood," he said to the Council, making sure to keep his voice even. Turning, he walked toward the portal waiting to transport him back to New Orleans.

No two ways about it. Brynn was still in peril…which meant he was seriously fucked.

CHAPTER SIXTEEN

Keegan downed another shot—his fifth one so far—and set the empty glass on the worn and dented wooden countertop. Just his luck. A city of over a million people, and he'd somehow managed to stumble upon a bar that catered mostly to demons. The waves of energy vibrating off the others buffeted his senses, forming a deafening cacophony that almost drowned out the stench of his own failure.

Almost.

How had he managed to become such a total fuckup? He couldn't do anything right. Not only had he not been able to protect his brothers when they'd needed it most, but now he'd let himself become responsible for yet another person. Just one more on the long list of people he couldn't help.

Someone rubbed against his shoulder. He looked to his side and watched a pretty demoness take a seat on the barstool next to him. She was all lush curves and sly glances, and there was no mistaking the interest in her eyes.

"You look lonely," she said in a sultry voice.

"Yeah?" he replied bitterly, motioning to the bartender for another round.

"What's the matter, baby? Having some problems?"

Keegan chuckled into his empty shot glass. "You could say that."

"Maybe I can help." She leaned in closer to him, near enough that he could see down her blouse. "I've been told I'm very good at solving problems."

The invitation in her voice was all too clear. And he couldn't be less interested. While he might have found her alluring once, right now all he could think about were laughing green eyes and hair the color of honey.

"I have a place down the street from here," the demoness continued, fluttering her lashes as she ran a teasing finger down his arm. "We could go grab a drink there, and you can tell me all about it."

Her touch awakened a glimmer of interest in Keegan's cock. After yesterday's close call, that wasn't too hard to do. He ached to get off, to be buried inside warm, willing flesh.

He considered her offer for all of half a second. While going home with her would certainly solve a lot of his problems, he couldn't bring himself to do it. Not when he'd be imagining it was someone else the entire time.

Shit. What had he been thinking yesterday? He'd almost made love to Brynn. Worse, he still wanted to, even though he knew it couldn't happen.

"This is ridiculous," he muttered.

The demoness's eyes widened and she sat back with a look of affront on her face. "What?"

"Sorry, uh...forgot I have to go somewhere."

He ignored her angry sputter and threw some cash onto the

counter. If his time with Brynn was limited, he wouldn't waste it here. Who knew what would happen tomorrow? Tonight, he was going to take her out. Let her have some fun. After all, it was the least he could do.

Maybe it wasn't the best idea, given he was halfway drunk and didn't know how he'd keep his hands off her, but right now he didn't care. He needed to see her.

℠℟℠

Keegan had been gone since she'd woken this morning. Brynn had tried convincing Ronin to tell her where he'd disappeared to, but he wouldn't budge. In fact, he hadn't left her alone all day, other than when she went into the bathroom. He sat next to her the entire time, plugging away on his laptop.

Right now, he was on the phone with Taeg.

"Yeah, he's still gone." Ronin aimed a sidelong glance at Brynn before he stood and turned to face away from her. "I'm thinking we should just start in the necropolis. It seems the most likely place… Yeah, well, it doesn't look like we're going to get much help."

Ronin sighed and began pacing as he listened to whatever Taeg was saying. "Maybe I should fly in to help. What about Dagan? You should make him do something."

Brynn gave up trying to watch television. She clicked it off and walked to the sliding glass door that led to the balcony. Even from inside, she spotted the heavy crowds on the street.

"What? What do you mean, he hasn't come back yet?" Ronin said. "Damn it, Taeg, we're on a mission here, and it's not to see how many chicks we can bang."

Her cheeks flushed at his crude language, but she didn't

BLOOD OF THE DEMON

turn around. Maybe he'd think the sights occupied her and he'd keep talking. Maybe she'd find out where Keegan was.

"I don't know, but we need to—"

Ronin broke off at the sound of the door to their suite opening.

Brynn whirled to see Keegan striding in, a grim look on his face. The heavy weight in her chest eased a fraction. "Keegan."

"Hey, Keegan just walked in," Ronin said into the phone. "Yeah, I'll call you back later."

"Everything okay?" Keegan said, stopping in front of her. Something about his voice sounded off. Sad.

Brynn nodded. "I'm fine."

Ronin dropped his cell phone on the table and stood next to Keegan. "How did it go?"

"We'll talk later." After a moment's pause, Keegan added, "What about you? Any discoveries? Anything on Taeg's end?"

"Nothing new," Ronin said grimly.

Keegan nodded and turned to Brynn. "Want to go out for a while?"

She hadn't expected that, but she wasn't about to turn it down.

"I'd love to." She snatched up her coat and slipped it on before he could change his mind.

"I'll go, too." Ronin headed for his jacket, but Keegan stopped him with a shake of his head.

"You stay here and keep working."

For a second, Ronin looked like he would argue. But as if he and Keegan shared some sort of silent agreement, he merely nodded.

Brynn followed Keegan outside their suite and to the elevator. She waited until they headed down to start questioning him. "Where did you go?"

"I went to see the Council."

"Really? In New Orleans?"

He chuckled at her obvious confusion, a fraction more relaxed for the first time since he'd returned. "The Council isn't really anywhere. It convenes on a plane between dimensions."

Between dimensions. There he went, astounding her again. "So how do you meet with them?"

"Through an inter-dimensional portal. There's one in every major city. It can take you from one world to another, or it can bring you to the Council's plane."

Why did she still expect a "gotcha" somewhere after the things he said? But it was quite clear he wasn't toying with her. This was real. "Oh, God. This is crazy."

His smile was sympathetic. "Too much?"

She paused for a long moment, then shook her head. "No, I want to know. How does it work? Can anyone use it? Do people stumble into it by mistake?"

Keegan draped his arm around her back and led her through the lobby, out into the chilly air of the street. "No, but you need clearance from the Council. It's invisible, but it emits a repellant force that steers most people away."

"Wait a second. If there's a portal in every major city, how come we couldn't just use that to get here instead of flying?"

"Traffic control," he said, straight-faced.

"Are…are you shitting me?"

"No." He uttered a short laugh. "The Council would never have time for anything else if it had to monitor use of its portals within dimensions. So all travel within any given world has to be done according to that world's means."

"Even when you're trying to catch a sadistic madman

who's in danger of taking over an entire world?"

"I never said the Council didn't have a twisted sense of logic."

Apparently, that couldn't be more true. "What did you talk to them about?"

"I asked for some help digging for the book in Memphis."

"And?"

"They blew me off." Though the words were said in a casual tone, she got a sense of just how pissed he was.

"Why would they do that?"

"Stupidity. Politics." Keegan shrugged. "Whatever the reason, it appears we'll need to solve this problem ourselves."

That was crazy. If he wasn't going to be angry, then she'd do it for him. "That's ridiculous. Why bother sending you here to guard me at all? Why not just have me killed?"

Keegan averted his eyes, and her stomach did a panicked flop. She froze in place so abruptly that he kept walking, and she lurched when his arm on her back pushed her forward. "Wait. You *were* sent here to kill me, weren't you?"

He stopped and turned to face her, two bright spots of color appearing on his cheeks. "If I had been, you'd be dead already, wouldn't you?"

Well, he had a point there. He was far stronger and quicker than she was, and her number one defense mechanism didn't even work on him. Still, something about this made her very uncomfortable.

"I suppose you're right," she finally said.

Keegan gave her a curt nod, then led her toward a bar advertising hurricanes, New Orleans's classic rum punch. "Come on. A drink should warm you up a bit."

Three hurricanes later, Brynn definitely felt warmer,

even though night had already fallen. The citrus punch was deceptively mellow-tasting. She was also well on her way to becoming shitfaced.

Somehow they ended up migrating to one of the countless night parades, and to her surprise, even Keegan seemed to enjoy it. She stood on her tiptoes to speak into his ear. "Guess they don't have anything like this where you come from, huh?"

"Like this?" He glanced toward several women who stood nearby, baring their breasts as a float sailed by. His gaze stuck there for a long moment before flashing back to her. "No, not quite."

Brynn laughed and shook her head. Keegan might be a demon, but in many respects, he was still a typical male.

Crowds of people swarmed around them, adding to the street's pulsing energy. Even though they kept getting jostled around, she didn't feel unsafe. No doubt it had everything to do with the demon standing next to her. Practically speaking, that blew her whole demon assassin theory right out of the water.

"Hey, babe." A drunken college-age kid sidled up to her, holding up a few strings of beads. "Show me your tits, and I'll give you some beads."

"Fuck off," Keegan said, shoving the kid to the side.

"Hey," he protested. But then he sized up Keegan—who towered at least an entire head taller—and must have realized he wasn't *that* drunk.

"Thanks." Brynn gave him an appreciative smile and he grinned back before tugging her in front of him. He wrapped his arms around her and suddenly, she wasn't at all cold anymore. Not when she had her own personal furnace, heating her in more ways than one. Her heart gave a little thump in her chest before resuming at a staccato beat that warmed her blood and flushed her cheeks. Despite all the craziness of the past few days, it almost seemed worth it to have this one moment in time.

With a sudden, blinding intensity, she realized she'd begun to fall for Keegan. Hard.

If anyone had told her last week that she'd be falling for a demon, she would have laughed him or her all the way to the insane asylum. But now that it was happening, it felt right. Destined, even. Demon or not, he was more like her than anyone she'd ever met. He understood what it was like to be different. He knew what she could do, and he didn't care.

She held him tightly against her, and settled in to watch more of the parade. Concentrating wasn't easy, though, with Keegan pressed to her back. Having him so close turned her on in ways she couldn't even explain. And if she wasn't mistaken by the hardness she felt at her back, he felt the same way.

The parade ended after what seemed like hours. Keegan grabbed her hand and gently tugged her along. "Come on, we'd better head back."

They walked a few blocks before she stopped him. "Wait." She didn't want to have this conversation with Ronin in the next room.

"What's wrong?"

Sliding her hands in her pockets to calm her sudden shivers, she moved close enough that he could easily hear her. "We need to talk. About yesterday."

Keegan adopted a disgruntled expression and leaned against the wall, closing his eyes. "Brynn…"

"Don't blow me off again." She took a deep breath, as if that would help calm her nerves. It didn't. "We need to talk about what happened."

He opened his eyes and shook his head. "We lost control. That's all that happened. Situations like this...life and death... they tend to work up your emotions—"

"Oh, come on. You're not going to tell me that none of what happened was real, are you? Because I know what *I* felt, and it was most definitely real."

"It's not. Think about all you've been through these last few days. It's natural that you would—"

"That's bullshit, and you know it."

"Brynn..."

She inched even closer, so close that Keegan's heat penetrated her coat, and lifted a hand to his cheek. "I'm being chased by a sadistic madman who wants me just because of who I'm apparently related to. You're doing a great job of protecting me, but who knows what the future holds? For all I know, I may very well be dead tomorrow. Is it wrong for me to want a little something good in my life right now?"

He pressed his cheek deeper into her palm, his expression softening, though he didn't respond.

"I like you," she continued, because now that she'd started, she might as well get it all out. "And it must be obvious that I want you. No complications. No strings. What's wrong with that?"

Keegan inhaled, his eyes glazing over with a hint of lust she didn't want him to contain. "Damn it, you don't know what you're asking."

"I know *exactly* what I'm asking."

"You..." His eyes narrowed into slits while his jaw clenched in an obvious battle for self-control. For a moment she thought he would pull away. But then, with a muffled curse, he reached for her.

Yes.

Grabbing her waist, he hauled her to him, crushing his lips to hers, heating her from the inside out. She threw her arms around his neck, unable to stop herself from undulating against him. Keegan severed contact, then led her into a little alleyway between two buildings a few feet away. It was damp and dark and smelled like piss, but she didn't care about that right now. At least it was empty.

He pushed her back against the wall and kissed her again.

"I want to *feel* you," she whispered, uncaring how brazen she acted right now. She wanted him and she wasn't afraid to say it.

Sucking in his breath, he unzipped his jacket and pulled it open. With deft fingers, he unbuttoned her heavy coat and pulled that open, too. Stinging cold whipped through the air, buffeting her body. But then he moved closer and pulled the ends of her coat around his sides. It acted as the perfect shield.

"This is wrong," he rasped, skewering her with the intensity of his gaze. If his eyes hadn't told her he wanted her, the hardness of his arousal pressing against her would have.

"No." She shook her head in denial. If he stopped now, she'd kill him.

"It is," he insisted, even as he hungrily ran his gaze over the upper swell of her breasts. His voice sounded tortured and resigned, all in one. "But I still want more."

Lowering his lips to hers, he slid his warm hands under her sweater and up to her breasts, where he cupped them over her bra. He slipped his thumbs underneath the fabric and rubbed them across her nipples, and his rock-hard erection burned a hole where it pressed against her hip.

"You feel so good," she confessed. She pushed her hands underneath his shirt, warming them on his hot flesh. Like silk over steel. She couldn't get enough.

"Brynn." He breathed her name like it was a prayer. Like she was his salvation. He tugged her tight jeans open and tugged them down until they were low enough to slide his fingers inside her panties. His nostrils flared as he inhaled. "Already so wet."

He found her clitoris and used the tip of his index finger to rub against it in a way that made her immediately squirm and pant for breath. She moved her hands to the fly of his jeans and clumsily unzipped them, dropping them low to free his erection. He was so hot and hard in her hands, and merely looking at him made her mouth water.

He groaned as she moved her hands up and down on him. She slid lower to hold his testicles, as his fingers slid between her slickened folds. He thrust one of them inside her. Unable to help herself, she cried out, and he bent his head to swallow the sound.

His fingers moved in and out of her, each upward thrust bringing her to her toes. She let loose a throaty moan and, after one final thrust, came apart in his arms. Arching her back, she tightened her fist around his arousal and sucked his tongue into her mouth. Lord, she longed to be closer to him, as close as two people could get.

He held her tightly as she rode out her climax. Her legs shook so badly she wondered if they'd ever support her again. Keegan made her feel so incredible. So invincible. She wanted to make him feel like that, too.

Her breath came out in harsh pants as she worked him once again, and he'd become so rigid he pulsed in her hand.

Breaking their kiss, he buried his face in her hair. "If you don't stop, I'm gonna come."

"I want you to come," she whispered, cupping and squeezing his testicles. Right now, she wanted it more than anything.

With a low cry, he gave in, jerking his hips as he climaxed into her hands. She moaned and licked her lips. Even though she'd already come, the simple act of getting Keegan off made her hot all over again. She tightened her grip, continuing to slide up and down while he shook with the aftermath of his orgasm.

Finally, he lifted his head to give her another deep, open-mouthed kiss.

"Next time you come," she confessed to him huskily, "I want to taste it."

He hissed and shuddered, his eyes glazed with desire. "I—"

They started as a dry voice with a New Orleans accent drawled, "Excuse me, sir, madam…"

Brynn tipped her head toward the figure standing less than ten feet away, at the entrance to the alley. Oh great. A police officer.

Thankfully, her long coat shielded much of their bodies. Keegan drew it tighter around him as he addressed the cop. "Good evening, officer."

"I'm sure it is," the officer said, his tone amused. "While I understand and appreciate how much you may be *overcome* with the joy of these festivities, you need to take it back to your hotel room, okay?"

"Sorry, officer," Keegan choked out. "We'll be gone in just a moment."

"You do that now."

Brynn hid her flaming face in Keegan's chest while the

chuckling police officer turned and walked away. "Well, that was just a little embarrassing."

"At least we were wearing most of our clothes," he said. He rifled in the pocket of his jacket and pulled out a napkin, then used it to wipe her hands clean before tossing it and zipping up his jeans.

She'd been so into him that she'd forgotten about their surroundings. Worse, she wasn't the least bit sorry about it. Even though it had happened in a foul-smelling alley, it *still* counted as one of the best sexual experiences of her life.

Keegan smiled, then took her hand and led her out of the alley. They took a few steps before he put his arm around her and pulled her closer to him. "Come on, we'd better get back."

She couldn't help but be happy. She'd never felt closer to anyone than she did to him right now. And the fact that he was one of the most gorgeous men she'd ever met only made it better.

He's mine. For now, at least, he's all mine.

She brushed aside that little part of her that insisted on pointing out that he wasn't a man at all, but a demon. What did that matter?

"Will you come to my room later? After Ronin is asleep?" Asking it that way made her feel like a schoolgirl with her first crush. It was embarrassing and exhilarating, all at once.

He hesitated a moment, but then he gave her a soft nod.

Her nerves calmed. Maybe, just this once, she'd get what she wanted.

As she'd half expected, Ronin waited up for them back at the hotel suite. He seemed frazzled, like maybe he'd patrolled the suite the whole time they'd been gone. Upon seeing them, he stopped and scowled. "Where the hell have you guys been?"

"Out walking around." Keegan frowned. "What's wrong?"

"Taeg and I have both tried calling you, man."

Keegan reached into his jacket and retrieved his cell phone. "Battery's dead. What's up?"

Ronin sighed. "Dagan's missing. It's been almost a day since Taeg last saw him."

The stony silence in the room was almost deafening.

"Could he maybe be with a woman?" Brynn asked. "I overheard you saying he does that a lot."

"No," Ronin said, shaking his head, his eyes grim. "He would never be gone this long."

Keegan frowned at the ground, voicing their general fear. "It's possible that Mammon got to him."

Swearing, Ronin strode over to the nearest wall and punched it. As he pulled his hand out of the drywall, his phone rang.

"It's Taeg," he said before answering. "Hello? Yeah, they just got back… You did? Man, I was so worried."

"What is it?" Keegan said, striding forward to take the phone from Ronin.

"Wait." Ronin lifted a hand to stop Keegan and sidled away before he could grab it. "Hold on, Taeg." He looked up at Keegan. "He found Dagan. He's fine. He got himself into a bit of a mess with a woman."

"That fucker," Keegan snarled.

"What's that?" Ronin said, turning his attention back to the phone. "Yeah?"

He gave Brynn and Keegan a funny look, then moved away again before continuing in a flat tone. "Yeah, I understand. Yeah I know…I know, man. Okay, that's a plan. All right, I'll do that."

"What is it?" Keegan said as Ronin hung up.

"Nothing. Just Dagan and his bullshit." Avoiding Keegan's glare, he forced a laugh. "Taeg promised him a real beating if he ever pulls something like that again."

"Ronin," Keegan said in a warning tone, slowly backing up, "quit messing with me. What's going on?"

Ronin took a deep breath. "I—"

He cut off abruptly, cocking his head to the side. "Do you feel that?"

Keegan froze. He turned to Brynn, his eyes wide. *"Shit."*

Her breath hitched as she took in his fear. A sudden burst of adrenaline pumped through her veins, skyrocketing the beat of her heart. If he, of all people, was frightened, then it couldn't be good.

"What is it?" she gasped.

"Demons," he said grimly.

"A whole shitload of them," Ronin added. "And they're approaching fast."

Brynn had time to do no more than take a deep swallow before Keegan grabbed her hand and rushed them toward the door.

CHAPTER SEVENTEEN

Keegan raced Brynn toward the elevators, Ronin only steps behind. About halfway there, the elevator doors opened and a small army exited. The acrid stench of boarg demons assaulted his senses. Why did they always smell like they'd rolled in their own piss?

"Shit."

"The stairs are back this way," Ronin called.

Keegan spun Brynn around to follow his brother, tugging on her arm to move her faster as they hastened toward the stairwell. Seventeen floors were a lot of stairs to take with an army of demons at their backs. But as it turned out, they didn't make it down one flight before they ran into another group of demons heading up the stairs toward them.

Ronin halted, staring down at them as if debating whether or not to try and fight his way through anyway. "Son of a bitch."

Any other time Keegan would have said, "Hell, yeah," but he counted at least ten of them, more than he and Ronin could take on without risk of injury. That wasn't an option now, not when they had Brynn to consider.

"The roof," he ordered, doing an about-face and dragging Brynn up the stairs. They'd just reached the top of the landing leading out to the roof when the first group of demons converged with the second, barreling up after them.

Keegan tried to open the door, but it was locked. He backed up and hurled his body forward, throwing his shoulder against it and easily busting the lock. Closing his hand around Brynn's, he all but carried her into the frigid night air.

He froze halfway between the door and the edge of the roof. Brynn let out a harsh gasp beside him but was otherwise silent. The night was dark, but enough artificial light drifted up from the street lamps that the three of them saw what was on the roof—four winged figures. They were hideous, with their leathery gray flesh; webbed, bat-like wings; backward-bending legs; and hooves where their feet should be. Compounded with their seven-foot height and wide, muscular bodies, they were a menacing sight.

"Guess Mammon anticipated us heading up here," Ronin said.

Keegan nodded. Of course he had.

"What are they?" Brynn whispered, her voice raspy with fear.

"Rayamara demons."

"They...*fly*?" she choked out.

"They fly," Ronin said.

They were also very rare, but Mammon had somehow managed to not only locate, but retain, a small number of them. They surrounded the roof, and a small contingent of demons now gathered at his back. They were cornered.

Just my luck.

Keegan whirled to face the demons at his back. Scattered across the roof, they slowly stalked forward with devilish smirks on their faces.

"What now?" Brynn cried.

"Make a getaway," Ronin said. "I'll hold 'em off."

"Getaway?" Brynn squeaked. "How can we possibly go? There's nowhere *to* go from here."

"No," Keegan said to Ronin. "I'm not leaving you."

"There's too many to fight," Ronin said.

His brother was right. They were surrounded by at least fifteen demons.

"Even if you *could* hold all of them off, I can't just abandon you," Keegan said.

"Can you...*you know*?" Ronin asked him.

Brynn turned to look at Keegan sharply. "Can you what?"

He ignored her. Now wasn't the time to answer questions. "It's never come to me at will before, only by accident."

That was the rub of his most powerful ability. It had a mind of its own.

"What are you talking about?" Brynn asked.

Ronin ignored Brynn, too. He gave Keegan a look fraught with meaning, reaching out to clasp his shoulder. "Then what choice do you have, man?"

Keegan fought back the sudden stinging behind his eyes. His brother would gladly give himself up for him, for their cause. But he wasn't about to abandon Ronin.

"Come, now," one of the demons said, stepping apart from the rest of the phalanx. "This is such a touching little family gathering. Why the gloomy faces?"

"Fuck you," Keegan snarled.

"Aw, come on." The demon laughed. "Why treat me that

way? After all, I'm almost family, too, considering I'm here on behalf of your father."

"Your…father?" Brynn cried. She wrenched her hand out of his and turned to plaster him with a confused, semi-accusing glare.

"Later, Brynn," Keegan said.

The demon turned his attention to Brynn with an evil grin on his face. "You're almost family, too, pretty girl, after all the help you've been. By the way, Daddy says thank you for helping him find you."

"Don't you look at her," Keegan said. But then the meaning of the demon's words hit him. "What?"

He turned to Brynn, but she stared at him with wide, confused eyes. "I don't know what he's—"

"Oh, she really doesn't know," the demon interrupted with a sinister laugh. "That's what makes it so great. I only found out about it myself just now, when your father told me."

What the fuck was he talking about? Keegan was sure the confusion on his face read as loud as Brynn's.

"I'll tell you what." The demon inclined his head and gave Keegan an appraising once-over. "I'll let you fight me one-on-one. If you win, I'll let you leave."

One of the other demons hissed and edged forward. "But Vhen, the boss said to—"

"Shut up," Vhen roared. "I'm the boss here."

The protester stepped away without another word. Leave it to demons to do whatever the hell they wanted, regardless of their orders.

"What about the heir?" Keegan asked, though he didn't believe for one second Vhen would let him leave if he won.

"She stays." Without further warning, he dropped his

glamour, growing taller and wider, taking his true demon form. Another rayamara demon.

Vhen lunged toward Keegan. Pushing Brynn toward Ronin, Keegan leapt for the demon, meeting him halfway. His fist connected with Vhen's face even as he fell backward, the larger demon landing on top of him. The other demons shifted about, as if wondering what to do, given the unexpected turn of events. But in the end, they all just stood there, watching the scene unfold.

Vhen lifted off him and slammed one of his clawed hands into Keegan's face, tearing large gouges into his flesh.

"Keegan," Brynn screamed.

He grabbed the demon's wrist before the creature could slam his hand down. That familiar twinge of pain told him his flesh was already repairing itself. He shoved Vhen and the demon flew, which gave him enough time to get off the ground before Vhen sprinted back for more.

Keegan ducked under one of Vhen's massive wings as it lashed out at him. He whirled around and delivered a roundhouse kick to his spine. Vhen fell hard on his knees, but used his wings to catapult himself into the air. Faster than Keegan could begin to process, Vhen landed behind him, grabbing him by the throat in a brutal chokehold. Vhen wrapped his other hand around Keegan's throat, his claws digging in deep and cutting off his air supply.

"No," Brynn yelled. "Ronin, help him."

Ronin shushed her while Keegan struggled not to fall to his knees. His vision blurred, the tiny black dots lining his sight warning him he was about to pass out if he didn't do something *now*. One of Vhen's wings wrapped around him, enveloping him like a lover's caress.

Perfect. Keegan knew all too well the weaknesses of that particular appendage. It was Vhen's mistake not to have thought about that. He seized the demon's wing and yanked hard, rending the wing almost in two.

Vhen screamed, releasing Keegan's throat and retreating in agony. Keegan spun to face Vhen, sputtering for breath as his throat healed itself. Even the process of healing was pure torture.

"What are you waiting for, idiots?" Vhen said to the demons huddled along the roof while he nursed his damaged wing. "Kill them. Get the girl."

Keegan inched toward the edge of the roof, stopping next to Brynn. She found his hand and squeezed tightly, her breath wheezing out in frantic, ragged exhales that clouded the frigid air. Terrified as she was, she stood tall as she followed him.

Sudden fury coursed through his veins, boiling his blood. Damn these demons for doing this to her. Damn Mammon for using a clueless woman as a pawn in his sick quest for power. It wasn't fair. Not to her, nor to him and his brothers.

Rage built in his chest, heating his very core until he became so hot he could have been made entirely of fire. Steam escaped his pores, fogging the air.

Oh shit. It was happening.

Ronin flicked his gaze toward him, eyes widening. "Is it… Are you doing it?"

Keegan was too steamed to respond. Literally. It built up like a furnace until there was only one way to release it.

"Duck," Ronin yelled to Brynn, grabbing her hand and yanking her down to the rooftop.

Keegan whirled to face the winged demons guarding the edge of the roof, feeling his eyes blaze in his sockets.

He opened his mouth and breathed out, but it wasn't air that escaped. Instead, a heavy stream of fire coursed from his lungs, spraying the area in front of him.

The winged demons stopped fighting, mouths open in shock, as the fire spread over them, incinerating their flesh quicker than they could react. They fell backward into the air, their bodies already nothing more than blazing bones. By the time they landed on the ground below, they would probably be no more than powder.

Brynn's harsh scream abruptly cut off. But he couldn't worry about her right now. Not when demons still lined the roof and his fury boiled over inside of him. He breathed again, his flames spreading over the demons who'd scattered across the rooftop. Within seconds, their burning bodies fell to the ground, a few of them lucid enough to utter agonizing screeches before their lungs dissolved to ash.

Finally, there was nothing but smoking piles of dust and the putrid stench of charred flesh.

He was out of juice. The fire receded, sliding down his throat and contracting into a ball of liquid heat somewhere in his chest. His mother's legacy, a gift he'd never been able to control.

Exhaustion spread over his body, making his knees go weak.

"Brynn," he practically choked. She'd seen what he could do, what lived inside him. Would she shriek and cower in terror? Would she run from him now that she'd seen his dark power?

Dreading her reaction, he turned to face her. But she wasn't cowering in fear. Rather, she knelt, with Ronin's arms still wrapped around her, and gazed up at him, a mix of awe and fascination covering her face. There wasn't a glimmer of fear or revulsion anywhere.

She wasn't afraid of him.

Keegan's heart did a lazy spin inside his chest.

Ronin slowly stood, pulling Brynn with him. "That was a close one. You really waited until the last second there."

"You know I have no control over it," Keegan said.

"What *was* that?" Brynn asked.

Keegan took a breath. "I—"

He cut off as the door leading onto the roof cracked open and spun around to face it. It was Taeg, who panted as if he'd raced all the way up here. Seeing them, he bent over, nursing a stitch in his side.

Keegan's momentary relief morphed into suspicion. "What are you doing here?"

"I…" Taeg straightened, still breathing heavily. "I flashed to your suite, caught the stench of demons in the hallway, and followed the residual energy up here. Are you all okay?"

"Yeah," Ronin said. "Keegan did his fire-breathing routine and fried them all to a crisp."

"No shit?" Taeg said, impressed. "Good timing, huh, bro? Sorry I missed that."

"What are you doing here?" Keegan repeated. He focused in on Ronin, whose face was set as grim as a funeral director's.

But then it all clicked into place: Ronin's terse conversation with Taeg, the demons' attack, and Taeg materializing here on the roof.

No. Oh, fuck, no.

Mammon had found the book.

Which meant Brynn had to die.

No. He gasped for air, only to find he couldn't take enough in. Not Brynn.

All these years of blind faith and duty to the Council. All

his admonitions to his brothers that they must do what was right, at all costs. And now, because of fate, because of his father, he was supposed to kill the one woman he'd ever had real feelings for.

It wasn't fair. And, even if it meant saving the world, it wasn't *right*.

No. He wouldn't do it.

They could defeat Mammon another way. Somehow.

"Listen," Taeg said, moving deliberately, "we need to talk about what—"

Faster than anyone could blink, Keegan sucker-punched Ronin. Hard. His nose shattered into pieces with a loud *crack*. He crumpled to the ground, knocked out cold.

"Keegan," Brynn cried in a mixture of shock and censure. She dropped to the ground beside Ronin, grasping his shoulder as she peered into his battered face.

Yeah, that was an asshole thing to do, but Ronin would heal. By the time he woke up, he'd probably have no more than a slight headache. Brynn, however, would suffer far worse than that if Ronin and Taeg succeeded in their mission.

Taeg dematerialized, and a fraction of a second later he reappeared right in front of Keegan. Taeg's fist caught Keegan's jaw. "You prick. Why did you do that?"

"You know why." He grabbed Taeg's shoulders and held on tight. There was no way he would let go.

Taeg grabbed onto Keegan's shoulders in a similar lock, his face red with fury. "Come on, you dickweed. We warned you over and over."

"I know," Keegan yelled. "I can't help it. She's innocent."

"Mammon has the book," Taeg said. "Innocent or not, she's the key to the fucking apocalypse. And if that happens, a lot more innocents will die."

"She shouldn't die because of something she has no control over."

"That's our fucking *job*, man."

"I—" Anything else Keegan might have said died with Brynn's loud gasp. Keegan pushed Taeg around so he could see Brynn, who'd risen to her feet.

"I knew it," she whispered, her eyes wide. "I knew that had to be it, but I didn't want to believe it. My gut told me you wouldn't do such a thing."

"I…I can't," Keegan ground out. "I can't do it, okay?"

"You dick," Taeg muttered, shoving him back about ten feet. They continued to wrestle. "You have to do it. We have no choice."

Keegan shook his head. "No, Taeg, it's not right. Listen, we can find another way to stop Mammon. We have to."

Taeg stopped struggling long enough to look at Keegan, a compassionate expression on his face. "We can't. It's too great a risk."

"You said it yourself: Things go better when we work together," he said. "We can find a better way…"

"There is no other way, brother. I'm sorry. Really I am."

Keegan's stomach rolled and his head pounded like it had been hit with a hammer. He contemplated his choices, pissed there were so damn few of them.

He would have given anything—even his life—not to have to do this. But he had to. He had no choice.

"You're right," Keegan said to Taeg. He stilled and slightly relaxed his grip.

Taeg threw him a look of utter relief and started to do the same.

"You're right, Taeg," Keegan repeated. "And I'm sorry, too."

Before Taeg could react, he shoved his head forward, ramming his forehead against Taeg's jaw with a deafening *crack*.

"Ow." Taeg grabbed his jaw, lobbing a shocked glance at Keegan before dropping to his knees like a rag doll.

Keegan raced to Brynn, who'd crept backward toward the exit during their struggle. Now she hovered there, as if debating what to do. He stopped just a few feet in front of her. "Brynn."

She stared at him uncertainly. Then, after what seemed like a lifetime but in reality was no more than a second or two, she gave him a slow and hesitant nod.

His heart gave a pained twinge. Trust shone in her eyes, telling him she believed in him, even if he didn't believe in himself.

He wouldn't let her down.

"Take my hand."

Brynn hesitated for only a moment before placing her hand in his.

He gave her a soft smile. "You trust me, right?"

She nodded. "Yes."

"Then hold on tight."

He pulled her close, and she circled her arms around his neck. *Here goes nothing.*

With a practiced flick of his shoulders, his leathery red appendages tore through the fabric of his T-shirt and jacket. They flapped hard, generating heat as they sliced through the air.

"Oh my...God," Brynn said. Her eyes grew wide as her gaze skipped from his face to his large wings. With a gentle shove, he took off into the air.

"Keegan," Taeg yelled below. "Keeg, come back. Please,

bro."

Brynn wrapped her legs around his waist, holding on tight. An expression of pure wonder lined her face. "What *are* you?"

"Brynn, I didn't know how to tell you before," he said. "I'm only half demon."

"And the other half?" she asked.

"The other half…is dragon."

CHAPTER EIGHTEEN

Back at the hotel suite, Taeg clasped his hands to the back of his neck while he paced the length of Ronin's bedroom. He'd passed the hour since Keegan had fled alternating between fury and dread. Try as he might, he couldn't see a happy ending in this for his big brother, and that just about killed him. They were really up shit creek this time.

"Where the hell could they be?"

"Who knows?" Ronin wearily replied from inside the closet, where he packed up their meager belongings.

Taeg touched his hand to the jaw Keegan had recently broken. It was already fully healed, thanks to Ronin. "I can't believe this is happening."

"Can't you? We both saw it coming. We just didn't know how to stop it."

He let out his breath in one long rush. "Yeah. Yeah, you're right. Now we're seriously *fucked.*"

"True," Ronin muttered.

"Aw, devil's balls." Taeg stomped over to one of the beds

and kicked the wooden footboard. It shattered into pieces, the mattress thumping to the ground.

Ronin stepped outside the closet and eyed the mess he'd made. "The Council is going to blow its stack when it gets the bill for this place."

"Screw them." Taeg swiveled around to confront Ronin. "Why didn't you do it, man? Why didn't you kill her when you had the chance?"

Ronin looked him straight in the eye. "I couldn't. You knew I wouldn't be able to. That's why you came."

"Damn it." Taeg's anger at Ronin melted away as quickly as it had come. He leaned back onto the dresser behind him. "None of us should have had to. It was a sucker's mission from the very start, one the Council knew we wouldn't turn down, thanks to our father."

"They never gave us the resources we needed to fight him," Ronin pointed out.

Taeg let out a deep sigh. "It just doesn't make sense."

"Yeah. So what now?"

"Now?" Taeg said. "Now we go out and get wasted. Drink ourselves into oblivion. Party down until the fucking apocalypse."

Ronin lifted a brow. "No, really."

What choice did they have? They couldn't abandon Keegan. Would *never* do that. Which left only one option.

"Now, little brother, we come up with another game plan."

❧❧❧

Brynn couldn't stop staring. It was incredibly rude, but she couldn't help herself.

"Half dragon," she said.

Keegan threw her a smile from the driver's seat of the car he'd stolen after they touched down on the outskirts of New Orleans. "Dragon-shifter, to be exact."

"Dragon-shifter? What does that mean?"

"Well, one of the other dimensions contains a shifter world. It's called Enevora. Everyone on that planet can shift forms, from humanoid to animal—wolf, jaguar, dragon, you name it."

Brynn sat up straight in her seat. "Wait—there are all types of shifters there? What about monkeys? Mice? *Insects*?"

Keegan chuckled. "You name it, there's a shifter for it. Even some animals you've never heard of. That's not all, either. There are gargoyles, gremlins, trolls."

"All on the same planet?"

He nodded. "There's also a water dimension with mermaids, harpies, and sirens."

Mermaids? How many times as a child had she dreamed of being one, and now she learned that they actually existed?

"Even the immortal beings your world has mistaken for Greek gods exist, on a world called Olympus," he continued. "They aren't quite all-powerful, as is written into the mythology, but they do have the ability to control the weather, death, and regeneration, and they can only be killed by beheading."

"Whoa. Will you ever stop surprising me?"

"Not today." He tapped his fingers along the steering wheel in a gesture that belied his anxiety. "I'm sorry I didn't tell you sooner. I just didn't know how."

"I don't blame you." Still, considering that Brynn knew about his demon heritage, how did one bring up the topic of dragons? Even more amazing was that she fully accepted it, without any resistance. Well, okay, not *too* much. After everything she'd seen the past few days, dragons were just one more crazy thing to add to the list of weird. Not only that, but she had to admit that in a strange way, it sort of turned her on. The man could fly. He was like her very own Superman.

"Can you actually morph into a dragon?"

He shook his head. "Full shifters can. But since I'm a half breed, I only have a few abilities. I can partially shift, creating wings, which you saw."

Yeah, those were weird. Leathery red appendages that probably spanned twice as wide as he was tall. But they weren't like the rayamara demons' wings, not by any means. They were beautiful, in their own way. Majestic.

"That was amazing," she confessed, "to soar in the air, above the city. It was so…exhilarating."

"Some might find it frightening."

"Not me." When the corners of his mouth ticked up, she asked, "What other abilities do you have from your dragon heritage?"

"My ability to heal."

Brynn lifted a brow. "So that's not a demon trait, but a dragon one?"

"What I told you about demons is true. We do have preternatural strength and speed, and the ability to heal quickly. But it's nothing compared to what dragons can do. Dragon blood heals, and incredibly quickly."

"You're pretty much invincible, huh?"

"Oh, I can be killed," Keegan said. "Beheading kills about anyone. And if I were to somehow lose all of my blood, I wouldn't be able to heal myself."

"So vampires are dangerous to you, then," she joked.

"They could be," he answered.

"Wait…what? Vampires exist, too?" She gulped at his patronizing glance. "Okay, let's leave that topic aside. For now. What else can you do?"

Keegan snickered. "I have a slightly enhanced sense of smell, and, well, you already saw the fire-breathing."

"Yeah. Why didn't Mammon anticipate that you would wipe out his men that way?"

"He never knew about it. In fact, it's only happened twice before, and both times by complete accident."

Huh. In that case, they had gotten pretty lucky tonight. But wait…

"Oh, and *Mammon is your father*?" She turned to glare at him. "That one would have been really nice to know."

"It's not very easy to explain. How do you tell someone that your father is a psychopath but still expect them to trust you?"

"Good point," she grudgingly admitted.

Keegan tapped on the steering wheel a little longer before curling one hand into a fist and beating it against the base of the wheel. "How the fuck did Mammon find us? The book?"

"I don't know. That demon said I told him, but I…" She broke off as the dreams of the past several days came back to her in a flash. Shooting up in her seat, she said, "Wait a minute. I've been dreaming about your father."

His expression was baffled. "What?"

"Ever since I had that vision when I touched your talisman. At first, he was just there. But then he started talking to me. I might have…I think I—" She broke off with a loud groan, burying her hands in her face. "In my last dream of him, I mentioned Memphis and New Orleans. Oh crap, have I been communicating with him in my sleep?"

"If he has that ability, it's something I never knew about."

"But...that has to be it, right? I mean, how else could I have led him to us?"

"Don't know." His brows drew together. "I'll look into it, see what I can find out."

Seeing the exhaustion written all over his face reminded her how tired she was. She fought a heavy yawn but ultimately lost the battle. "I want to know about you and your father. Tell me your family history."

"I will. *After* you get some rest."

"But Keegan," she protested.

"I'm serious. You look exhausted. Get some rest while you can. Just...if you dream about Mammon, don't tell him a thing, okay?"

She thought about protesting some more, but her eyelids were growing awfully heavy. Leaning her head back against the seat, she asked, "Where are we going, anyway?"

"Don't know. Somewhere safe. Which reminds me." He reached into his jacket pocket and retrieved his cell phone. He rolled down the window and tossed it out. "Don't want to be tracked."

What he meant was that he didn't want his brothers to find them. Brynn closed her eyes as gut-wrenching guilt washed over her. Keegan had chosen her over his brothers, whom he obviously loved very much.

"I don't regret my decision," he said, as if he could read her thoughts.

"Thanks." She reached across the seat and closed her hand over his.

He flipped it over and laced his fingers with hers.

Here they were, holding hands like high school kids and running away to destinations unknown. It might have been romantic if their lives hadn't been on the line.

Even if Keegan didn't regret it, as far as his brothers were concerned, he'd committed an act of betrayal. He'd gone against his word. For her.

And now they were being hunted, not only by Keegan's father but possibly by his brothers.

Oh, sweet heavens, what were they going to do?

𝕰𝕺𝕮𝕾

After a fast-food stop and a trip to the gas station, where Keegan had bought a cheesy New Orleans Saints sweatshirt to replace his torn jacket and shirt, Brynn had finally fallen asleep. Keegan snuck a peek at her. For the past few hours she'd slept with her head against the window of the car, her neck awkwardly scrunched. She'd probably wake up with one hell of a crick in her neck if she didn't shift position soon.

Amazing how, in the midst of all this, she managed to look so peaceful, with long eyelashes fanning down above her cheeks and her mouth slightly open. The air was scented with the sweet fragrance he'd come to recognize as Brynn, making him hungry for something he couldn't articulate.

Damn it. How was he going to protect her?

He grasped her shoulder and shifted her onto the seat, so that her head fell backward onto the headrest. She didn't even twitch. Her last sleep had come too long ago, back at the New Orleans suite.

Just thinking about New Orleans, and his brothers, made him frown. What were they doing now? How disappointed in him they must be. He'd always impressed upon them the necessity to live up to their obligations, and here he was, fleeing his own.

But if he'd done the wrong thing, then why did it feel so right?

Keegan lifted his hand to Brynn's cheek and caressed it before returning it to the steering wheel.

"Shit," he muttered. What was he going to do? Keep running from place to place, fleeing both Mammon and his brothers?

But what choice did he have if he wanted to save Brynn's life?

He passed an exit sign for Daytona Beach.

Keep driving. That's what he'd do for now. Drive until he couldn't drive anymore. Then rest a bit while he considered their options.

There was only one thing he couldn't do now. One thing he *wouldn't* do.

He wasn't about to give Brynn up.

CHAPTER NINETEEN

The first thing Brynn noticed when she awoke was the glowing green of the dashboard clock. It read 4:34, and from the daylight streaming in through the car window it was clearly afternoon. She'd slept for well over ten hours. She lifted her head to look around. It didn't look like they were even in the same country anymore. The narrow highway they drove on was bound by sparkling blue waters on either side.

"Where are we?"

"Just outside of Marathon, in the Florida Keys," Keegan said. "We're about to stop. Any weird dreams?"

"No dreams at all." Thank God for that. She must have been more exhausted than she'd realized.

True to his word, when they pulled into the small town, he stopped at a restaurant, where they enjoyed a long, leisurely lunch that almost made Brynn feel like she was on vacation. Then he drove to a state park and stopped the car.

"Are we…camping?" she asked as she followed him out of the car.

"Not exactly." He led her toward the water, where a few other couples walked along the beach. As he stared out at the calm ocean, a wistful expression crossed his face. "I've always wanted to see this."

Brynn placed her hand in his. "Guess there isn't anything like this in your world, huh?"

"No." Keegan shook his head, a ghost of a smile on his face. "Not even close."

The weather was perfect, warm even, in her winter clothes. The aquamarine waters of the ocean lapped gently against the shore. There wasn't a more romantic sight. If only she could enjoy it more. "So, what do we do now?"

"Now we wait."

"Wait?" Brynn blinked. "For what?"

"You'll see."

What they waited for was apparently for people to clear out. As soon as there was no one else around, Keegan wriggled out of his sweater and tucked it into the back of his jeans. Brynn's eyes flicked down to his smooth, muscled chest, marred by nothing other than the dragon talisman dangling around his neck. Her eyes stuck there for a long moment. She couldn't help it. The man deserved to be stared at.

"What are you doing?" she finally asked.

"This." Without another word, his wings grew out of his back. Before she could react, he grinned and snatched her up. Zooming out over the water, he flew low in the sky.

"What if someone sees you?" she choked out. Not that she was complaining. She liked having his arms wrapped around her, no matter the reason.

"They'd probably just think they were seeing things. You'd be amazed at what people can pass off as a trick of the light."

Okaay. "So where are we going?"

"You'll see," he said again.

You'll see turned out to be a tiny private island several miles off Marathon Key. A large two-story house on concrete stilts took up most of the space on the island, with a dock built outside the front and a small boat moored to it.

Keegan slowed down, waves of heat emanating from his wings as he flapped them in broad strokes. He touched down onto a second-floor balcony. A moment later, his wings disappeared and his back appeared normal once again, not even a ridge or groove to mark the spot where his wings had grown.

She finally managed to tear her gaze off him long enough to glance out at the view from the balcony. "Wow, this is amazing."

"Isn't it? I read about it somewhere." Keegan paced the length of the balcony, edging around the small seating area and two deluxe lounge chairs as he took in the sights from all corners. With his chest bare and his sweater tucked into his waistband, he resembled some sort of medieval pirate, set to plunder his next port of call.

"How do you know this place isn't occupied right now?" she asked.

"I have my resources. I was looking into it as a vacation spot on the odd chance the Council granted me one if we stopped Mammon. Owners shouldn't be back for a couple of months. Come on." He grabbed her hand and led her to the French doors, which opened without any difficulty.

"Guess they don't anticipate many break-ins here," Brynn said.

"Or they figure anyone who goes to the trouble of getting here deserves a payday. Let's go look."

The doors opened to a large bedroom with a metal-frame

canopy bed draped in netting. An adjoining bathroom sported a large Jacuzzi tub. They found one other bedroom on this floor with feminine décor, and another adjoining bath. The main floor housed a great room, a half bath, and a kitchen, as well as a wraparound veranda with more sweeping ocean views.

This was heaven. Brynn sighed as she sunk onto the white down cushions of the rattan couch. They were so soft she might have been lounging on a fluffy white cloud. "I could get used to this."

"Don't," Keegan said, his tone grim. "You never know when we'll have to leave."

He was right. Still, except for the insane demon chasing her, it was almost like being on vacation.

"I could use a shower," she said. "Better yet, a long, hot bath."

"Me, too." Keegan sat on one of the matching rattan chairs directly across from the couch and exhaled loudly as he closed his eyes and put his feet up on the coffee table. Somehow, he managed to look enticing, even while clearly exhausted.

When he didn't look as if he would go anywhere, she quietly rose to her feet. The least she could do was give him a few minutes of peace. Especially since just being around him had her hormones in overdrive. Something about zipping through the sky in the arms of a magnificent winged dragon made her long to stay there.

She took the stairs up to the smaller bedroom and snooped in the closet. Whoever the owners were, one of them was a woman close to Brynn's size. She grabbed a silky light-blue robe that hit her at mid-thigh. For one second, she considered using her ability to learn more about the robe's owner. But then, why bother with someone else's memories? Right now she had enough of her own to deal with. She filled the Jacuzzi in the smaller bathroom, added some lavender-scented bath salts, and soaked.

Half demon, half dragon-shifter. What an amazing being Keegan was. She'd thought she had it rough, growing up with abilities. They were nothing compared to what Keegan could do.

How had he managed to grow up into such a good man? Having seen Keegan's father in her visions, she knew how evil he was. Now, knowing that he and Mammon were one and the same, she didn't know how Keegan had made it.

One thing was certain: she was determined to have no more secrets between them.

She crawled out of the tub, tugged on the robe, and searched for Keegan. She found him on the balcony where they'd initially landed, looking out over the water. His hair was wet, and he had only bothered to put on his jeans. The muscles of his bare back rippled with every breath he took.

Good Lord, he was breathtaking.

Even from behind, he was a sight to behold. The way his broad shoulders tapered into a trim waist, the muscular arms, the sharp curve of his backside in his jeans. He might be half demon and half dragon, but he looked all man.

Mine, that selfish inner devil of hers said. That was the part of her that wanted to taste him, to hold him. Maybe even keep him.

She shook herself out of it and moved to stand beside him. "There you are."

He didn't turn her way, but the corners of his mouth lifted. "Just taking in the view."

It was so quiet out here. So peaceful. Not another soul

around. Not for miles.

"What are you thinking?" she asked.

Keegan didn't speak for so long she thought he wouldn't answer. "I'm wondering what my brothers are doing right now."

She slid her hand along the concrete balustrade until it covered his. "Oh, Keegan, I'm sorry."

"Me, too."

"Do you think they're looking for us?"

"I don't know," he responded.

It must be killing him. After everything the four of them had been through, their father had finally managed to tear them apart.

Don't forget your role in this whole thing, Brynn.

Yeah, right. As if she could.

"Tell me about your father," she said.

Keegan sighed, withdrawing his hand from her grasp. "It's hard to talk about."

"I want to know," she insisted.

His features lined with weariness, he turned to face her head-on. "Okay. But you first. I know you've been keeping something from me."

When she threw him a blank look, he clarified. "How did you find out about your ability to drain energy?"

"Oh, that." *Crap.* But hadn't she just vowed there would be no more secrets between them? That worked both ways. Turning so her side pressed into the balustrade, she took a calming breath and met his expectant gaze. "I...I found out about my other gift when I was eleven."

Ordinarily, she pushed these memories into the recesses of her psyche, not wanting to relive anything about that day.

Now, for the first time ever, she was going to talk about it. "I was walking home from school one day when a man drove up in his car and snatched me."

Keegan gave a pained wince and touched her hand. "I'm sorry."

The remembrance of the event inundated her with recollected sights and sounds. The stifling heat of the closed-in space. The utter absence of light. The fear that she would die in this prison. Then, the realization that what was *about* to happen was a million times worse than being locked in a trunk. She swallowed back the pained moan that threatened to burst from her lips. It was all in the past. She had survived, and she was strong enough to tell this story. With Keegan by her side, she might be able to do anything.

"He threw me into his trunk and took me to his house, locked me in the basement."

His jaw dropped and his eyes clouded over with unmistakable anguish. "I had no idea. You must have been terrified when I took you."

She shook her head, driven by the inexplicable urge to reassure him. "No, it wasn't the same thing. I think…somehow I knew you wouldn't hurt me. I sensed that you were a good man." Or maybe she had just grown that much stronger since that horrible event of her youth.

Keegan looked away, guilt written clearly on his face. He didn't believe her words, and it didn't take a genius to determine that he was mentally berating himself for his actions. Knowing what she now knew about him, it broke her heart that he judged himself so harshly. After all the hell he'd endured as a child, he was still a good man.

Brynn forced herself to continue her story. "He left me

there in the dark for a few hours." Waiting and sick to her stomach with fear. She'd tried to escape but the basement door had been locked and the windows had been too high, with nothing in the dank room for her to climb on. The recollection of the damp, moldy smell in the basement assaulted her nostrils. It had been so large, so dark, that she'd imagined a monster lurking behind every column and in every corner…even while instinctively knowing that the biggest monster of all was the one who'd imprisoned her there to begin with.

"This is horrible," Keegan said, swallowing hard.

She barely heard him, caught up in the frightful memory. "When he came down again, he started to say horrible things about what he was going to do to me. He was so big, so scary."

"You don't have to tell me—"

"It's okay. There's a happy ending, I promise." Taking a deep breath, she continued. "He tore my dress and…and touched me." Had tried to do things to her that no man should ever contemplate with a child. "In that moment, I just knew. It was like I felt this thing inside me, wanting to come out. I put my hands on him, closed my eyes, and just concentrated. It was so crazy—I felt the energy drain out of him. He collapsed to the ground almost instantly. I kicked him a few times to make sure he was unconscious, then ran to one of his neighbors' homes. They called the police."

What a relief to get that part of the story over with. Not only that, but she actually felt better now that she'd shared it. Maybe the wound from that day was finally healed. "They said he had a minor stroke, but I knew it was me. And I tested it a couple of times after, with guys who wouldn't take no for an answer."

"You're very brave." Keegan's tone made it clear he was 100 percent sincere.

"Somehow, I have a feeling that what I went through was nothing compared to you, was it?" When he looked away and didn't respond, she touched his cheek and gently nudged his gaze back in her direction. "Tell me, Keegan. About your father. What did he do?"

ଚଠ୪ଔ

Keegan mentally traced the curves of Brynn's face. She was so lovely, with her curious gaze trained in on him as she waited for him to speak. But where to begin? His past wasn't something he liked to revisit, but she deserved to know. She *needed* to know.

"I told you before that Mammon is a scientist and was once an adviser to the Council, right?"

She nodded. "Yes."

"Well, he decided during one of his cataloging missions to experiment with cross-breeding for personal gain. He was in the shifter world at the time and, being the self-centered demon he is, decided to pick the most majestic and elusive race: dragon-shifters. He captured my mother and used drugs to keep her insensible, unable to shift. He raped her repeatedly, only letting her go when he knew she was pregnant."

Brynn's eyes full of unspoken emotion, she touched his shoulder. It was soft and warm, and just the slightest touch of her fingers drove him crazy. How was that even possible?

"I'm so sorry," she whispered.

"I don't remember her," he confessed. "I only know the story because my father told me." Coldly and without a care in the world. His mother had been nothing but an instrument for Mammon. Just as he and his brothers were meant to be instruments. "Later, when I was almost a year old, Mammon returned to that world and took me from my mother. She struggled, and he killed her. He brought me back to Infernum with him to be raised by a successive string of wet nurses. He had a habit of burning through them."

"But…but you said permission is needed to travel through the portal," Brynn sputtered. "Didn't the Council find out about him killing her? Didn't they care at all?"

Keegan gave a humorless chuckle as he began pacing the length of the balcony. "They found out and disciplined him, but it was nothing more than a slap on the wrist. Like I told you before, to the Council, evil is relative. They didn't condone his actions, but he was valuable to them at the time, and so they let it slide."

"How could they do that?" she asked, her voice thick with horror. "How could they care so little about a woman's life? About a child?"

"They are what they are, Brynn." He'd stopped trying to figure out their agenda ages ago. What was the point? "Later, on another world, he captured a faerie. An—"

"Oh my God, *faeries*?" Brynn took a shaky breath, visibly composing herself. "Sorry, keep going."

"The faerie was an air sylph, to be exact, one of the most innocent species among the fae. After studying the race, he managed to ground her so she couldn't dissipate into the air or flash away to escape."

"Flash?" Brynn asked.

"Some faeries can manipulate space," Keegan explained. "Travel from one spot to another in the span of an instant. They call it walking the fae path, or flashing. After Mammon captured the sylph, he raped her until she was pregnant, and he later came back for the child. Taeg."

"Whoa." Brynn shook her head. "So even though you and Taeg are brothers, you're very different, aren't you?"

"In some ways," Keegan said. "We're all half breeds, byproducts of Mammon's crazy experiment. Dagan's mother was a siren. Same story with him. But Ronin...he's a little different. His mother was an angel."

"One of the beings from your planet?"

"Right. She got away after he raped her, and she was harder to catch. But eventually, he tracked Ronin down, when he was a young boy. Ronin's mother wasn't there at the time. Mammon told him he would kill his mom unless he came to live with him, so he did. But he was always disobedient. He hadn't grown up with Mammon like the rest of us did."

"So Mammon beat him," she finished.

Keegan nodded. "All the time." The horror of the night he and Taeg had returned home to find Ronin beaten, bleeding, and half conscious on the floor—along with a bloodied Dagan, who Mammon had sliced open for daring to defend his brother—was what had finally driven him to escape Mammon's household with his brothers. He would never forget the helpless fury he'd felt at knowing that their father, the man who was supposed to guide and shelter them, could so cruelly torture his own sons. He'd known then that Mammon was incapable of love...and that was how he and his brothers differed from the man who'd given them birth.

Keegan had sworn that fateful night to protect his brothers from their father. To teach them to be the exact opposite of him. And every day since, they had embraced their love for one another, because it was the one thing that set them apart from their monster of a dad.

Brynn tilted her head to the side. "What abilities do your brothers have?"

"Taeg can flash, as well as charm."

She laughed. "I'm familiar with the latter, thanks. Wait, if he can flash, does that mean he can find us anywhere we go?"

"No, he has to know where we are."

"Well that's a relief. What else?"

"He can change from his normal form to air and become intangible and invisible."

"Invisible?" She let out a delicate shudder. "Creepy."

But extremely useful, unless you were someone like Mammon who anticipated that and took steps to ground any air sylphs within a certain range. "Ronin can also grow wings, though they look very different from mine. He can heal himself or others by touch. He also has this really annoying ability to calm others with his presence."

"I sort of noticed that."

She was more perceptive than he'd even realized, then. "Dagan, like all sirens, can breathe underwater. He's got an incredible singing voice, though he'd kill me if he heard me say that." He let out a laugh. "He also... Well, like sirens, he seems to have sex appeal that many women can't resist."

"Really? I hadn't noticed that." She actually seemed surprised. Then she gave him a sheepish grin. "I suppose I was too busy looking at you to notice much."

Her frank admission caught him off guard. To his chagrin, his face heated, along with other body parts.

"Your father was trying to create his own army of people with special abilities."

Very perceptive of her. Again. "That's right. It threw a big wrench in his plans when we left instead of falling in line with him."

"I'm sorry you had to grow up that way. But more than anything, I'm so proud of the man you are in spite of it."

His breath caught at her words. He moved away and turned to look out over the balustrade before he went and did anything stupid. Like lose his heart. "I've been thinking more about these dreams you had of my father. Have you had any other strange dreams since you met me?"

"Strange dreams?" she asked in a choked voice. "I guess I've had some vivid ones, but…"

She moved beside him and pushed his arm so that he was forced to turn and face her. Damn she was beautiful, with her flushed face and her slightly dilated pupils. Like a goddess.

"Wait a second. That first night after you took me from the gallery, do you think you might have been communicating with me through my dreams?"

That first night? He froze. His dreams that first night were nowhere near G-rated. "Why? What did you dream about?"

"You and me. In my bedroom?" She flushed, but rather than look horrified or embarrassed, she looked almost like… well, like she might be a little turned on.

"I had dreams like that, too," he admitted. "You think it was telepathic communication?"

"I think so." She cast her gaze downward and nodded fervently.

"It wouldn't be the first thing Mammon held back from the Council." Damn that bastard.

Her chest rose and fell as she took a deep inhale, then let her breath out slowly. Despite himself, his gaze was drawn downward. Did she have anything at all on under that tiny excuse for a robe? From the way it dipped between her breasts, he didn't think so.

What would she do if he untied the sash of her robe? Just thinking about it made him grow hard. He wanted her, with an intensity he'd never felt before.

"What are we going to do about Mammon? About your brothers?"

"I don't know," he answered honestly. "But I'll figure something out."

"No, *we* will," she said, her eyes intense. "I don't know how we ended up here or why you chose to save me, but I'm thankful for it. We're in this together."

Together.

Why did that very word make his heart rate accelerate and his limbs go weak? Devil, but he wanted her. Given the gravity of the situation, the last thing on his mind right now should be the creamy expanse of her skin visible above the neckline of her robe, or the little pearls of her breasts budding underneath the silky fabric. But he couldn't help himself.

As if sensing his thoughts, she peeked up at him from underneath her long, curly lashes. "So what do we do now?"

"Now?" His voice came out raspier than he'd intended. "Now we rest here for a bit. You're safe here."

"Do you really think we're safe?"

On an island in the middle of the ocean, almost a thousand miles from where they were last located? "Yes."

Maybe not forever, but for now they were.

She shot him a seductive smile and just like that, his body was ablaze. "Then I know a few things we can do."

"What?"

Brynn took a deep breath. "Keegan, make love to me."

CHAPTER TWENTY

If she weren't so turned on, Brynn would have laughed at the shock evident on Keegan's face. She wanted him. Knowing about his father, about the way Keegan was conceived and raised, only made her want him more. He was a survivor. Selfless. And for right now at least, he was hers.

"Brynn," he said in a choked voice, "I don't know if that's a good—"

She pressed her lips to his before he could finish his protest. Lord, he was warm. So incredibly warm.

He crushed her to his body with a muffled groan. Even through the fabric of his jeans, his erection pressed hot and hard against her side. She ran her hands from his neck down to his back. His muscles tensed and pulsed under her fingertips, a testament to just how taut he was right now. If ever a man needed loosening up, it was him.

She slipped her hands in between their bodies, fumbling with the zipper of his jeans. He broke away long enough to say, "Wait, I—"

"No more holding back." She unzipped his jeans, rising to her toes for another kiss. Then, sliding her hands up his chest, she broke the kiss. She trailed her lips down to his throat and farther down to his waist, where she swirled her tongue around his belly button, much as he'd done to her before.

"Brynn," he groaned.

"Shush. Let me." She knelt in front of him, watching his anticipation build. But then she saw what he wore under his jeans. Nothing.

One gentle tug freed his cock from the confines of his jeans. It angled toward her, as if eager for her attention. He was so hard and so incredibly arousing. So perfect. She wrapped her hands around his erection and took him into her mouth, swirling her tongue around the head before sucking.

"Oh…damn." He groaned and clutched her head, letting her go on for several moments before tugging her away. "Stand up."

She obeyed, panting as she rose to her feet. He visibly collected himself. Just when she thought he would protest, he lifted his gaze to hers. The hunger in his eyes was undeniable, and it took her breath away.

He motioned toward one of the lounge chairs. "Go sit down."

Her lips curled into a satisfied smile. *At last.*

∞∞∞

Keegan watched Brynn walk to one of the chairs, which was covered with thick padding. She sat on it and waited, licking her lips while her hungry gaze devoured his stiff arousal. He knew she feared he'd change his mind, but he wasn't about to back down. Not now. He couldn't.

After tugging his jeans all the way down and stepping out of them, he joined her.

"You're so beautiful," she whispered.

He chuckled and knelt in front of her, untying her robe. One tug was all it took to pull the robe open, slowly unveiling her to his view like a priceless work of art. His breath caught. "You're the beautiful one."

And she was, with her small, firm breasts topped by dusky, beaded nipples. He took one in his mouth, tugging and sucking on it until she moaned and arched her spine. Then he greedily lavished the same attention on the other. Finally, he trailed kisses down to her stomach and parted her legs, exposing her to his view.

"Keegan," she gasped.

"Lie back," he whispered. She obeyed, and he slid a finger between her legs, flicking and pressing against her clit. When he sucked it into his mouth, she cried out, her hips lifting off the lounge chair. The sound of her pleasure was beyond arousing.

Rearing back, he rubbed along her slit, spreading the moisture, and slowly pressed one finger inside her. She was so wet, so hot. *So tight.* He couldn't wait to be there.

"Oh, please," she gasped, pulling his hair.

"Shush," he whispered, blowing lightly over her flesh. Bit by bit, he slid another finger in with the first. Then he moved them in and out, keeping time with her heavy moans. His cock twitched, eager to take their place. He was so hard he ached. But he wanted to make her come first.

He had to taste her again. Arranging her legs over his shoulders, he replaced his fingers with his tongue. Delicious. She tasted so sweet, he didn't ever want to stop.

"Keegan," she screamed, her whole body arching upward.

That's it. He groaned in satisfaction as she came apart beneath him, her thighs tightening around his head. Then, when her spasms died away, he rose over her.

"Please," she said, her gaze down between their bodies as she grasped his erection and pulled him forward. He groaned at the almost painful pleasure of her hand enclosing him. She guided him to her, trying to press him in. "I want you so much."

"Yes," he growled, bracing himself on his elbows as he pressed down. The head of his cock slipped in, the heat and pressure making him gasp. "So tight."

He brought his lips to hers, giving her a deep kiss as he pushed, slow and steady, all the way inside. She was so incredibly tight, and from the way she panted against his mouth and wriggled under him, he sensed she was a little uncomfortable with his fullness inside her. Still, he didn't stop until he had completely seated himself within her. He couldn't.

His balls were so heavy and full it felt like he might explode. But not yet. Not yet.

As he kissed Brynn and waited for her to adjust to him, his mind was consumed with one thought. Just one.

Home. She felt like home.

☜☞

Brynn breathed in and out, holding on tightly to Keegan while he kissed her. She'd come so hard against his tongue, had gotten so wet, that she would have thought he'd slide right in. But still, his size took a little getting used to.

"I'm good now," she whispered.

He shifted, gazing at her from half-lidded eyes. "You sure?"

"Yes." She gasped as he pulled almost all the way out, then thrust back in. Then again and again, tensing his hips each time. Lifting all the way up onto his hands, he angled his hips even more for maximum penetration. She felt so amazingly full. So great. *This* was what she'd been missing.

"More?" he asked between thrusts.

"Oh…yes," she gasped, digging her fingers into his ass and drawing him deeper into her. Already, her body shuddered and spasmed like it would fall to pieces. Each silky, gliding thrust brought her that much closer to the edge.

With a low growl, he lifted one of her legs over his arm and angled himself so that she felt each and every thrust all the way to her core.

She came apart again with a scream, her legs shaking from the force of her orgasm.

"Brynn," he cried as he followed her into oblivion, pumping his hips deep inside her. Only after she'd milked every last drop did he fall on top of her. She wrapped her arms around him, hugging him tightly to her. That had been so incredibly intense. Even now, she had residual pulses where his flesh still met hers.

"That was…wow."

He lifted his head to shoot her a lazy, satisfied grin. "Yes, it was."

When he lifted off her, she rolled to her side and scooted backward to give him some more room next to her. Not that it helped. The lounge chair was so narrow he still threatened to topple off it, but he didn't seem to care. He just stared at her, smoothing her hair down. "You're incredible," he whispered, then bent down to kiss her.

No—they were incredible together. When he gave her an

inscrutable look, Brynn asked him, "You aren't having any regrets, are you?"

"Just one."

Disappointment washed over her in waves. She hadn't expected him to say yes. "What is it?"

"This lounge chair is too damned small."

"Oh." Relieved, she let out a little giggle.

He rose and lifted her into his arms in one easy movement, shooting her a naughty grin.

"What?" Brynn asked as he carried her inside and gently laid her on the large bed.

"Again," he said, covering her mouth with his.

Full dark had already fallen by the time Keegan awoke from his deep slumber. Moonlight streamed in through the French doors, illuminating Brynn's sleeping form. She lay on her stomach, the silk sheets covering up to her waist. Her skin was a shade of pale cream under the light of the moon.

"My moonlight goddess," he whispered. Damn, he was becoming a total sap. If Taeg could hear him now, he'd laugh him all the way into the next dimension. But he didn't give a shit.

He hadn't slept this deeply in ages. And it was all because of Brynn. She was the light to all the dark that warred inside him. Practically, he knew he should feel bad about what happened. She relied on him to save her life and probably believed she was indebted to him. He couldn't bring himself to regret anything that happened between them. Brynn made him experience things he'd never felt before, things he never expected to feel.

Like hope. For the first time in a long time, he saw a glimmer of hope.

Now all he had to do was figure out exactly how Mammon was communicating with her, see if he could use it to find a weakness, and figure out a way to kill him.

Easier said than done.

Demons were unable to kill their own parents. Apparently, that was nature's way of ensuring demon offspring didn't do the parents in. Too bad nature never gave a fuck about how those parents treated their children.

That was the thing that sucked the most about this whole mess. If it had been any other man, Keegan would have stopped him. Nothing would get in his way. But he'd never been able to defeat his father, no matter how hard he'd tried. Now that he was older and stronger, if he had the rest of his brothers to help him, they might stand a chance against Mammon. But the way things were now...

"Shit," he muttered.

One thing was certain.

He would fight until the bitter end.

CHAPTER TWENTY-ONE

Taeg waited impatiently for Ronin to exit the terminal at Cairo International Airport. "Come on, come on," he muttered, glancing at his watch. Not like they were in any particular hurry. He just wanted to get the hell out of there so they could figure out what they were going to do.

"Finally," he said as Ronin walked out of the terminal area, a weary look on his face.

"We can't all just teleport," Ronin said.

Taeg grunted. It wasn't like he could blame Ronin for being on edge. They all were.

They hopped into a taxicab outside the airport.

"I hate the fucking morning," Taeg grumbled. It was way too damn early.

Ronin fought back a yawn. "Yeah, me, too."

"Humph." After a moment's silence, Taeg said, "We had to switch hotels, since Mammon tracked us to the one we were staying at before."

"Do you have any clue how he did it?"

Taeg shrugged. "Beats me, bro."

"I don't understand." Ronin rested his head against his seat and closed his eyes. "I mean, why would Mammon go to the trouble of planting a demoness at the hotel bar to lure Dagan and drug him insensible?"

"Because he wanted to keep us occupied trying to find our missing brother while his goons snatched the book out from under our noses."

"Yeah, but why not just order her to kill him while she had him? Our deaths seem to be his overall intent, so why not?"

Taeg let out a deep sigh. "He's fucking with us, that's why."

Ronin shook his head, a look of distaste crossing his face. "I really hate him."

"You're preaching to the choir, man."

Ronin lifted his head to look at him, one eyebrow arched in question. *"Preaching to the choir?"*

"What? It's a human phrase I learned," Taeg answered defensively.

Ronin chuckled. "You sure are taking to Earth, man. *Like a fish to water.*"

"Fuck off." But Taeg couldn't help his grin as he turned to look out the window. Things couldn't be that bad yet if Ronin still had enough of a sense of humor to rib him about his colloquialisms. "I like it here."

"I do, too," Ronin said. "Have you heard from Keegan?"

Taeg's light mood faded as quickly as it had come. "Not a word. Tracked the GPS on his phone to the side of the freeway on the outskirts of New Orleans. He must have tossed it on their way out of town."

"I don't blame him. We tried to kill his girl."

That pissed Taeg off, mostly because it made him feel so

damned guilty. "He knew that we might have to."

"I know, man. I know."

Taeg's anger and guilt faded under the calming influence of Ronin's ability.

"I hate it when you do that," he said.

"Yeah, I know that, too."

The taxicab pulled up to their Cairo hotel. Taeg dragged himself out of the car and led Ronin through the lush lobby and up to their top-level suite. Dagan and Cresso already waited for them in the large sitting room.

Ronin glanced around the space. "This is…gaudy."

Taeg let his gaze drift over the muted animal-print rug and couch, gilded coffee table, and two-tone metallic entertainment center housing the fifty-eight-inch LCD television. "This is the finest in Egyptian luxury, bro. Enjoy it."

Cresso chuckled from where he sat in a striped armchair. "Is the Council springing for all this?"

Taeg let out an amused snort. "Yup."

Cresso rose and crossed the room to clap Ronin on the shoulder. "Good to see you, man."

"You, too." Ronin's gaze moved to Dagan, who sat in a chair that matched Cresso's. "And you, too, little brother. Glad to see you're still in one piece."

Dagan colored at the obvious references to his run-in with the demoness. "Fuck off."

Ronin chuckled as he took a seat on the large, elegant couch. "Speaking of the Council, anyone contact them?"

"No," Taeg said as he sat next to Ronin, "and screw them, anyway. They won't lift a finger for us, so they don't deserve to know squat."

Cresso nodded with a casual lift of his brow. "Don't blame

you for feeling that way, man."

Dagan leaned forward, his elbows on his knees and his hands clasped. "So, what now?"

"Exactly," Taeg grumbled.

"Are we going to go after the girl?" Cresso asked.

"No." If Keegan had chosen to risk it all for Brynn, then Taeg would respect that. His duty was to his brother. He should have remembered that before, when Keegan was practically begging for his help on that damned New Orleans rooftop. If he had, Keegan would have been here with them now. Instead, he'd been forced to run and hide from the very people who loved him the most. And they really could use Keegan now.

"We're going after the book."

Three sets of eyes jerked in Taeg's direction.

"Serious?" Dagan finally asked him.

"Serious as cancer. Ha, that one's for you, Ronin."

"How do you plan on getting it?" Ronin asked him.

"Since we've been a little busy, Cresso's been keeping an eye on Memphis for us."

Cresso nodded and jumped in. "Mammon's workers cleared out of Memphis right after he found it. Most of them were sent home. But a number of them went back over to the Valley of the Kings. They've been setting up an elaborate system of tents out there."

"What?" Ronin lobbed a confused glance in Cresso's direction. "What the hell for?"

"Think about it, man," Taeg said. "Mammon's already got the book. All he needs is Brynn and he'll become the ultimate ruler of this world. The king."

Dagan chuckled dryly. "Mammon's got the biggest ego of anyone I know. He would find it fitting to begin his rule on

Earth at the Valley of the Kings, right underneath one of this world's greatest wonders."

"Plus, let's not forget how many stiffs must be buried out there. Perfect place to raise an army of the dead." Taeg shook his head. His bastard of a father had always been a clever one, he'd give him that.

"You think he's planning on permanently taking over the whole site?" Ronin laughed and leaned forward in his seat. "That's ambitious, even for him. I can't see him bedding down in one of the dusty old pyramids."

"Hence the tents," Taeg said. "Knowing him, they're probably heated. He'll have enough workers there to cart his necessities in."

"In other words, all of his luxury items," Dagan said with a smirk.

Taeg snorted. Dagan was right, no doubt. "He's probably planning on building something more permanent once he takes over. Hell, he might even plan on knocking down all the damned pyramids and building a massive monument to himself."

Cresso rubbed his chin, letting out a little chuckle. "That does sound like your father."

"He'll have guards set up all around the site," Taeg continued. "Demons, of course. The regular guards were likely paid off when he first started digging in the Valley."

"Shit." Ronin rose and paced throughout the room. "So how can we get to the book? Odds are, Mammon will already have wards in place to prevent anyone from flashing in and out of the site."

Taeg cast a pointed look at Ronin. "Don't forget we've got a set of wings."

Ronin's glance was dry. "How could I forget? They're mine, after all."

"Yeah, well, you could support my weight. We could get as close as possible to the place. Then Cresso and Dagan could cause a distraction while we fly in."

Ronin's eyes widened. "What about the rayamaras? He's bound to have them all over the place."

"That's what the distraction is for," Taeg said. "We'll do it at night, too, when we're less likely to be spotted."

Ronin stared down for a long moment, then sighed. "Once we get in?"

"We find the book. My bet is that it will be wherever Mammon is."

"We can't fight him," Ronin said. "Not if we expect to win."

"You don't have to fight him," Dagan said. "Just get the book away from him somehow. If you can do it quickly enough, you could fly yourself and Taeg out of there before he can stop you."

"A lot of *ifs* to this plan," Ronin noted.

Yeah, and didn't Taeg know it. "I won't lie to you, to any of you. It's risky as all get-out. But what are our other options? We can either keep trying to find Keegan so we can kill his girl, or we can do nothing. If we do nothing, the Council will find out soon enough that Keegan's gone. They'll take him out, too. You know they will."

"Only if they can find him," Ronin said.

Taeg shook his head. "Now that he's gone into hiding, he's got no money. Nowhere to go. Brynn's surely not used to living like that. How long do you think they'll last out there?"

"You're right," Dagan agreed.

"When would we plan on doing this?" Ronin asked.

Yeah, that was the kicker. Taeg took a breath. "Tonight."

"Tonight?" Cresso asked. "Why so soon?"

"The longer we wait, the more time Mammon has to get his resources in order, to figure out the weak spots in his security. Our best bet is to do it right away, while he's still setting things up over there."

"Good point," Dagan said.

Taeg leaned forward. "Keegan's never asked us for anything, never dared to want anything for himself. He deserves a chance at happiness. The odds are slim, but maybe we can give it to him."

Dagan shrugged. "I'm in."

Ronin nodded with a deep sigh. "I'm behind you, too. But Taeg, it's practically a suicide mission."

"I know." But he was going to do it anyway.

There was a long moment of silence before Cresso spoke up. "Hell, I've lived long enough. Count me in."

"Thanks, man." Taeg gave Cresso a grateful nod. "Really."

"Eh, your dad's an ass. I'd love to help take him down. As a matter of fact, I've got some thoughts on how we can cause a distraction…"

めのら

One good smack was all it took to bring the insolent demoness to the ground.

"I told you, only one-thousand-thread-count sheets on the bed."

The demoness rubbed her cheek and gave him a fearful look. "But my Lord, they are—"

"They are not!" Mammon shouted. He turned to pace

about the large, luxurious tent that had been set up for him. Truly, he was growing impatient with this whole scene.

The demoness scrambled to her feet. For one moment he thought she would slink away, but then she stiffened her spine and addressed him again. "I checked the label myself. These are what you asked for."

Mammon stared at her in mute amazement as fury fueled his veins in a fiery flood. No one ever dared talk back to him... not if they expected to live, that was. In fact, he almost admired her for her bravery. Almost.

Quick as a shot, he sped across the room and grabbed the demoness by her throat. She croaked in protest and closed her fingers over his in an effort to pry them away, but her strength was no match for his own. With a squeeze and a jerk, he twisted her neck, severing the tendons. He released her and she fell to the ground, sightless eyes staring up toward the tent's ceiling.

His murderous rage faded as he examined the body of the demoness. He hadn't taken her head, but the damage was so extensive that he wasn't sure she would be coming back from this one. Pity. Now they would have to find a replacement for her.

"Guard," he yelled. When one of his men, a brute boarg demon, entered the tent, he pointed at the demoness's body. "Take her out, and those bed linens as well. Make sure someone returns with the correct bedding or it will be your head."

The boarg demon gulped. "Yes, Lord."

Mammon barely noticed as he gathered the body and linens, and then scurried away. He was too busy rethinking the wisdom of his decision to move his operations to the Valley. Even though this tent was the fanciest of its kind, more akin to a luxury cabin than a mere tent, the hotel suite had been so much more lavish. But it was only fitting that he begin his reign over Earth in such a powerful place. The message it would send to the world was a strong one. He would be the first king of all the Earth.

The only problem was that he'd expected it to happen already. Keegan had thrown a serious wrench in his plans by taking off with the heir, and he was truly annoyed about that.

"He'll pay," he muttered.

He was willing to admit that some small part of him had held out hope his sons would return to him once he began his rule over Earth. After all, he'd spent so much time cultivating them, breeding them for their specific abilities. He'd sired other half-blood children, of course…too many to count. The female offspring he'd automatically discounted. He'd needed strong sons, not weak women. But none of his sons had been as promising as those four, which was why he'd chosen them to come live with him. A few of the offspring he'd kept track of over the years had seemed equally strong, but they had been less than perfect for other reasons. Like the half-breed vampire. He shuddered at the memory of the child's cold, observant eyes. Even though it had been an infant, Mammon could tell it would one day become too difficult to control. But he'd never expected that of Keegan, Ronin, Taeg, or Dagan.

The simple fact was that Mammon had thought he would be able to mold in his image the four sons he'd collected, to use their abilities for his benefit. They would have been his ultimate weapons. That they had betrayed him, slipping away in the night and seeking protection as employees of the Council, still infuriated him. If there was one thing he regretted, it was losing control the night they'd fled. He'd almost killed two of them. But they shouldn't have left him.

They were *his* sons. If it hadn't behooved him at the time to continue his role as adviser to the Council, he would have collected them straightaway, and damn the consequences. Yet he hadn't been ready to do that then.

And now...now they were as good as dead to him. All was not lost, however. Once he took the place of the Council, he would simply make more. His position would allow him to garner the most gifted females of each species. And this next time, he would take a firmer hand to ensure that his sons never questioned their loyalty to him. Clearly he'd been far too lenient on his sons.

"Damnation." He stalked over to the small, elegantly decorated dining table that had been set up in one corner of the massive tent and furiously swept all the expensive china off it. The dishes clattered to the floor, shattering into tiny bits.

Being a scientist, as well as a former adviser to the Council, had certainly had its upside. He'd discovered during one of his Earth assignments that demons possessed the ability to communicate telepathically with humans through their dreams, a process he'd termed dreamscaping. How easy it had been to withhold that information from the Council, which made it a potential tool—one he'd used on Brynn. But he hadn't been able to dreamscape with her since the night she'd fled with Keegan, and now it was as if she slept too deeply for him to reach her.

Even though she'd likely already realized she had been communicating with him through her dreams, he still wanted to visit with her. Humans could be so amazingly foolish when it came to inadvertently imparting information in their sleep.

No matter. He would find her sooner or later. Or he would find a way to make her come to him.

Mammon strode out of his tent, ignoring the guards that snapped to attention as he sought a good view of the Great Pyramid. When he was king, he would use his slaves to build a monument ten times larger than this. It would become the symbol for his might, an object that struck fear in the hearts of all Otherworlders. Because they would know that, unless they obeyed his every command, he'd be coming for them, too. Eventually they would come to thrive under his rule. They would realize that, unlike the Council, he knew best.

Mammon smiled.

It wouldn't be long now. Whether she knew it or not, Brynn was as good as his.

CHAPTER TWENTY-TWO

When Brynn awoke, she was lying in bed alone. But the door to the bedroom was open, and Keegan's whistled tune carried all the way from downstairs. He sounded happy. Arching her back into a deep stretch, she let out a wide grin. She could relate.

Her achy muscles protested when she sat up. Lord, she was tender.

Keegan had felt badly about the way he had made love to her last night. He thought he'd been too rough with her, no matter her assurances to the contrary. In fact, he'd only become convinced otherwise after she'd thrown him onto his back and straddled him this morning, riding him so hard that they'd both almost passed out.

That was fun.

It took her a few minutes of searching before she remembered Keegan had discarded her robe outside yesterday. She quickly retrieved it. Even though she knew no one was around to see, it still felt scandalous to parade outside naked. Tugging on the robe, she made her way downstairs, where Keegan stood in front of the stove, flipping something in a pan. The smell of pancakes scented the air, eliciting a low growl from her stomach. How long had it been since her last meal?

He must have heard her soft steps, because he turned to grace her with a sexy grin. "Morning."

He'd borrowed a pair of pajama bottoms from the home's owner. They were light blue and a little too wide for his frame. Even though he'd tied the drawstring tight, they still rode low on his hips, in danger of sliding down his body.

"Yummy," Brynn said, though her gaze was stuck on his chiseled torso and the faint trace of hair beneath his belly button that disappeared into the waistband of his bottoms.

Keegan sobered, devouring her with his hungry gaze. "Stop that, or we'll be having more than pancakes for breakfast."

"Sorry." She diverted her gaze with a blush. When had she become such a hornball? They practically made love all night and it was still all she could think about.

"Me, too," Keegan said.

Was he reading her mind?

"This is all new for me, too," he clarified.

"Oh."

Keegan laughed, then turned to load a plate with pancakes. "I thought we could eat outside on the veranda. It's beautiful today."

"Sounds wonderful." She grabbed a plate and headed outside to the cozy dining table. The sun blazed down on them, a perfect complement to the soft, cool breeze. For the first time she noted that it was more like afternoon than morning. But then, her conception of time had been all screwed up since they'd arrived.

Keegan sat across from her, appearing more relaxed than she'd seen him…well, ever.

I did that, she thought with a burst of pride.

"How'd you sleep?" he asked. "No dreams about Mammon, right?"

"No dreams at all lately, not that I can remember. Do you think he's tried?"

"Don't know." Keegan's brow creased. "I wish I knew more about this ability, but I don't."

"It's nothing you've ever heard of before?" she asked.

"No." Keegan sighed. "I need to speak with my brothers, tell them about it. I'll head over to the mainland later today and borrow someone's phone."

Though he didn't say it, he was worried about talking to them. Brynn clasped one of his hands. "I'm sorry."

He squeezed. "I know you are. None of this is your fault."

That was true, but for some reason she still felt guilty. He'd chosen her over his brothers. Over his duty to the Council. It wasn't fair that he'd had to, but she was sure glad he had. "Thank you."

Keegan opened his mouth, as if he was about to say something. But in the end he just smiled. Somehow, it managed to convey all the wicked things he was thinking about doing to her.

Sucking in her breath, she did everything she could not to read his thoughts. If she did, they'd end up in bed again, and there was still so much they hadn't talked about.

"Do you think the Council knows yet?"

"Don't know," he said evenly. "Doesn't matter either way."

"What will they do when they find out?"

He gave her a reassuring smile. "It'll be fine."

"They'll order your death, won't they?" Somehow, she knew that would be the end result, and it frightened her.

"It'll be fine," he repeated. When she didn't respond, he tugged on her hand. "Come here." She rose and sat on his lap. He enclosed her in his arms and pressed a kiss to her forehead. "I'll be okay. I promise."

Wrapping her arms around Keegan, she buried her face in his neck. He smelled like soap and spice and the indescribable scent that was unique to him. So warm. Wrapped in his arms, she almost believed it would be okay. Almost.

"We can't run forever," she said.

He tugged her head backward so he could stare into her eyes. His gaze was bright and earnest. "Brynn, I can fly. We'll soar all over this world, if that's what it takes."

Wow, that was the most romantic thing anyone had ever said to her.

She stroked a hand through his silky hair and traced her fingertips down his straight nose to the center of his full lips. Her heart swelled and filled with emotion, burning a hole in her chest until she could no longer hold back the words that longed to escape. "Keegan, I want you to know I—"

He cut her off, his lips crushing hers, devouring her with his heated kiss. One hand deftly untied the sash of her robe and he pulled it open, baring her breasts to the gentle breeze. "I could never get tired of looking at you."

As if to prove it, his gaze warmed her, and her nipples hardened even more under his stark perusal. He lifted his fingers to pluck them and lowered his head to lap at the stiff peaks. One hand crept down to her waist and he lifted his gaze to hers. An unspoken question glimmered in his eyes.

He wanted her. Again. And God help her, she wanted him,

too. Desperately. After all, who knew how long they would have together? They had to savor every moment.

Keegan's eyes narrowed in on her as if he could read her thoughts. His thumb reached out to brush across her taut nipple. "Tell you what. Why don't you eat something first, then come back inside with me?"

"What about…" She couldn't even think when he touched her like that. Didn't want to think. Only wanted to feel. "What about the mainland? Your brothers?"

His eyes flashed with equal parts promise and desire. "They can wait."

CHAPTER TWENTY-THREE

Full dark had fallen over the Valley of the Kings some time ago. Tents had been set up along—hell, even *through*—the archaeological dig sites. Mammon must have greased a lot of human palms to get this setup going without being questioned. He already had security measures in place, too, like wards that prevented Taeg from dissipating or flashing. Just as they'd expected.

Taeg adjusted his earpiece from his spot at the highest cliff overlooking the Valley. "Can you hear me, Cresso?"

"Loud and clear," Cresso's voice called over the earpiece.

Taeg used his binoculars to look down to the cliff below, which jutted out directly over the Valley. "I see ten rayamaras, all keeping watch. Who knows how many demons there are on the ground?"

"Gotcha. I'll send the ishtari demons in now."

Ishtari demons could fly. Female ishtari had large breasts and were a particular weakness of male rayamaras, especially since the ladies loved to play hard to get. Luckily, Cresso knew two of them, and they'd agreed to fly in to play a couple of horny demons looking for a good time. He'd also flown in a group of succubi from London, and at this very moment he drove them toward the entrance to the Valley.

"Where are you?" Taeg asked him.

"Should be pulling up with my lady friends in about five minutes."

Taeg watched through the binoculars while the two ishtari made an entrance, flying onto the cliff where the rayamaras patrolled. They touched down and sauntered to the nearest demons. The remaining rayamaras took note and, like flies scenting honey, flew to their side.

"Are you sure this will work?" Doubt and concern colored Ronin's tone as he paced back and forth between Taeg and Dagan. "I mean, isn't it a little obvious, sending horny chicks to the flying demons and to the ground demons all at the same time?"

"Of course it's obvious," Taeg said. "And of course it'll work. There's nothing like a smoking-hot, horny chick to make a guy's big brain check out and his little brain take charge. As Dagan can attest with that haknasa demon who got him the other night. Isn't that right, baby bro?"

"Fuck you," Dagan grumbled.

Taeg snickered while keeping his eyes on the scene below. Sure enough, the rayamaras surrounded the two ishtari, watching them with unwavering intensity as the ishtari flirted and struck poses intended to show off their generous curves.

"We're here," Cresso whispered into Taeg's earpiece.

Taeg shifted his binoculars downward and saw the RV pull up to the front gate. The guards at the entrance rose to attention, prowling toward the vehicle. Cresso opened the door and exited, looking for all the world like a friendly tourist.

Taeg heard one of the guards growl to Cresso, "What are you doing here?"

"Hey, I was just driving through the area with the ladies here, and we figured we'd stop by to see the pyramids," Cresso said, adopting a carefree tone. "You got something special going on here?"

"Don't mess with me," the guard snarled. "I can feel that you're all demons."

"Yeah." Cresso chuckled sheepishly. "Fire demons. We do a traveling show, you know, fire and acrobatics and all that shit. Humans love it. They think it's some crazy magic act. Makes us tons of money."

"Fire demons, huh?" the guard said dubiously. "Why don't you show—?"

"What do we have here?" a woman's coy voice crooned. One of the succubi scrambled out of the vehicle, her long blond hair flowing behind her. Taeg recognized her as one of the demons from back at Cresso's place. She sauntered up to the guard and trailed a finger down his chest. "Hello there, handsome."

The guard lost his defensive posture. He let out an uncertain chuckle. "Hi."

Taeg laughed to himself. "See? Nothing like a hot piece of ass to make a man go brainless."

Cresso cleared his throat, as if silently warning Taeg to shut up lest he risk being heard over the earpiece.

The other guards surrounding the RV shuffled in place as the remaining succubi piled out, cooing about how excited they were to be at the site of the pyramids. The succubi approached the guards, engaging them in conversation. Sure enough, within less than five minutes, the place more resembled happy hour at a singles' bar than a heavily guarded entrance. And Mammon was no doubt sitting imperially in his tent, dreaming about what he'd do once he ruled the world, clueless as to what was going on outside. The ass.

Cresso covered his mouth and murmured, "Sublime."

The code for them to proceed.

Taeg glanced toward the rayamaras, who were still preoccupied with the ishtari. Dropping his binoculars, he clicked off the earpiece and turned to Ronin. "Showtime."

Ronin nodded and sprouted his wings, flicking them open. Full, soft, and white, they were pretty damn spectacular, though Taeg would sooner die than admit that to his little bro.

"I can't believe I have to stay here," Dagan grumbled.

"Ronin can't carry the both of us down there." Taeg clapped him on the back. "Besides, we need at least one person to report to the Council if we don't make it out alive."

"Don't say that, jerk," Dagan said. Despite his angry words, an undertone of fear colored his voice.

I shouldn't have said that. No need to make his little brother worry more. "Kidding, bro. I'm not planning on kicking it anytime soon, okay?"

At Dagan's terse nod, Taeg turned and spread his arms perpendicular to the ground.

"This is really fucking annoying, you know," he admitted to Ronin, "to have to be carried around like this."

Ronin laughed. "Well, that's just about the only bright spot in my entire day."

He moved behind Taeg and hooked his arms under and around him, holding on tight as he zoomed up into the air.

"Shit." Taeg swallowed hard and closed his eyes as they flew over the cliff ledge. He'd almost forgotten what this felt like.

Ronin chuckled into his ear. "This is nothing like riding the fae path, huh?"

Not even close.

They soared over the camp undetected. So far, their plan was working.

"There." Taeg pointed to one tent, the largest by far. Bigger than many small houses, it had Mammon written all over it.

Ronin changed direction with one practiced flip of his wings. A few seconds later, they touched down next to the large tent. Taeg sighed with relief. Flying was a whole lot scarier when one took off from the ledge of a cliff.

Flipping the earpiece back on, Taeg whispered, "We're in."

"Got it," was Cresso's terse reply. What he was thinking, but *didn't* say, was loud and clear—it would be a hell of a lot harder getting out than it was getting in. Taeg clicked the earpiece off. Cresso didn't have to say it. He already knew.

Ronin motioned to one side of the tent and Taeg toed along the outer wall, keeping as far in the shadows as possible. Not surprisingly, two demons stood side-by-side at the entrance to the tent—boargs, by the looks of them.

Well, Mammon may have personal wards to keep from being charmed, but Taeg was willing to bet that didn't extend to his minions. For one, fae wards were far too valuable to waste. For another, Mammon was so sure of himself he probably thought there was no way Taeg could break in here.

That was his mistake.

Taeg slid unnoticed, only feet away from the boargs, then flipped around to face them. He gave them a cocky grin. Their eyes widened with alarm one millisecond before he placed his hands on them. His gaze bored into theirs, charming them into submission. Boargs were so easy, probably because there was such little brain to charm. He leaned in close, fighting the urge to gag at the foul stench of rot pouring out of their mouths.

"Relax," he whispered. "Go to the side of the tent and take a two-hour nap."

The boargs blindly obeyed, and Ronin stepped up beside Taeg. The entrance to the tent was open but covered by heavy mosquito netting. Taeg shot Ronin a look that warned him to keep an eye out, then carefully lifted the netting and stepped inside.

The interior of the tent, though hard to see in the dim light, was just as luxurious as he'd expected. He was even standing in a small foyer. Off to his right, separated by more netting, was a great room with seating and dining areas. It was empty, but angry voices drifted from farther in the back. He crept into the great room.

"...growing impatient," Mammon said to someone. "Keegan sorely tries me with his antics."

"We'll find him, my Lord."

Taeg gritted his teeth at the sound of Leviathos's voice. It still burned his ass that his former childhood friend had aligned with his father, after all the stuff Leviathos had seen him do as a child and after all the misery Mammon had put Taeg and his brothers through. One day, Taeg would hold him accountable for his actions.

But today was not that day. He had more important things to do right now.

Taeg edged toward the back room where Mammon and Leviathos stood.

"I hold you responsible for this, Leviathos," Mammon

seethed.

"But, Lord—"

"If you had retrieved the heir's name from the scholar before the Council determined it, we would not be in this situation. I should skin you where you stand."

"But...but, Lord," Leviathos blubbered.

You deserve it, asshole, Taeg thought with satisfaction. Something on the dining table caught his eye and he froze. His heart gave a sick *plop* and then settled into a faster rhythm. It was a thick book, made of some sort of metal with a golden clasp.

The *Book of the Dead*. It had to be.

"We *must* find the heir," Mammon continued from the other side of the tent.

Taeg stole across the room, focused on the book. He was so close to it. So damn close.

He reached for it and ran his fingers along the cool metal before lifting it. His heart gave a triumphant squeeze. He'd *gotten* it.

"You never fail to disappoint," his father's smug voice said from behind him.

Taeg whirled around. Mammon and Leviathos stood at the entrance to the back room, staring out at him. Mammon wore a pompous look on his face, but Leviathos's expression was one of bitter hatred.

Son of a bitch.

Taeg adopted a casual pose and flashed them a cocky grin. "Fancy seeing you here."

"Oh, I knew you'd come," Mammon said. "I knew as soon as Keegan absconded with the heir that you'd try to steal it out from under me. Your loyalty to your brother makes you weak and predictable."

Well...fuck.

"Your loyalty to no one but yourself makes you sick and pitiful," Taeg retorted, feeling smug satisfaction when the smirk faded from Mammon's face.

"You're one to talk," Leviathos growled, stepping in front of Mammon. "Where was your loyalty when you betrayed me?"

Ouch, that stung. Mostly because it was true. Taeg had betrayed Leviathos once, when they were supposed to be best friends. He'd been young and incredibly stupid. But that didn't excuse what Leviathos had done. "How could you join him? You grew up beside me. You *knew* how evil Mammon was."

"All I know is that he tried to keep you and your brothers in line. He should have beat you more, as far as I'm concerned."

Leviathos's words had their intended effect: to piss Taeg off. He let out a snarl and Leviathos tensed, clearly ready to pounce.

"Leviathos," Mammon snapped, and the demon jumped as if he'd forgotten Mammon was there before turning back to him. "You forget your place. It's *behind* me."

Taeg would have laughed at the incensed look on Leviathos's face, but he had more important things to focus on right now. Like getting the hell out of there. "Well, it's been fun catching up, Dad, but I gotta hit the road."

He swung around and grabbed the book, then ran toward the exit.

"Stop." Leviathos rushed at him, an expression of pure rage on his face. Taeg let him come close, then swung around in a flying kick that brought Leviathos to his knees in front of him. He lifted the book and smashed it over Leviathos's head. The demon slumped to the ground in a daze.

"*Damn*, that felt good." He leered at Mammon and

whipped toward the exit again but stopped dead short when four demons staggered in. One held Ronin in front of him, a dagger to his throat. He struggled against them, but he stopped when the weapon cut deep into his flesh, releasing blood down his neck.

"Sorry, Taeg," Ronin said without emotion. "They snuck up on me."

Fuck. Fuck, fuck.

Taeg lifted his hands. "Take it easy, boys."

"Drop the book, Taeg," Mammon said in a bored voice.

Oh, shit. He was so fucking close...but he couldn't abandon Ronin. He would never leave a brother behind, no matter what else was on the line. Gritting his teeth, Taeg obeyed. As soon as the book left his hands, four more demons marched into the tent, snatching Taeg and yanking his arms behind his back. "Easy, pansy-asses," he ground out.

Mammon laughed, and even after all these years the sound made the hair on the back of Taeg's neck stand on end. "I was beginning to wonder how I would manage to snag the heir. Thank you, sons, for making it easy. Now that I have you two, you'll lead Keegan—and her—right to me."

"Bite me," Taeg spat at Mammon.

Mammon scowled and approached. "You never should have left me. You'll live to regret that."

"I doubt it." Taeg snorted.

The last thing Taeg saw was Mammon's evil smile, a second before he lifted his fist and smashed it down on Taeg's face with enough punishing force to knock him out.

CHAPTER TWENTY-FOUR

She was so beautiful while she slept, with her hair fanned out to one side and illuminated by soft rays of light from the early morning sun. Like a sea of honey.

He could watch her sleep for hours.

Keegan rolled onto his side and ran his fingers down Brynn's stomach. What would it be like to wake up next to her every morning? To grow older with her? To watch as her stomach swelled with child—his child?

He yearned for that with an intensity that took his breath away. But it would never be. They were from different worlds. Too different. Even if, by some miracle, he managed to defeat his father, he would have to return to Infernum.

Even if Brynn couldn't be his, he had to do everything in his power to save her. He needed to go to the mainland and find a phone to call his brothers. Maybe this time they'd be willing to listen, willing to help him concoct a plan. Hell, he'd beg them if he had to. She deserved a good life. A normal life.

A life without him.

Her brows furrowed and she shook her head from side to side, though she was still asleep.

"No," she whispered.

Keegan's heart constricted. Was she dreaming? He reached out to shake her, when she awoke by herself. She sat up in the bed, panting for air.

"What's wrong?" He touched her chin, turning her face to him.

Brynn's eyes welled with moisture. She swallowed heavily before whispering, "I had a dream about Taeg and Ronin. They were captured by your father. There was someone else there, too. Mammon was…torturing them."

Keegan stopped breathing. His gut twisted and wrenched as if someone were squeezing his innards and trying to yank them out.

No. It couldn't be.

"Could that really be happening?" she asked, wearing an expression of horror.

No. Please no.

Keegan carefully schooled his expression into one of reassurance. He spoke the words even while he slid off the bed and searched for his jeans. "If anything, Mammon is likely trying to trick you."

"Where are you going, then?"

"To the mainland. To call them. It's past time I did, anyway."

She bit her lip, looking uncertain, but he couldn't give her any more reassurance. He didn't have any more to offer. That sick feeling in his gut told him that, somehow, her dream was all too real. "I'll be back soon, okay?"

Brynn nodded. "You'll be careful?"

"Always." Keegan bent down and pressed a kiss to her lips. Then he grabbed his shirt, walked to the French doors, and tossed them open. Unfurling his wings, he took off fast.

Could Mammon have gotten to his brothers? If so, would they even still be alive? Worse, would it be better for them if they weren't? His father had inflicted unimaginable torture on him and his brothers as simple punishment for childhood misdeeds. The thought of the things he would do to sons who had dared betray him made Keegan sick to his stomach.

After arriving on the mainland, it was easy enough to head to the nearest boardwalk and relieve an unsuspecting passerby of his cell phone. Dread unfurling in his chest, he dialed Taeg. It rang several times before a gravelly voice answered, "Hello?"

Keegan's heart squeezed, practically cutting off his air supply. "Mammon," was all he said.

The voice chuckled. "Well, hello there, son. I was expecting your call."

"If you've hurt them, I swear I'll—"

"I don't think you're in any position to be making idle threats, are you, son?"

Keegan clenched his fist, biting down on his teeth so hard that a molar cracked, and then immediately healed.

"Not to worry. Your brothers are still alive, along with that incubus friend of theirs."

Cresso.

"Though they hardly deserve to be after they tried to steal the book from me in a harebrained attempt to save the heir's life," Mammon added.

There was a scraping sound, then a second later, a scream. It sounded like Taeg.

"Don't," Keegan said. He instantly cursed himself. Show

his father weakness would only result in more torture for his brothers. He took a deep breath before continuing in a more even tone. "What do you want?"

Mammon laughed. "You know what I want. The heir." When Keegan didn't respond, Mammon added, "I tell you what. Though I'm still put out by the way you and your brothers ran away in the middle of the night, if you bring me the heir we'll let bygones be bygones. Just think—when I am ruler of this world, you will be its princes."

"No thanks," Keegan replied caustically.

"So quick to refuse, hmm? You think you are so principled, don't you? Well, how about this to sweeten the deal? Once I am done with the heir, you can have her to do with as you wish."

Keegan froze. "What do you want to do with her?"

"I simply need her to resurrect the army. Once she has done that, I have no use for her. She will come to no harm by my hands."

Somehow, he doubted that. "How do I know you're telling the truth?"

"I will swear a blood oath. You can save your brothers and your woman. You can even revel in my power. It's too good a deal to pass up."

Yeah, it was. Keegan asked the obvious question. "Why would you agree to this?"

"You are my sons. I've bred you to be powerful. Useful. Why would I destroy such works of art if I could instead have you on my side?"

So that was it. Nothing to do with love. Not that Keegan was still foolish enough to believe Mammon had any of that for them. They were tools to him, and nothing more.

What was he going to do? He couldn't let Mammon take over this world. The consequences would be far too deadly. But he couldn't let him torture his brothers to death, either.

Keegan absently paced. "Let me consider it—"

"I'll give you two days," Mammon said. "You know where to find me. At least, Dagan does."

"Dagan?"

"You didn't know? The littlest one got away. He's off licking his wounds somewhere, no doubt."

"Two days," Keegan finally said. "Give me your word that you won't hurt any of them until I get there."

"Done," Mammon said in a tone of supreme satisfaction.

The phone clicked silent.

"Shit!" Keegan yelled. He ran to the boardwalk railing and smashed it with his fist. The wood splintered and crumbled to dust underneath his hand.

If only he had called Taeg as soon as they'd left New Orleans. If only he had tried to reason with him more before stealing Brynn. His brothers had sacrificed themselves to save Brynn's life. They had sacrificed themselves for him. He couldn't let them die because of it. He wouldn't. Saving them was the only option.

Damn, he hated this. No matter what he did, he'd let someone down. But there was one thing he could do, at least. One way to right the wrongs he'd done these past few days.

Collecting himself, Keegan dialed Dagan's cell phone.

"Hello?" His brother's voice was rough, as if he'd been crying or screaming in frustration.

"Dagan, it's Keegan."

"Keegan?" Dagan gave a semi-hysterical chuckle. "Nice to hear from you, brother. I'd put Taeg or Ronin on the phone, but they're off *being tortured* right now."

"I know. I just spoke with Mammon."

"You did?" Dagan audibly collected himself. "What are we going to do?"

"I have a plan. Listen carefully. And Dagan, *don't argue with me.*"

CHAPTER TWENTY-FIVE

For the millionth time since Keegan had left, Brynn tried to concentrate on reading the novel she'd found on the coffee table. It was no use. She could barely read a word. She didn't allow herself to think about the possibility of her dream being real. With a shudder, she recalled the way Mammon had stood by and watched while his henchman flayed strips of skin from Taeg's and Ronin's flesh, then forced Ronin to heal them both so he could do it all over again.

No. It was inconceivable. No father would order that to be done to his children. Not even Mammon was that great a monster.

A *thump* sounded out from above. *Keegan.*

She rose and headed toward the staircase, expecting to find him on the second floor. But then he appeared at the top of the steps. Something in his expression stopped her cold. "Keegan?"

Instead of answering, he raced down the steps toward her. She backed up a little at the intensity blazing on his face. "What's wrong?"

He stood in front of her, and without saying a word he pushed her against the wall next to the staircase and kissed her thoroughly. The kiss went on and on, growing more and more heated, until she trembled with the force of her passion. She finally gasped and pulled away. "Your...your brothers?"

Burying his head in her neck, he licked and sucked at her sensitive flesh while his fingers roamed down her body.

"Does Mammon have them?" she tried again.

"They're fine," he mumbled against her neck, then kissed his way down her throat.

"Keegan," she persisted, pulling his head away, "I can tell something's wrong. Did you talk to them?"

"Yes. Everything's fine." But he wouldn't look her in the eye.

"Something's up. Tell me."

"I'd rather not talk about it right now." He gave her a smile that didn't quite reach his eyes, then bent down for another kiss.

Their conversation didn't go well. Her heart broke a little for him. Keegan had probably asked his brothers for their help in keeping her alive. They must have said no. Again.

She was tearing his family apart.

She opened her mouth to speak, to say something, but before she could, he untied her sash and drew her robe open. Leaning down, he closed his mouth around one of the hardened peaks of her breasts. She shuddered at the sudden temperature change. His body heat, combined with the wicked things he was doing to her, set her on fire.

"We should talk about it—"

"Later," he said. Clearly, he only had one thing on his mind right now. His lips trailed hot kisses down her stomach as he lowered to his knees. Then, before she could utter another word, he lifted one of her legs and drew it over his shoulder.

Her fingers tangled in his hair as his tongue found her center and delved in. She moaned. The man was a master. Within seconds, he made her entire body tremble on the verge of orgasm. All thoughts of talking fled as he flipped her other leg over his shoulder, fully bracing her weight. He rose to his feet, sliding her back up against the wall.

"Keegan," she gasped. She had the discomfiting sensation of flying, which wasn't altogether a bad thing.

His tongue laved expertly at her flesh, each silky stroke driving her to new heights of ecstasy. Unable to help herself, she undulated against him. She was almost there. *So close.*

One of his hands left her body, and his zipper rasped as he unfastened it.

"Are you sure you're okay?" she asked before she could lose all thought.

"Just…" He slid her back toward the ground. "Just let me love you," he said in a voice tinged with desperation.

Just let me love you. Those five simple words drove her to the edge. Because it would be easy, so easy, to let him do that very thing.

He was right. Now wasn't the time for talking.

She grabbed his hair and yanked him toward her, kissing him while she pressed into him. He tugged his jeans lower and lifted her body flush to his so the tip of his arousal slid along her folds, spreading her moisture. He apparently sensed she was more than ready, because he dipped into her, and with one hard thrust, seated himself all the way inside.

"Keegan," she cried. Her climax tore through her with all the ferocity of a runaway train.

He ground against her with hard, powerful thrusts that quickly drove her to the precipice once more, as if he was determined to drive her crazy with his lovemaking. If so, it was working. She tightened her legs around him, reveling in the way the muscles of his ass flexed under her calves with every pump.

Right now, she felt crazy. Out of control. And she wanted him to feel that way, too.

"Wait." Unhooking her legs from around his waist, she shoved him back, breaking apart their bodies.

"What's wrong?" he asked, a frown on his face.

"I…" She blushed as she was overcome by—of all things—a sudden burst of shyness. "Have you ever made love while flying?"

His hunger-filled eyes widened a fraction and he wordlessly shook his head.

"Do you…do you think it's possible?"

"Yes."

That was all she needed to hear. "Come on."

She grabbed his hand, starting up the stairs. In the master bedroom, she shrugged completely out of her robe, then turned to help him take off all his clothes.

"You're amazing, you know that?" He snatched her into his arms before she could respond and carried her out onto the balcony. The bright afternoon sun shone down on them, even as a cool breeze made her shudder.

His eyes glittered with unspoken emotion as he set her down. He obviously wanted her, but still he looked so…sad.

"Are you sure you're okay?"

He smiled, his gaze raking up and down her body. "Right now, I'm perfect."

Kneeling in front of her, he spread her legs and used his lips and tongue to ready her for him again. In one smooth motion, he flexed his wings out wide, so every ridge and groove was visible, and she traced the spot where they grew out of his back. "Does it hurt?"

"No." He lifted his head to shoot her a blazing look. "Feels good."

"Oh. *Oh.*" She'd never considered that he might actually get pleasure from her touching them. She rubbed outward, starting where they met his back. They felt like hot leather beneath her fingertips. Not at all unpleasant.

"That feels so good," he groaned. "Don't stop." He buried his face between her legs once more, driving her insane. Just when she thought she couldn't take it anymore, he rose.

"Now." He lifted her and pushed up off the ground. His wings flapped against her back while his cock unerringly found her entrance. Before she could so much as catch her breath, he thrust forward, driving all the way into her. The heady pressure of him inside her, the erotic slap of his wings against her flesh, was too much to bear.

She screamed his name, wrapping her legs and arms around him. Her body entwined so tightly around his that she didn't know where one ended and the other began.

There was no space between them anymore.

✇

Brynn. Right now, nothing mattered but her. This moment was something he would never forget.

Keegan held her to him as she rode out her pleasure, flapping his wings to keep them soaring above the water. His cock jerked and stiffened, but he ignored the urge to come. He wanted to make this moment last forever.

Finally, her awareness returned and, with it, her sense of caution. "Wait," she gasped, looking down to the water far below.

"I've got you," he reassured her. When she nodded, he pulled his hips back, then forward, using his wings to give him momentum as he built up a rhythm inside her once again.

She would never know how special this moment was to him, to soar so high with her. He would forever treasure this experience, and he hoped that she'd do the same.

Emotions surged within and threatened to overwhelm him. Reining them in, he flew toward the balcony. He sat her on the narrow balustrade, holding on tight as he found his footing and spread her thighs wide. Then, with single-minded intensity, he set about making her fall apart in his arms once more.

She cried out, grabbing onto his shoulders and arching into him.

He sucked on the taut little peaks of her breasts, pink and ripe like berries. He would make her come so hard that she would never, ever forget him.

Planting his feet, he ground into her. "Come for me, baby. Again."

With a high, keening cry, she did. She slid her hands down, grabbing his ass and holding him to her as if she would never let go.

Closing his eyes, he lost himself in her. With a harsh shout, he came hard and deep.

He knew there was no Heaven. But even if there had been, this was the closest he'd ever get. Keegan bit down on his lip as his emotions threatened to burst forth, manifesting themselves in words he could never live up to and promises he could never keep. He had no words to give her. He'd already given all he had.

CHAPTER TWENTY-SIX

Brynn woke to a quiet, darkened bedroom. Was it night already? With all the craziness, her internal clock was screwy. And it didn't help that Keegan had worn her out by making love to her for hours. He'd acted as if nothing else in the world mattered.

For a time, it hadn't.

Now that the haze of passion had worn off, she realized they hadn't talked about his conversation with his brothers. He was obviously torn up about it. But she couldn't just let it fester. It would kill him.

She would make him open up whether he wanted to or not.

Brynn rolled onto her back and stretched. For the first time she noticed the other side of the bed was empty. The sheets didn't appear ruffled, as if Keegan hadn't slept there.

No, wait. The bed wasn't empty. A scrap of paper lay on his pillow.

She sat up and flipped on the bedside lamp. Prickles of

dread broke out over her body, coalescing into a heavy lump in her throat. This wasn't good. Even without reading it, she knew that. Heart racing, she picked up the paper and read it.

Brynn,

Someone will be coming for you tomorrow. He's promised to watch over you, keep you safe. Please go with him.

Don't try to find me. Your safety is more important than anything. Not just to me, but to the world.

Just promise me you'll take care of yourself.

Keegan

"No." Brynn crumpled up the paper and threw it across the room. "No!"

She jumped off the bed, barely pausing to yank on her robe before she threw the French doors open and ran out onto the balcony. "Keegan. Keegan!"

Nothing. Only silence.

She rushed back inside and peeked into the spare bedroom before flying down the stairs.

She darted toward the front door and threw it open, stopping long enough to flip on the floodlights before she raced out into the night. "Keegan. Where are you? Please, answer me!"

There was no response. Nothing but silence. She headed toward the boat dock and ran until she reached the edge.

Empty.

Her heart slammed up against her ribs with all the force of a sledgehammer.

He'd left her. He'd taken the boat and abandoned her here so that he could save his brothers, and he'd mostly likely gone to his own death.

That was why he hadn't told her about it. That was why he'd marooned her here.

Panting, Brynn fell to her knees in the sand. She lifted her head and tried one more time. "Keegan, please!"

Nothing. Nothing but the damning silence.

Bowing her head, she blindly stared down at the sand in front of her. She couldn't believe he'd left her without a good-bye, knowing he would probably never see her again.

She blinked back the moisture from her eyes, willing a sense of numbness to kick in. But it wouldn't come. The pain was all too real.

Damn you, Keegan. Damn you.

80C8

By the time Keegan arrived, it was early morning in Egypt. He found a concealed ledge that overlooked the Valley. The flight alone had taken almost an entire day. The two days Mammon had given him were just about up.

If Mammon had broken his promise not to hurt them…

He concentrated on breathing evenly, trying to calm the rage and despair churning around in his gut.

Earlier, he'd told Brynn there was no such thing as Hell.

How wrong he'd been. There was a Hell, and he was in it.

Thinking about her brought the crushing weight of hopelessness down on him. He would never again know her warmth or feel her arms around him. For the first time in his life, he'd found someone worth fighting for, and worth dying for. But she would never be his. They'd had no more than a few stolen moments in time together.

It had been so unexpected, so sudden. So unavoidable.

Keegan picked up the cell phone he'd taken from an unsuspecting man at the airport and dialed Taeg's number. As he'd expected, Mammon answered.

"Where are they?" he said to his father.

"Keegan." Mammon's voice was jovial. "I was beginning to think you'd backed out. Your brothers' guards grow antsy."

"You mean their torturers."

Mammon laughed. "Should I inform them to prepare for disappointment?"

"We're here," Keegan responded.

"Excellent." There was a moment of quiet. Keegan lifted his binoculars. As he'd expected, mere moments later the rayamaras lifted off, circling the area. "Will you be coming to join us, then?"

"Don't bother with your flying demons," Keegan said. "They won't find us."

"Ah…that close, hmm?"

"Yes. But you won't get what you want until you bring out Taeg, Ronin, and Cresso. I want to ensure that you've kept your word not to harm them."

"So distrusting?" Mammon asked. He didn't sound too upset about it, though.

"I learned from the best."

"Indeed. Very well. Just a few moments."

He spotted movement from the largest tent on the grounds and shifted his binoculars as Leviathos headed to a smaller tent.

"I trust you've explained all of this to the heir?" Mammon said.

Keegan didn't bother answering. Instead, he said, "I want you to swear a blood oath."

"I've already given you my word," Mammon said in a disgruntled tone.

"And we've already established just how much that's worth. Jack shit," Keegan ground out. "Swear a blood oath that you will let them leave unharmed, and that you won't ever again cause harm to any of us. Or to Brynn, for that matter."

"You ask for too much," Mammon said.

"Think of what you'll get in return, *Dad*. An entire world to rule as you wish." When silence answered on Mammon's end, Keegan pressed, "You've already promised me as much. This makes it official."

"Fine," Mammon finally spat. "I swear to you that I will leave them and your precious heir unharmed. But you haven't even revealed yourself to me. I won't guarantee your safety until I see that you have delivered what you have promised."

No more than he'd expected. And Keegan was willing to live with it. Or, in this case, die for it.

"Done," he said.

The flap to the smaller tent opened and Leviathos exited, followed by Taeg, Ronin, and Cresso. Though they staggered, that was probably due to the guards hauling them around with their hands tied behind their backs. Compound that with the fact that this was probably the first time they'd walked in days, and it was a miracle their feet supported them at all.

With the exception of their tattered, frayed clothing, they appeared relatively unharmed. But he knew better than anyone that appearances were deceiving. Knowing Mammon, he'd probably forced Ronin to heal himself and the others so he could torture them over and over again. The sadistic bastard.

The flap to the large tent lifted and Mammon stepped

outside.

Hatred churned within Keegan at the sight of his father, threatening to bubble over into pure rage. He forced it back. Now was not the time to go berserk. Even if he *did* summon his fire-breathing ability, he couldn't save all three of them. Not before Mammon got to them.

"Do you see them?" Mammon said into the phone.

"Yes. Now your oath."

"Knife." Mammon spat out the terse order to one of the minions guarding the tent. The guard hastily dug a knife out of his pocket, and Mammon used it to cut a shallow groove into his arm. "I swear by my blood, in exchange for your presence, no harm shall come to your brothers, your friend, or the heir. The prisoners will be free to go, as will the heir once she's satisfied her mission."

Mammon threw the knife to the ground. "Satisfied?"

He was. A blood oath was unbreakable to one of his kind without dire consequences. "Be right down."

He stepped out of his hidden recess, sprouted his wings, and glided toward the camp. He ignored the rayamaras, who spotted him and circled behind, blocking his escape. They didn't understand that he wasn't about to escape. He'd freely accepted his fate: one life for many. There was no choice to be made here.

Mammon's expression grew from baffled to suspicious to downright livid when Keegan touched down alone. "Where is the heir?"

Keegan cast him a toothy grin. "Not a clue. She's not with me."

"But you said *we*," Mammon said in a low, furious tone.

"You said I'd be a prince." Keegan gave him a casual shrug. "I was using *we* in the royal sense."

"Deceiver!" Mammon yelled. He moved lightning-fast and struck Keegan full on in the face, dropping him to his knees.

Shit, that hurt. Mammon always did have a stone fist.

But then again, it was all too familiar, being in this position in front of his dad. Just some old father-son bonding time. Nothing new here.

"Keegan!" Taeg called, but when he tried to rush forward, the guards held him back.

Keegan rose to his feet, spitting out blood. His nose cracked as it mended itself. Instantly, four of Mammon's guards surrounded him, yanking his arms behind him while his father furiously walked back and forth.

"You think you're so clever, don't you?" Mammon said.

Keegan shrugged. "You swore an oath to set them free without harm."

"Keegan—" Ronin said.

"Shut up!" Mammon shouted. He turned back to Keegan, a tight smile on his face. "But you don't have the same protection, do you?"

Keegan adopted a bored expression.

"Bro," Taeg said in an alarmed voice, "what the fuck are you doing?"

Mammon gritted his teeth and whirled to face Keegan's brothers. "You are all eternal disappointments. It's beyond me how any of you could be children of my loins."

"We often wonder the exact same thing," Ronin said in a dry tone.

Ignoring that, Mammon took a cell phone that Keegan recognized as Taeg's out of his pocket and tossed it in front of Taeg.

"Deposit them in the back of a vehicle," he said to the guards holding them captive. "Drive them to Cairo and then let them go."

Leviathos's expression grew anxious. "But Lord—"

"I swore a blood oath, you idiot. Besides, they are no longer of any use to me." Mammon turned, dismissing his lackey and ignoring Ronin's and Taeg's shouts as they were dragged away.

Keegan ignored them, too, keeping his focus on Mammon. It didn't matter what they had to say. Now they were safe. As their big brother, he had a duty to protect them, and that was all that mattered.

Mammon studied him for a moment, then gave him a sly smile. "You think you are doing the noble thing, sacrificing yourself for your brothers?"

Damn right, he did.

"We'll see," Mammon said, reading the look on his face. "You believe you've won, but you've only postponed the inevitable. You see, now I have the one thing the heir wants most."

"You're wrong," he said, keeping his voice level.

Mammon barked out a laugh. "You underestimate the power of love."

Love? Keegan ignored that foolish little kernel of hope that rose in his chest. He didn't want her love. He wanted her to live, to be happy—even if his heart wrenched at the thought that it wouldn't be with him. "Brynn doesn't love me."

"Are you so very foolish that you don't recognize love when you see it?" Mammon shook his head, his eyes dark with pity. "I recognized it solely from invading Brynn's dreams. But then, I've always recognized love. It is the best of all emotions because it makes those feeling it the weakest. What better thing to exploit than that? The heir will come for you, and when she does, I'll get what I want."

"No." Keegan shook his head in denial. "She won't."

After what he'd sacrificed, what they'd all sacrificed, she couldn't possibly consider giving herself up for him. And if there was even the smallest chance she might, he'd taken precautions to ensure she didn't.

Mammon turned to the guards who held Keegan captive. "Take him to the holding area."

"What should we do with him?" one of them asked. He gave Keegan a vicious poke in the ribs.

"Use your imagination." Mammon whirled about and started back toward his tent. He turned at the last second and gave Keegan a long, slow look before shaking his head in clear disappointment. "Such a waste."

"Glad you think so," Keegan couldn't help but respond, even though he knew he should be keeping his mouth shut if he wanted things to go easier on him.

Mammon pursed his lips and turned back to his men. "Start draining his blood slowly. We want to give the heir motivation to come sooner rather than later, don't we?"

After Mammon left, the guards unleashed their fists on him with blow after blow. He fought back, relishing in each jab and hit he landed, taking perverse pleasure in the scream one of the guards let loose when his arm broke with a loud *snap*. He ignored his own broken bones and the pain as they healed. Nothing existed but this fight and releasing as much ass-kicking as he could before they inevitably brought him down. Yeah, he'd pay for it in the torture tent, but right now, he didn't give a fuck. They continued hitting and kicking him until he stopped fighting altogether, his strength completely zapped.

It's no more than I'd expected, he thought as they dragged him toward the torture tent. Mammon knew his weakness—that he would no longer have the ability to heal himself once he'd been fully drained. He knew he would die.

At least my brothers are safe. Brynn is safe.

At the very least, he had that.

CHAPTER TWENTY-SEVEN

By the time Brynn heard the rumble of a motorboat approaching, she'd already tried to think of a million different ways to get off this stupid island. After all, it had been well over a day since Keegan had left her. But short of swimming to the mainland, there was no way out. To think that such a dreamy safe haven could so rapidly become a prison.

Where was Keegan now? The mere thought of him in Mammon's grasp was beyond horrifying. If his father got ahold of him, she had no doubt the torture he'd endure would be unbearable. Why hadn't he stayed? She understood his loyalty to his brothers, but why did he have to go it alone? Together, they might have found another way.

Brynn rose to her feet on the dock and watched as the boat came closer. She didn't see anything at first, as it was close to midnight, and even with the floodlights from the house the night was still dark as hell. Squinting, she shaded her eyes from the bright light on the front of the approaching boat.

Who would Keegan have sent for her, anyway? With the

exception of his brothers—who, as far as she knew, still wanted to kill her—and his father, she didn't think he knew anyone else on Earth.

The engine cut, and the person inside looped a rope over the dock post. At last, its spotlight dimmed and the figure stepped off the boat.

Brynn blinked as her eyes adjusted to the change in light. Then, once she made out who it was, she gasped. "You!"

"Brynn—" Dagan started, but she didn't let him finish. She turned and sprinted toward the house.

"Brynn," he yelled. His footsteps pounded hard on the sand behind her.

She panted as she flew toward the front door, trying to ignore the stitch forming at her side. If she could just get inside, she'd... Well, she didn't know what she'd do, but at least she'd have a few extra moments to think.

"Wait!" A second later, he tackled her to the sand.

She went down hard, biting her lip in the process. The metallic tang of her blood filtered onto her tongue.

"No," she cried, grabbing two handfuls of sand as he twisted her around to face him.

He pinned her with his body. "Listen—"

She closed her eyes and threw the sand in his face.

He reared back. "Shit."

Brynn swung her palm at him. When it connected with Dagan's chin, he yelped, but before she could fight him further, he grabbed her hands and trapped them high over her head.

It was no use. He was far too strong.

"If you hurt me, Keegan's gonna kill you," she spat at him.

"Damn it, Brynn, that's what I'm trying to tell you," he said. "Keegan sent me."

Shocked, she stopped struggling. "Why would he do that? He knows you're trying to kill me."

"Not anymore. If you'd listen for a moment, you'd know that." From the way he shook her for emphasis, she figured he was more than a little pissed about the whole sand thing.

She opened her eyes, blinking them furiously, and shook her head to clear off the remaining grains of sand. Admittedly, if he had wanted her dead, she probably would be by now. "You're not trying to kill me?"

A drop of blood trickled from the corner of his mouth. "Okay, how would I even know to find you here if Keegan didn't tell me?"

He had a point. Brynn relaxed under him.

"Are you going to stop attacking me now?"

"Sorry," she said.

Dagan pushed off her with a curse, sitting on his heels. He rubbed the grit from his eyes and spat some blood to the side. "Shit. You managed to blind me *and* make me almost bite off my tongue."

"Really?" *She* did that?

"I can see you're torn up about it," he said dryly. "Don't worry, I'll heal."

Yeah, well, he'd wanted to kill her before, so he could suck a big one. Besides, she was absurdly proud she'd managed to hurt him. If she could injure a powerful demon even without her abilities, maybe she was stronger than she thought.

"I promised I would keep you safe," he told her grimly. "So that's what I'm going to do."

That was what Keegan had said to her in his Dear John note. The memory of it came back to her in one searing flash, sending an echo of pain slicing through her gut. Brynn sat up.

"Keegan really sent you here?"

Dagan dropped his hands from his face. "Yes."

He lifted to his feet, then offered her his hand. After a moment's hesitation, she took it. "What made you change your mind? About killing me, I mean?"

Dagan laughed, the bitter sound slicing through her. "If he's sacrificing himself to save your life, the least I can do is honor his wish to keep you alive."

"Sacrifice?" Brynn stared at Dagan, her eyes going wide. Pain sliced through her midsection like a punch to the gut. "He's exchanging himself for Taeg and Ronin?"

"It's what he wanted."

"No, we can't just let him give himself up. We have to stop him."

"It's already done."

Brynn clamped her mouth shut. She stared at Dagan for a long moment. He stared back, unflappable. "We can't just stand by and do nothing."

Dagan's eyes softened, and he reached for her hand. "Keegan wants you to be safe. Don't forget the consequences if Mammon gets ahold of you, Brynn. He made a decision. We need to honor it."

Could he really be suggesting that they do nothing? *Nothing?* "So what's your plan, then?"

"I have a friend who owns a condo in Miami. He's agreed to let us borrow it indefinitely. We can go there. You can make a new life, if you want. Start over—"

Brynn yanked her hand away from his. "You actually think I'm going to be able to *forget* about him? To just go on with life as if nothing happened? Are you crazy?"

"I expect it because Keegan expected it," Dagan said.

"Don't let his sacrifice be in vain."

"No." She pushed away from him, but he caught her by the waist. "No, I won't."

"It's time to go."

"No!" She slapped him. When he did nothing, she made a fist and punched him in the chest. She wanted something from him. A flinch. A curse. A promise that he would do *something*. When she got nothing, she struck him again, taking out all of her anger and frustration on his chest. He barely budged, and he allowed her to hit him over and over before finally grabbing her and holding her tightly to him.

"No, let go!"

She tried to push him away, but she surprised herself by instead wrapping her arms around his neck. Anger and frustration gave way to despair. Agony.

"It's okay." Dagan squeezed her tightly, rocking her back and forth as he stroked her hair. "It'll be okay."

She clutched his shoulders, bitter sobs tearing out of her throat. "We can't just let him go. We can't."

He pressed her tighter to him. "We have to."

80C3

Dagan strode aimlessly around the living room of their borrowed Miami Beach condo. Though the sweeping ocean views from the large windows were stunning even at this time of night, he barely paid them notice.

Brynn had closed herself off in one of the condo's three bedrooms as soon as they'd arrived. Her eyes had been nearly swollen shut from the heavy tears she'd cried, and she'd clutched her stomach as if she was in pain. A broken heart hurt beyond belief…that he well knew from past experience.

"Shit." Kicking off his shoes, he threw himself onto the brown Ultrasuede couch. He'd gone from facing the possibility of losing two brothers to the certainty of losing one.

Worse, what if Mammon tricked Keegan somehow and ended up keeping them all?

Ever since he could remember, Dagan had heard music inside his mind—a byproduct of his siren heritage, he supposed, since sirens spent the majority of their lives expressing emotions through song. Rich chords ebbed and flowed in his head, the harmony changing and the volume lowering or increasing dependent on his frame of mind. The occasional popular song would seep in there, too, if the lyrics were particularly appropriate to his mood…

But there was always music.

Right now, harsh, discordant tones that spoke of pain and suffering echoed loudly in his head. Intense, clashing rhythms melded with fierce, pounding beats, sparking a symphony of soul-numbing regret. If only they could have done something differently. If only *he* could have acted differently. Then he wouldn't be sitting here, wondering how the hell he was going to comfort the woman who clearly loved his brother when it was so obvious that Keegan wasn't going to be coming back. Not in one piece.

He bent forward and wearily dragged his hands across his face. Damn, but he hated feeling so uncertain, so beaten. He wanted to help his brothers, but he knew he couldn't. Keegan had asked him—practically begged him—to take care of Brynn. The least he could do was honor this one last wish.

The sudden ringing of his cell phone made him jump. Only three people had his number, and he'd be glad as hell to speak to any one of them right about now. He hopped off the couch, rushed to his jacket, and fished out the phone.

Please. Please let this be them…

When he answered, Taeg's tired voice replied, "Man, am I glad to hear your voice."

"Taeg! Thank the devil. Where are you?"

"In Cairo. Keegan exchanged himself for us, bro."

Dagan took a breath. "Yeah, I know. He told me what he was doing."

"And you *let* him do it?"

"He was going to do it with or without me," Dagan said.

"Fuck." Taeg sounded too tired to be angry. "So, where are you?"

"I'm with Brynn."

"What?"

"Keegan asked me to take over her protection, and I agreed."

Dagan expected an argument from Taeg. Instead, he sighed. "I understand. If he thinks saving her life is worth dying for, then we need to respect that."

His thoughts exactly. "What do we do now?"

"I don't know," Taeg replied. "We can't get Keegan back. Not without the Council's help. And we can't go to the Council if we're going to protect Brynn. We're up shit creek, no paddle, you get the drift."

The door to Brynn's room opened. She walked out, even more puffy-eyed than before, if that was possible.

"Who's that?" she asked.

For a moment, Dagan debated not answering, but it wasn't like she would stop asking. "It's Taeg. Keegan was able to get him and Ronin freed."

She covered her mouth with her hands, then stumbled toward him on shaky legs. "Let me talk to him."

Devil, did she want to know what Mammon had done to him? What he was going to do to Keegan? The very idea made Dagan's heart pound in tune with the desolate chords ringing in his head. She shouldn't have to think about it. "Brynn—"

She stopped directly in front of him and held out her hand. "Let me talk to him," she repeated, her voice hard as steel.

After a moment of hesitation, Dagan obeyed.

Brynn placed the phone to her ear, not bothering with a greeting. "Are you still trying to kill me, too, or have you given up on that?… Well, I need to talk to you, then… Can you come here? I know you can flash. Keegan told me about it… Yes… Okay."

She recited the condo's address and hung up before returning the phone to Dagan. "He'll be here in a sec."

Sure enough, moments later the air shimmered with Taeg's path and he appeared out of nowhere. He was obviously wearing a fresh set of clothes, not looking like a man who'd been tortured for the last two days. But Dagan detected the exhaustion and the undertone of horror in his eyes, and he had no doubt he'd suffered greatly at their father's hands.

For a while there, he thought he'd never see him again. "So glad to see you, brother."

"Me, too." Taeg clasped him in a tight embrace.

Dagan held on for a long moment, then pulled back. "Ronin?"

"He's fine. He's at the hotel with Cresso."

So they all were free, then. All except for Keegan.

"Taeg." Brynn approached, grabbed Taeg's arm, and turned him around to face her. "You have a plan to get Keegan out of there, right?"

Taeg exchanged a glance with Dagan. "The site is heavily guarded. There's no way we could infiltrate it without more people. I think it's pretty clear that we can't expect any more help from the Council."

Brynn shook her head. "We have to do something. There has to be a way. Maybe we can pretend to set up an exchange."

"No." Taeg took her shoulders and looked her in the eyes. "Keegan went to a lot of trouble to make sure you were safe. We can't endanger your life."

"I thought you, of all people, would understand." Brynn scrunched Taeg's shirt in her hands in an unconscious gesture of pure desperation. Tears welled in her eyes but she blinked them away.

That simple act of bravery broke Dagan's heart, and he knew why Keegan had fallen in love and given himself up for her. He would honor that sacrifice if it killed him.

"I dreamed about what he did to you," she said to Taeg. "You know Keegan's probably going through worse than that right now. You can't just leave him there."

Taeg cast Dagan a frantic look, as if his resolve were wavering. Well, if it was, he would be strong for all of them. For once. "I'm sorry, Brynn. There's nothing we can do."

Brynn flinched and took a shuddering breath. Then she drew herself up, untangling her fingers from Taeg's shirt. "I see I was wrong about you guys." She wriggled out of Taeg's grasp and backed away. "I thought you were brave, but you're not. You're both cowards."

With one last death stare, she turned and stomped back to her room, slamming the door behind her.

Taeg watched her go. He turned to Dagan, his eyes red

and swollen from the tears he held back. In an uncharacteristic moment of weakness, he asked, "There isn't anything we can do, is there?"

Dagan felt the heavy weight of his own tears pressing behind his eyelids. So pointless. Crying would accomplish nothing. He fought them as he shook his head. "Not this time, big brother. Not this time."

CHAPTER TWENTY-EIGHT

Brynn was surrounded on all four sides by sand, rock, and pyramids. Although it was dark, a world-class lighting system illuminated the area. Ahead of her, dozens of white tents were set up in all shapes and sizes.

This wasn't any normal dream. She stood in the Valley of the Kings.

Rooted to her spot, she willed the ice in her veins to heat. Something bad was going to happen here. Part of her longed to wake up before she saw what it was, but she had to know.

The canvas tents rustled in the breeze as she strode forward, farther into the camp. Other than that, eerie silence filled the open space. She headed for the largest tent but stopped when, out of the corner of her eye, she spotted a mottled tent.

No, not mottled. Stained.

From the inside.

"Oh, God." She covered her mouth with her shaking hands. No denying what that was. Blood. Lots of it.

"That's the one," said the now-familiar rasping voice.

When she whirled around, Mammon stood directly behind her, a polite smile on his face.

"You." She ran at him, struck his cheek with her fist.

His head snapped to the side. He laughed and turned to look at her again. "That almost hurt, little Brynn."

"Go to hell, you monster," she spat.

"Hell?" Mammon's lips curved even wider. "This *is* Hell, and I am its master. Come see."

Brynn's world spun, and suddenly she stood in front of the bloodstained tent. Pure dread unfurled in her stomach, rising in her throat and threatening to suffocate her.

No, she didn't want to go in there.

But when she tried to stumble back, she couldn't. No way to go but forward.

The tent flap rose of its own volition. Brynn swallowed hard and stepped through the doorway, fighting the urge to vomit.

She stood inside a torture chamber. Blood was splattered everywhere, even on the low table that held a variety of wicked-looking devices—knives, daggers, rods, weapons her mind couldn't even process. The tangy smell of blood permeated the air, threatening to choke her.

Keegan was there, lying on what appeared to be a gurney. Heavy iron manacles strapped his hands and feet to it, and his clothes clung to him in tatters. And in front of him stood a large demon, who lifted the knife and sliced Keegan's stomach.

"Keegan," she screamed.

She tried to run toward him, but she couldn't do anything but watch as his flesh immediately wove itself back together, his guts sucking back into his body with an audible *slurp*. From the way he groaned and convulsed, it appeared the healing process was almost as painful as the wound.

"No, Keegan," she sobbed.

He didn't look at her, didn't appear to hear her at all. The demon slashed again, drawing another guttural yell from Keegan.

"No, please, no," Brynn whispered. Tears rolled down her face, blinding her.

"I'm afraid he can't hear you, dear. He's quite lost in his pain."

She turned her head toward the voice.

Mammon had appeared beside her.

She tried to lunge at him, but once again she couldn't move or rake her nails down his face the way she longed to. There wasn't a damn thing she could do to destroy him. "You monster. How could you do this to your own son?"

Mammon inclined his head toward her, giving her a speculative glance. "You can stop this, you know. You have the power. Simply turn yourself in to me, and I'll set him free."

"No," Keegan cried.

Brynn whipped her head toward him.

"No, Brynn," he said through gritted teeth. Agony was etched all over his features. "You need to stay away. Promise me. Promise—"

"Shut up," Mammon yelled, pure rage contorting his face.

The demon put the knife down and picked up an iron poker. He lifted his hand and a ball of fire appeared in his palm.

"Fire demon," Mammon said conversationally. "I found it fitting."

The demon heated the poker in the fire, then plunged it into Keegan's side. The stench of cooking flesh burned her nostrils. Brynn turned away, choking on her own bile as Keegan screamed.

"Make him stop," she pleaded with Mammon.

"Only you can do that, Brynn. Come to me and his agony will end. But I give you fair warning. You have no more than a couple of days before it is too late."

"What…what do you mean?"

"Do you see that apparatus at his side?"

He motioned toward what appeared to be a sharp iron spike digging into Keegan's flesh. Attached to it was a red hose that snaked all the way underneath the gurney.

"What is that?" she whispered.

"Blood. Once he is fully drained, there will be no coming back. Remember that."

"How could you—?"

"Brynn." Keegan gave her an entreating look. "Promise me. Promise you won't come."

"I said be quiet," Mammon screamed. He flew toward Keegan, and she felt the sudden sensation of being thrown backward. She flew out of the tent…and jolted awake in her bed.

"Oh, no," she moaned. "No, Keegan."

Brynn buried her face in her hands.

She couldn't sit idly by while the man she loved was tortured to death.

She loved him. Oh, God, she loved Keegan. Somehow, it had snuck up and smacked her on the face, but it was indisputable. The man she loved was dying. And she was the only one with the power to save him.

Brynn remembered some of Mammon's first words to her. *That almost hurt*, he'd said. And Dagan, back on the island, had been hurt, too.

Demons were strong and powerful, yes, but they weren't almighty. Keegan had told her demons couldn't defeat their parents, but that didn't mean the parents were indestructible.

Could she do it? Was she crazy to even contemplate it?

The odds were that she'd probably die. But she couldn't wait in Miami and do nothing.

Decision made, she bounded off the bed.

ഒ

Taeg sat slumped over on the end of his bed, facing the large wall of windows overlooking the ocean. It was a fabulous view. Why was he the one here seeing it instead of Keegan?

He was responsible for this. If only he hadn't decided to try to get the book. He'd made so many mistakes, and Keegan was the one who'd paid for them. Deep inside, he knew the gruesome torture he and Ronin had undergone was nothing compared to what Keegan endured now. And that was killing him.

Taking in a deep sigh, he buried his face in his hands. He'd gladly trade his life for his brother's. But he wasn't going to get Keegan out of Mammon's grip alone, or even with his brothers' help, and the Council would sooner destroy Brynn than help them. What options did he have?

Taeg looked up at the sound of his doorknob turning. Brynn crept inside, then shut the door behind her. She wore the same clothes as before.

"Brynn, what's wrong?" He rose off the bed and started over to her, but she met him halfway. "What is it?"

"Listen…" She took a seat on the side of his bed.

"Do you need to talk, Brynn, because I can — "

"I don't need you to baby me. I'm here because I had a dream." She looked away for a second, then back at him. "More of a vision, actually."

"Vision?" Was she kidding? He walked back to the bed and sat beside her. "I didn't know you had visions."

"I think I know of a way we can save Keegan," she continued, ignoring his comment.

"What?" Taeg's heart broke out into a fierce gallop. *"How?"*

"Keegan said the resurrection spell gives power to the person in possession of the book. Well, I'll need to hold it in order to work the spell, won't I?"

Taeg frowned, not liking where this conversation was headed. "So what?"

"So, when I perform the spell, I'll have control over the army. I can order them to destroy Mammon."

Disappointment coursed through him. "Yeah, but, one, you'll have let loose an army of zombies, and, two, what are the odds of Mammon actually letting you hold the book while you perform the spell?"

"I'll tell him I *have* to hold it, and…and that it also contains a counter-spell. As soon as he's gone, I can order the zombies back into the grave." Brynn's gaze flickered down. "I saw it in my vision."

For one second, hope flared, but then reality set in. Taeg was all for saving Keegan, but not if the risk was too great. He'd already made one foolhardy decision this week. Well, several, actually. He couldn't afford another. "No way, Brynn. It's far too risky. What if he gets to you before the zombies get to him?"

"He won't." Brynn leaned forward. "Think about it. He's at the Valley of the Kings. Bodies are literally buried everywhere.

And they'll all do as I command."

"*If* it works. There's just as great a chance that you'll end up dead and Mammon will have control over the book and the army. Keegan didn't give himself up so you could walk into a trap."

"But it's not." Brynn put her hand on his arm, her fingers digging into his skin. "It would be one thing if I didn't already know how this was going to end, but I told you, I *saw* it. It'll work."

Taeg stared at Brynn, his defenses wearing down. He wanted to believe her. "Dagan won't go for it. Keegan has rarely, if ever, coerced him to do anything. He takes his vow to protect you seriously."

"I know," she said evenly. "That's why I'm here with *you* now."

Shit. *Shit.* If he agreed to this, he'd betray Dagan's trust. But if it meant saving Keegan's life…

"Please, Taeg." Brynn stared at him with beseeching eyes. "You know better than anyone what he's going through right now. We *have* to save him."

She went right for the throat. The mere thought of what they'd done to him, of what they were doing to Keegan, made him want to howl in agony. "You promise you're right about this? You're sure you'll be able to do it?"

Brynn grabbed his hand and squeezed tight. "Yes."

Damnation, if they somehow managed to make it out of this okay, Keegan would kill him and Taeg wouldn't blame him. But how could he live with himself if there was a chance he could save Keegan and he didn't take it?

"Fine," he said. "Let's do it. But we have to leave now, before Dagan catches on."

She smiled and rose off the bed. "I'm ready."

∞

Fresh out of his dreamscape with Brynn, Mammon rose off his bed with an angry growl. He barely noticed the frigid air as he stomped, bare-chested, out of his tent. At the moment, he had only one thing on his mind: his blasted sons. Why did they continually seek to destroy him? After all he had done for them, this was how they rewarded him?

He stormed into the tent where he'd left Keegan. One of the guards stood in front of his son, working him with a jagged knife. Ignoring the guard, Mammon asked, "Why?"

Keegan groaned.

"Leave us," Mammon ordered.

The guard dropped his weapon and left.

"Why?" he asked again.

Gasping, his skin slick with sweat and blood, Keegan turned his head. "Why what?"

"Why did you and your brothers desert me? Act against me? After all I've done for you. I *made* you, for devil's sake."

"You mean you raped our poor, innocent mothers."

His son was such a fool, always focused on trivial matters.

"They were mere tools for your creation. You wouldn't *be* here if not for me. So why betray me?"

Keegan actually chuckled, the insolent fool. It turned into a hacking cough. "Because you are an evil, sadistic demon with no care for anyone but yourself."

Mammon lifted a brow. "And?"

"And you actually have to ask why that's a problem." Though he must be in utter agony, the boy had the nerve to sound amused. Patronizing.

What a supreme disappointment they had all been to him. Good riddance to the four of them. His future progeny would put their talents to shame.

Mammon strolled to the weapons table and ran his finger along one of the bloodstained knives. "Was warrior service to the Council preferable to a life of power and luxury in your father's service?"

"Yes," Keegan said.

A burst of fury whipped through Mammon. He knocked the table to the side and it upended, knives flying everywhere.

"What about now?" he shouted. "Is even torture preferable to serving your father?"

Keegan laughed, leaving no doubt as to the sincerity of his tone. "I'd rather die."

Mammon rose to his full height. "As you wish, son."

He turned and stalked out of the tent. The guard waited outside. "Double the rate of his blood extraction," he told him. "Leave only the barest amount necessary to keep him alive."

From this moment on, his duty as a father was done. His sons had chosen another path and they must pay the price for it. Now it was time to focus on the future. On his reign.

And if he had to do it alone, then so be it.

Chapter Twenty-nine

Brynn and Taeg made it to the Valley of the Kings in record time, mostly because they knew they had to move quickly. If her dream was accurate—and she had no reason to believe it wasn't—Mammon was bleeding Keegan to death, and not even a half dragon could survive that.

Dagan had been calling Taeg nonstop, and she harbored no doubt that he'd found them both missing and put two and two together. He must have called Ronin to tell him, because soon enough, he joined in the calls to Taeg. Thank goodness Taeg refused to answer any of them. The last thing she needed was for him to start rethinking his agreement to help.

Taeg seemed pretty sure that Dagan trailed them, so that gave them something else to worry about. At least he'd done a moderately good job of masking his impatience over having to fly with Brynn rather than flashing over to Egypt.

Brynn sat next to him inside their rented car about a mile outside of the entrance to the Valley. He turned to her, uncertain. "Brynn, are you sure—?"

"I'm sure."

He handed her his phone. "Remember what I told you."

"Okay." Brynn took a deep breath, then dialed Keegan's number. A gritty voice answered. Though she'd never actually heard him in person before, she recognized him immediately. Just the sound of his voice made her shudder. "Mammon."

"Brynn." Mammon sounded delighted. "So wonderful to hear from you."

"Cut the shit." She made her voice as hard as possible. "I want an oath from you. A blood oath."

After a moment of silence, Mammon laughed. "A blood oath, hmm? Which of my sons is with you?"

"None of your damned business. I want you to swear that once I come to you, you'll let Keegan walk out of there unharmed. Promise you won't hurt him or me."

"How will you know I'm telling the truth?" he asked, his tone smooth as silk.

"Walk out into the middle of your camp. Out in the open."

"Ah, I take it you are nearby? How delightful."

"Stop stalling," she snarled.

"Fine. I'm going out now."

She put her hand over the phone and turned to Taeg. "Okay. He's doing it."

He nodded and then disappeared.

Brynn waited until Mammon said, "I'm here."

"Okay," she said. "Now promise."

"I swear on my blood that in return for your cooperation, Keegan will be allowed to leave unharmed, and that I will not harm you, either. Are you satisfied?"

Taeg flashed into the car, winded, like he'd been running. "He cut himself. It's done."

Brynn nodded. "I'm on my way."

She hung up, niggling tendrils of fear and uncertainty shooting down her spine. Too late to back down now.

Taeg read her thoughts. "Don't worry. You already know how it'll turn out."

"Yes." She turned away. "You'll wait for Keegan?"

"You know it. Brynn, please be careful. If anything happens to you…"

She forced a smile. "I will. I promise."

He seemed satisfied with that. "You got the dagger?"

"Right here." She patted the scabbard holstered to her stomach underneath her loose-fitting sweater. He'd given it to her after they touched down in Egypt, insisting that she take it for protection. But the bleak look in his eyes had said it all. He didn't think she would stand a chance of succeeding if she needed to use it. Still, she was grateful for the weapon. It would be the only one she had against Mammon, since her ability to drain energy didn't work on demons. And unbeknownst to Taeg, she truly *did* plan on using it.

"Well, then, good luck." With one last reassuring look, he flashed away.

Brynn slid into the driver's seat. She was on her own now. On her own and terrified. Apparently, she'd done a good job of convincing Taeg about her vision. Too bad she couldn't do the same to herself, since it was all one big lie. She didn't know how this would turn out. But she had to try something. With one last reassuring pat of the dagger, she started forward.

Please, please let this work. Her only advantage was that she was human and female and, therefore, undoubtedly weak as far as Mammon was concerned. She would have to exploit that at the best possible opportunity.

The entrance to the Valley crept up far sooner than she'd expected. Several armed guards waited outside the gate. They straightened as she pulled up, and then approached her vehicle.

She shifted the car into park and opened the door, sliding out of the seat. "Hello, I—"

"Come on," one of the guards said gruffly, grabbing her arm and yanking her forward.

Another guard slid into place at her other side, and a few men closed ranks behind her. Ah, so these were Mammon's minions.

They dragged Brynn through the barren entrance and all the way across the clearing in the camp to where Mammon waited. Just as they had been in her dreams, tents were set up throughout the space, with the pyramids looming in the background.

"You are as beautiful in real life as you are in your dreams," he said once she was within hearing distance.

"Save it." She kept her voice tough, even though inside she trembled. "Don't forget your oath. Where's Keegan?"

Mammon tipped his head sideways, toward the spot where Keegan struggled against a couple of Mammon's guards as they dragged him toward the exit.

Oh, thank God, he hadn't seen her yet. She stepped backward.

"You can't let him know I'm here," she whispered to Mammon. She didn't know what he'd do if he saw her.

Mammon appeared to think it over before nodding. He motioned for his guards to step in front of her, concealing her from Keegan's view.

Brynn watched the guards drag him toward the entrance.

Ragged sobs threatened to tear out of her throat, but she choked them back. She'd made her choice, and she didn't regret it. No matter what happened to her, he would be safe.

"Never fear, my dear," Mammon said, turning to face her. "He's been shown to the exit, as promised."

Brynn focused in on Mammon, on the rage and fury that bubbled up inside, threatening to consume her. "You'll pay for this, you evil monster."

He lost his oily smile. "No, you stupid human, for this I will be *rewarded*. Now, let us get started, shall we?"

⁋⁃⸃

Keegan stumbled as the guards hauled him through the entrance. What the hell was going on? Were they planning to kill him all the way out here?

He pushed against one of the guards and the demon fell, landing on his knees.

"You got lucky, idiot," the guard hissed, his face reddening as he rose to his feet. "Now get lost, before your luck runs out."

Lucky? Keegan edged backward, staring at the guards in confusion. He didn't understand. They were letting him *go*?

"Keegan!"

Stiffening, he turned toward the sound of the familiar voice. "Taeg."

Relief rushed through him, and he slumped forward. A wave of dizziness hit him. How much damn blood had he lost? Right now, it felt like most of it.

His brother caught him before his knees gave out. "Are you okay, bro?"

"Okay?" He didn't know how to respond to that. He wasn't

sure *how* he felt. Only that he was alive, and somehow it was thanks to Taeg. "How did you—?"

"Later." Taeg directed a meaningful glance toward the guards and supported Keegan's weight as he led him forward. "Let's get you in the car, man."

For the first time Keegan noticed the car a few feet away, its driver's-side door open. Taeg drove here instead of flashing? Why? Unless he did it to retrieve him, knowing he would be too weak to fly.

Taeg helped him into the passenger seat, then jogged to the driver's side, where the keys already waited in the ignition.

"How did you do it?" Keegan asked while Taeg started the car.

His brother's brow crinkled, and he examined the interior, looking at it as if he'd never seen it before. Then again, he'd never driven before today, so it made sense.

Taeg shifted the car into gear and they squealed forward, practically tumbling Keegan onto his brother's lap. The blood loss and exhaustion from the last few days' events slammed into him.

"How did you manage to drive this thing all the way out here?" he slurred.

"Get some rest." Taeg's voice seemed far away. "Try to recuperate. You're going to need all your energy."

Keegan nodded as sleep threatened to overtake him. But he couldn't help but wonder what Brynn would say when she found out he was free.

Brynn!

"Is she safe?" He lurched forward, unable to keep himself upright anymore.

"Everything's fine. Everything will be fine." Without taking his eyes off the road, Taeg pushed Keegan's chest, gently forcing him back onto the seat. "Now just rest."

Moderately reassured, he surrendered to an exhausted slumber. He wasn't sure how long he was out, but he was jostled awake when the car made a bumpy turn. Sitting up, he looked around. "Where are we?"

"Old gas station," Taeg answered, his voice clipped.

The dilapidated white shack was stained a dull brown from the sandy dirt of the road. There wasn't a soul in sight.

"Why are we—?"

"I called them earlier and told them I'd meet them here." Taeg put the car into park and opened the door, stepping outside without another word. He headed toward the shack.

What?

Opening his door, Keegan exited the car and started after Taeg. He was only a few feet away when Ronin stepped out from the side of the building.

"Ronin." His brother looked fine. They both did.

Ronin turned to look at him, and much to Keegan's surprise the expression that crossed his face was almost pitying. Why would he look at him like that?

Just then, Cresso stepped into view, followed by Dagan.

"Dagan?" He'd expected his little brother to be with Brynn. Did that mean…was she here?

Heart soaring, he waited expectantly for her to come into view. But nothing. His brothers all watched him silently, wary looks on their faces, and it all fell into place—Brynn wasn't coming. She wasn't even here.

His gaze drifted back to Taeg, and the guilty expression Keegan thought he'd imagined when he first saw him suddenly made sense. So that was the reason for the car. Not to transport him…but Brynn.

Taeg had helped her exchange herself for him.

Sudden fury slammed into him and he focused every bit of it on Taeg. "You. How could you?"

"Hey, wait a sec—"

Keegan lunged at him, practically flying those last few feet. His brother stumbled, holding onto him but not fighting back.

"Wait. Stop," the others yelled.

He ignored them, concentrating his rage on beating the shit out of Taeg.

"Stop it," Taeg finally yelled. "I have a plan."

A plan? Keegan paused. "Brynn…"

"We're getting her back," he said. "All of us. I promise."

"What are you planning?"

"We're going in. We're gonna stop this and get your girl back." Taeg gave him a measuring look. "I really hope you've got it in you, bro."

"What do you mean?"

"Well, whatever that mechanism is that triggers your powers, you're gonna have to figure it out fast. Because, dude, we're gonna need you to breathe fire."

CHAPTER THIRTY

The inside of Mammon's tent was every bit as opulent as Brynn expected, and just as creepy and disgusting. How was it even possible that this demon had fathered Keegan and his brothers?

After Keegan left, Mammon had directed the guards to bring her inside and guard her while he prepared himself for "ultimate rule." Whatever that entailed. That had been two hours ago. She'd spent the time searching for an escape, but guards manned every inch of the place, clearly prepared for her to try something. She was totally stuck in here.

This sucked.

Please, Taeg, keep Keegan safe.

It killed her to think she might never see him again. But maybe...just maybe...

No. She couldn't allow herself to hope. Right now, she had to focus on stopping Mammon. If there were no other possibilities, she knew the one thing that would stop him: her death.

But Mammon wouldn't kill her. No, he'd resort to torture

until he broke her. If it came down to it, and she was unable to destroy him, she'd have to take herself out of the equation.

Could she take her own life to prevent the apocalypse?

She took a deep, calming breath. *If there is no other choice, you'll have to.*

At last, Mammon returned. "I know it's a bit rustic, but this is only the beginning. Once my empire is established and the rubbish is cleared away, this will make an excellent base."

"Rubbish?" Brynn echoed in disbelief, rubbing her tender arms. The demons who'd deposited her in here were brutes. "You mean the pyramids?"

Mammon shrugged. "They are simply the relics of an ancient past no one cares about. The monuments that will be built for me will make these pyramids pale in comparison."

She stared at him for a moment, then laughed. "Wow, you really do have a big ego, don't you?"

He didn't seem the least bit offended. "I am merely confident in my ability to be the ultimate ruler, my dear." He headed to a small dining table and lifted the tablecloth, reaching underneath it for a medium-size wooden chest. He deposited it on top of the table, opened it, and took something out.

Her heart squeezed tightly when she realized what it was. "The book," she whispered.

"Lovely, isn't it?"

It was. Mesmerizing, in fact. She took several steps toward it before Mammon snatched it up. "Not so fast, my dear."

"What do you want from me?"

"I want you to tell me how to work the resurrection spell. I thought I made that clear during our dreamscaping."

"Dreamscaping?"

"The term I use for our telepathic communication. It is one of my best discoveries, and one I have kept secret from those fools at the Council."

Brynn shook her head. "I won't do it."

Mammon's amusement disappeared. The evil glint in his eye made her gulp and take a step back. "Oh, but you will. Or the demon you love will die."

"You swore you wouldn't harm him." Fear weakened her knees. Had Mammon not kept his word?

"I swore I would let him leave unharmed. But I didn't swear that I wouldn't have my men hunt him down once he'd gone or that I wouldn't kill him if he came back."

Anxiety and fury gnawed at her stomach. "You can't do that."

"Oh, but I can." Mammon laughed as he looked at the book and stroked it, his eyes glazing over for a moment. He refocused on her. "I can have them hurt you, too, darling. That's the problem with blood oaths. You are only bound to your literal words."

Brynn swallowed back her curses. "If you want me to perform the spell, you'll have to give me the book."

"I don't think so. I will open it for you, and you can read the spell."

"What makes you think I'll even be able to read it? It isn't written in English, is it?"

"You are the heir. It is meant for you to read."

"Yeah, maybe." She shrugged. "Or I might have to examine it closely to figure out how to use it."

Mammon frowned at the book, but he must have decided she had a point because he approached her. Brynn resisted the urge to back away, clenching her fists tightly. Every instinct in her body told her to flee, which was difficult to ignore.

He stopped in front of her and held up the book. There were only two thick metal plates, held together by gold hinges and a clasp. "What do you see?"

Brynn stared at it for a moment. "Nothing. Maybe if you open it?"

"Damnation." He turned it back toward him and clumsily worked the clasp, opening it before he flipped it back to face her.

Brynn examined the hieroglyphs engraved on the metal, trying to get a reading off them. But it was just a bunch of pictures she couldn't read. "Sorry. It's all Greek to me."

A low snarl rose from his chest. "If you are lying to me, I swear—"

"I'm not."

He lowered the book with a muttered curse. Brynn took an involuntary step back at the rage in his eyes. For a moment, she feared he would strike her. But instead, he whirled to pace about the tent, grumbling things she couldn't understand. At last, he turned to face her again, training his features into a calm mask.

"Hold it. Tell me what happens then." He held it out to her but kept a tight grasp on it.

She gasped as the cool metal made contact with her fingers. Its immediate pull urged her to use her senses to read its memories. She didn't dare think about resisting. She had to know…she had to.

Closing her eyes, she gave herself over to the book. She saw a man—Iyri—chanting in a language that was foreign yet familiar, while he etched the images into the metal. He uttered a spell of protection, making it indestructible. A gorgeous woman stood by his side, her belly softly rounded with child. He felt equal measures of love and despair for her. He must protect her at all costs. Not only her but his child. His bloodline.

"Use this gift, children of my loins. Ultimate protection. If needs be, ultimate power. Call it forth as you will, and use it wisely."

Iyri performed the spell, and the bodies of the resurrected rose from the earth around him. But he was caught before he could finish it; a dagger plunged into his heart. The bodies fell to the ground and crumbled to dust.

The memories stopped abruptly, flinging Brynn back to the present. She choked on her breath, phantom pain shooting in her chest at the spot where the dagger had struck Iyri.

Mammon's hands trembled. "What? What is it?"

So that was it.

It appeared Iyri had kept a little secret all of his own, something no one could determine by simply reading the incantations. No, only someone who read memories would know what the spell did.

Wouldn't Mammon be surprised when he learned the truth?

Steeling her gaze, Brynn glanced up at Mammon. "I can read the words now."

He breathed, an unholy light glimmering in his eyes. "Go on. Do it."

Fighting back the shadow of a smile that threatened to creep onto her face, she started to chant.

"From the bowels of earth I call to thee, to protect and shadow over me. Until the need for guard is waived, and you are called back to your grave."

She recognized the meaning behind the words even

though they weren't in any language she'd ever heard before. Immediately, the earth around her rumbled but she continued on, ignoring it.

Mammon tore his gaze away from the book, his attention drawn outside to the rumbling of what felt like a mini-earthquake. "Is it done?"

Oh, it was done. "Yes."

His lips curled back to reveal his teeth, and he yanked the book out of her hands, striding toward the exit. Curious, Brynn followed. She stepped outside the tent and gasped.

Knowing what was about to happen was very different from actually seeing it.

Bodies, no more than skeletons, dug themselves out of the earth. The ground not more than ten feet in front of them crumbled upward as dozens of mummified corpses rose from it. The scene was beyond terrifying, like the worst horror movie come to life.

"Oh, sweet heavens." Covering her mouth, Brynn inched backward.

Mammon's minions screamed and scattered at the sight of the zombies. One unlucky demon didn't move fast enough and was torn apart, the zombies feasting on his limbs. As they ate, flesh modeled itself over bare bones.

Beside her, Mammon watched in fascination, the book held tightly in his grasp. "Is it like this all over your world?"

"No, just in the vicinity of where the book is."

His lips curled into a grin. "And they all answer to me."

Well…

Several pig-like demons ran toward them, shadowed by a small group of zombies. Brynn instinctively jumped backward and moved to hide behind Mammon. He grabbed one of the demons by the neck.

"Kill her," he ordered, propelling the demon toward her.

He moved to obey, drawing a dagger out of its sheath. But that was as far as he got before three zombies leapt on him.

"Oh, shit!" Brynn screamed. She edged away, unable to avert her eyes as the zombies devoured the demon less than five feet away from her. Lord, they stank like ten-day-old road kill.

"What?" Mammon stared at the zombies in confusion. His attention darted back to Brynn and, pointing to her, he said, "Kill the girl."

They stopped eating momentarily, turning their gazes toward him while their bodies continued to regenerate. Then, as one, they returned to their demonic feast.

Mammon lobbed an accusing glare at Brynn. "What is this?"

"Oh, forgot to tell you. The book doesn't actually control the army," Brynn said, gracing him with an airy smile. "The heir does."

Mammon glared at her for a long moment, rage building behind his evil eyes. "What?"

"The army is meant to protect the priest's bloodline."

"No." He gripped the book so tightly his knuckles turned white. "No, how dare you lie to me?"

"I can't help that what you believed was wrong."

His chest heaved as he absorbed her words. Then, he moved in front of her and grabbed her neck, choking off her circulation.

The zombies lurched toward them. But Mammon must have heard them, because he shifted around to her back, keeping his hand on her neck, and used her as a shield. She screamed as the zombies got within inches of her, close enough that their stench burned her nostrils and their gore dripped onto her clothes. Recognizing the danger to her, they stopped.

"Stay back," Mammon ordered them, desperation thick in his voice.

They obeyed, edging anxiously, as if searching for his weak spot.

"Tell them to back away," he whispered in her ear.

She opened her mouth to respond…when the sky burst into flames.

CHAPTER THIRTY-ONE

An involuntary screech tore from Brynn's throat as streams of fiery red sprayed the air, creating thick plumes of smoke. A winged figure flew toward the camp.

Keegan.

With Taeg on his back.

Fire blanketed one corner of the camp, setting demons and zombies ablaze. But then, just like that, Keegan appeared to run out of fuel. The fire dissipated, though the carnage remained.

Through the thick smoke, Brynn barely made out the figures of Keegan and Taeg dropping to the ground. They pulled swords from their backs and fought her new army. They attacked, and the zombies mindlessly lurched forward to defend themselves.

She opened her mouth to scream at Keegan, but before she could say a word Mammon dropped the book and clapped his free hand over her mouth.

"Isn't that funny? Turns out they're fighting their own side."

Brynn kicked her heel against Mammon's shin and tried to

elbow him in the stomach. He muffled a curse and dodged her elbow, using the zombies' preoccupation with Keegan and his brothers to his advantage as he edged her backward into the tent. Once inside, he twirled her around and shoved her into the great room. She landed in a crumbled heap on the ground.

Mammon loomed over her, cruelty slashing across his face. "Are you going to cooperate now, my dear?"

She rose to her feet and circled the inside of the tent, staring at him in disbelief. "You can't command the army. Give it up."

Mammon scoffed at that. "I haven't lost. I merely have to reevaluate. I may not be able to command the army, but you can. And I control you."

Control her? He wished.

"Fuck you," she snarled. She made a run for the exit, but he caught her by the arm and his fist clipped her on the chin, dropping her to the ground. Agony erupted at the point of impact. The pain that spread across her face was so intense she feared her jaw might be broken.

"Fuck," he screamed, grabbing his face. A purple bruise had formed there.

Disoriented, Brynn peered up at him, noticing a thin row of bruises darkening on his neck. What on Earth? "The blood oath."

"Yes." He gripped her arm and dragged her toward his bedroom. "I've sworn not to harm you, so whatever harm I do to you will come back to me threefold."

"Let go." She tried to get to her feet, but Mammon hoisted her over his shoulder, not stopping until he reached the side of his bed and dumped her.

Hell no.

Brynn's fist flew out and connected with the side of Mammon's face, in the same spot as his new bruise. He flinched and drew away. She used that moment to reach inside her sweater and slide the dagger from its sheath. Then she lunged at him, swinging it toward his neck in a long arc.

The blade came within an inch of slicing him, but Mammon moved aside at the last second. Instead of cutting his neck, it grazed the top of his shoulder, leaving a shallow cut.

"Bitch. You'll pay for that." He snatched her wrist and squeezed.

She held the dagger for as long as she could, but intense pain spiderwebbed through her wrist, eliciting a ragged scream from her. The bastard had broken her wrist. The dagger fell to the ground with a dull *clang*.

Still holding her firmly in his grip, Mammon punched her, hitting her square on the jaw. Stars erupted in her vision. She must have blacked out, because when she came to, he straddled her and was fitting her wrists into a pair of manacles chained to the top of the metal-framed bed.

Her jaw and wrist were on fire, and the unpleasant tang of blood coated her throat.

"A warning," he said, his voice smooth and full of control. "I don't mind pain the way you so obviously do, and I heal a damn sight faster. So anything short of killing you is fair game."

Panic and desperation overwhelmed her.

"No. No, please." She stifled a scream as he jarred her injured wrist. It hurt so *freaking* badly.

"Hush." Mammon sat back, smiling down at her. "Don't like to be tied up, do you? I'll have to remember that. For later."

His words elicited deep-seeded horror. Although she tried, she couldn't hide it. All at once, she was that little girl again, whimpering in the trunk of the strange man's car, wondering what he would do to her.

No. She couldn't relive that scene. She couldn't be helpless again.

She bucked upward. "Stop!"

Ignoring her, Mammon tore a heavy strip off his sheet and gagged her with it. "Don't want you spilling our little secret, do we?"

He rose off the bed and walked to a small table in the corner. Lifting a large, heavy-looking sword, he turned back to her. Brynn struggled against her binds, biting on the gag to ease the pain of her shattered wrist.

Mammon looked on with an evil smile. "Perhaps if you had behaved, things would have worked out differently. Your lover is still my son, after all. But now, I'm going to kill him."

Keegan must still be weak from blood loss, and on top of that he was fighting demons and zombies. He'd be no match for his father.

No.

"Don't worry, dear." Chuckling, Mammon walked back to her and patted her face. "I'm going to let you watch."

৪৩৫৪

Keegan fought as if his life depended on it. As if Brynn's life depended on it. Because it probably did. He'd been too late to stop the army, but he could still save her life. Damn the Council. Damn Earth. All that mattered now was Brynn.

A zombie lunged at him, snapping its teeth as if it were dying for a taste.

He reared back, then swung his sword in a loose arc. It

caught the zombie across the neck, slicing off its head. The head and body fell inches from each other, but even then, the headless body rose and crawled toward its skull, trying to reassemble itself. Keegan kicked the head and it flew across the field like a soccer ball.

They wouldn't die, these fuckers. No matter how many times he hacked at them, the damned things kept putting themselves back together. And if the gory demon bits strewn about the camp were any indication, the zombies were hungry.

"You okay?" Taeg grunted beside him as he hacked away at a small group of zombies. Nearby, Ronin and Dagan, who'd flown in together, did the same.

"Yeah," Keegan replied. Still weak as hell, his arm ached so badly he wanted to cry, but at least he was alive. All that mattered now was getting to Brynn.

"At least we don't have to worry about the demons anymore," Dagan called beside him.

That was true. The few demons who hadn't hightailed it out of there were either currently fighting off zombies or being snacked on by them.

"Do you see Brynn anywhere?" Ronin yelled.

"No." Not that he could see much. The zombies appeared in waves, and residual plumes of smoke clouded his vision.

"Let's try to flank him so he can fly out of here," Taeg shouted.

Damn. He didn't want to leave them but he had to find Brynn. Devil only knew what Mammon was doing to her.

After much slicing and hacking, his brothers managed to get him enough room to safely fly out. "I'll be back."

"Just go get her," Taeg yelled as a zombie took a chunk of flesh out of his arm. He viciously hacked it in half. "Take that, you piece of shit."

Keegan sure as hell didn't want to leave his brothers in this position. But he took flight nonetheless. Brynn was here somewhere. He dropped in front of Mammon's tent, betting this would be the first place he'd take her. As he stepped inside, Mammon's gritty laugh drifted from the rear of the tent.

Mammon, you fuck.

He ran to the back…and stopped, his blood turning to ice.

Mammon stood in front of Brynn, a sword in his hand. He'd chained her to the bed and gagged her, and she watched him with utter terror.

"No," Keegan roared.

Mammon whirled, and Keegan focused all of his rage on his father. The bastard had tied her up. Made her afraid.

He was going to die.

"Keegan," Mammon said. "I've been waiting for you, son. Here I was, telling your delicious little morsel that it wouldn't be long until you came." He looked back at Brynn and deliberately licked his lips. "And I'll admit, she is delightful. Imagine all the fun we'll have once you're dead."

Keegan charged him, sword swinging. Mammon jumped back and lifted his weapon in time to block the swing. Their swords connected with a loud *clang* and vibrations rattled Keegan's arm, sending a jolt of agony spiraling upward.

"Why bother?" Mammon laughed. "You know you can't win."

Brynn struggled against her binds and mumbled something he couldn't hear. Keegan ignored her, circling Mammon, who jabbed his sword toward Keegan's throat. He blocked the thrust, staggering backward as Mammon advanced. Hitting the end table, Keegan kicked his foot up to shove Mammon away.

Mammon stumbled but caught himself before he hit the ground. Keegan rushed him, but his father swung his sword the opposite direction than he'd expected. He sidestepped it, but not quickly enough. A gash opened on his cheek, and it immediately and painfully healed.

"Ha." Mammon chuckled. "How does it feel to always be second best to your father?"

"You're nothing compared to me," Keegan growled. Again he attacked, but Mammon parried his thrust.

"So say you. You are merely a cheap imitation of my greatness." He bared his teeth. "I daresay your little heir will even think me a better lover."

Keegan tried his best to ignore his father's attempts to goad him into recklessness. Problem was, it was working. He advanced, swinging his sword in a high arc. Staggering back, Mammon blocked it. Keegan used the opportunity to move closer. He lifted his other fist and punched him, connecting solidly with his jaw.

Mammon untangled his sword and stumbled away, spitting blood to the side. "Lucky hit."

"I'm feeling lucky," Keegan replied. If only he really meant it. With his body bruised and sore and still weak from the loss of blood, he was certain he would pass out at any moment.

The sounds of the outside battle grew closer to the tent. Someone—one of his brothers—yelled, and the tent shook as the melee flowed inside. Mammon directed a momentary glance outside the bedroom entrance, then swung at Keegan with renewed vigor. He leapt back to block it.

"Keegan, we're getting creamed out here," Taeg called, his voice anxious.

Keegan stole a glance out at the great room and found Taeg, Ronin, and Dagan in there, fighting back the flood of zombies flowing into the tent. The creatures ripped and tore their way inside, and the entire canvas began falling down around them.

Shit. They were fucked.

Mammon laughed as he aimed his sword at Keegan. Although Keegan stopped it, his collarbone broke from the impact, buffeting his body with pain. He gritted his teeth as a hoarse yell tore from his mouth, and his sword clattered to the ground as he fell to his knees.

"Oops." Mammon's eyes lit up. He lifted the sword above his head and readied for a decapitating swing.

Oh, shit. *Shit!*

Keegan fumbled around the back of his jeans for the dagger he'd hidden there, knowing all the while that by the time he got it out, it would be too late.

Brynn uttered a muffled scream. "Stop!"

Mammon hesitated, lobbing Brynn a surprised glance.

Yes. Keegan's fingers closed around the dagger. He yanked it out of its scabbard and slammed it upward, through his father's belly. A loud *crack* sounded as the blade broke through Mammon's ribcage and lodged itself into his heart.

"Ugh…" Eyes widening, Mammon glared at the dagger embedded deep inside his chest. Keegan kept a tight hold of it as Mammon's sword dropped from his limp fingers and he slowly slumped to his knees in front of him.

Mammon's glazed eyes met his, echoing his shock at what had just happened. A thin line of blood dribbled from the corner of his lips.

After a moment of complete silence, Taeg uttered, "Uh…

what just happened?"

Keegan tore his gaze from Mammon, and his mouth dropped open.

The canvas separating Mammon's bedroom from the great room had all but disintegrated in the melee. Taeg, Ronin, and Dagan stood with their backs to one another, with zombies surrounding them.

Motionless zombies, who stood there staring at him. No, wait...

At Brynn.

CHAPTER THIRTY-TWO

Brynn, although still manacled to the bed, struggled to sit up. She spat out the rest of her gag and threw them a dirty look. "That's what I was trying to tell you the whole time. The zombies are mine."

Keegan choked on a cough. "Yours?"

"They were never meant to obey the holder of the book," she continued in a disgruntled tone. "It's *me* they obey. They were only fighting you to protect themselves. You attacked them first."

Keegan stared at Brynn in stunned silence. Taeg laughed behind him.

"They obey you?" he repeated dumbly.

"Yes. Now someone please get me free."

Ronin slowly backed away, his sword pointed at the zombies. When he seemed sure they wouldn't attack, he dropped his weapon and moved to Brynn. He rummaged inside the drawer on the end table and pulled out a key, then unlocked the manacles.

She let out a pained cry.

"What's wrong?" Keegan said.

"My wrist."

Ronin grasped her wrist in his hands. "I'll heal it. I don't think Keegan has any blood to spare right now."

Mammon made a choking sound, drawing Keegan's attention to him. "Kill me."

Keegan looked at Mammon. *Really* looked at him. He'd actually never been this close to his father before. At least, not when he wasn't busy defending himself from attack. Funny how weak he appeared now. Weak and old. Pathetic.

He barely noticed Taeg and Dagan move next to him. He slowly rose to his feet, pulling Mammon up with him.

"I'll bet that hurts like a son of a bitch," Taeg said coldly.

Dagan laughed. "Won't kill him, but more than enough to make him damn near paralyzed. Yeah, it's got to sting a little."

"Kill me," Mammon repeated, his eyes bright with pain. "Better dead now than a prisoner to the Council. Give me the honor of death, as I would have done for you."

Keegan turned to Taeg, who simply shrugged, then to Ronin and Dagan.

"It's up to you," Ronin said.

"He deserves to die," Dagan added, pure hatred etched on his face.

"You know I would do the same to you," Mammon gasped.

He was right. Mammon would have easily done the same to him, and he would have laughed while he died. No doubt, he would have raped Brynn right in front of his still-warm corpse. For that alone, he deserved to die.

Keegan gave him a cold, hard laugh. "No."

"What?" Mammon panted. His fingers dug into Keegan's

shoulder.

"I said no."

He swore he'd never be like his father, and he wasn't about to start now. As much as he wanted to see the man dead, he wouldn't give him the satisfaction.

Keegan shoved him backward. Taeg caught him and wrapped his fingers around the blade, twisting until Mammon screamed, eliciting a ragged chuckle from Taeg. "Can't have you breaking free, can we?"

"Keegan." Brynn threw herself into his arms. Staggering, he pulled her tight and closed his eyes. "Don't you ever do anything like that again."

He laughed despite himself. "I was going to say the same thing to you."

Brynn kissed him deeply, her tears scalding him where they landed on his cheeks. When she pulled away, her eyes glowed with emotion. "I was scared. So scared for you. Damn it, Keegan, I love you."

"I…" He trailed off without saying the three little words he so desperately longed to. What was the use? Break her heart now or break it even worse later? Because now that Mammon was captured, he'd have to return home.

She seemed to realize he wasn't going to, and her hurt and disappointment punched him in the gut. Composing herself, she stepped out of his arms and turned to face his brothers. "What now?"

"Can you get rid of the zombies?" Ronin asked.

Brynn nodded. "I think so."

"We need to get Dad here back to the Council for punishment," Taeg said.

"And once we do, we'll be sent back to Infernum," Keegan

added gently.

Her eyes widened and a myriad of expressions crossed her face as comprehension dawned.

"Oh. *Oh.*" She carefully studied each of Keegan's brothers. "But none of you wants to go back there, do you?"

"Fuck no," Dagan said. "That place is a shithole."

"Don't you think you might be able to petition the Council to let you stay here, now that you've caught Mammon?"

"Yeah, right. If only." Taeg snorted, tightening his grip around the dagger.

Mammon groaned.

"Well…" Her brow crinkled as if she were considering something. "Can you get me in front of the Council?"

"The Council ordered your death. I'm not letting you anywhere near them," Keegan said, surprised she'd brought it up.

"What are they going to do, kill me?" she countered. "They can't. They need me to get rid of the zombies."

"Still, only a fool would throw that in their faces, especially since it protects you only until the zombies are gone."

"I'm not a fool," she said. "And I've got an idea."

"No. No way." He crossed his arms, wincing at the residual trace of pain in his shoulder. With his low blood volume, damn thing was taking longer than normal to heal. "I'm not putting you in danger."

Taeg shifted, uncomfortable. "Um, I'm gonna take Daddy Dearest outside."

"Yeah, me, too," Ronin muttered, echoed by Dagan. The three of them hightailed it out of the tent, Mammon in tow.

Brynn shook her head as she watched them leave, then turned back to Keegan, her expression a cross between pleading and exasperation. "Can't you trust me?"

Her words twisted in his heart. "I trust you, Brynn, but…"

She took his hand in hers, her grip sure and tight. "For once, why don't we work together?"

Brynn's honest words wore down his defenses. The bottom line was that Keegan had never trusted anyone enough to help him, not even his brothers. In a way, that was what had gotten him here to begin with.

"Please, Keegan," she persisted. "I know what I'm doing. I promise."

He believed her. More than that, he believed *in* her. She was worthy of his trust, and he owed it to her to give her that. "Okay."

"Good." Brynn took a shaky breath. "Now, help me find that damned book."

⥁⥃⥀⥂

Leviathos watched from his spot hidden in the cliff side as Keegan loaded Mammon into the trunk of their rental car. The girl folded herself into the car, the book held tightly in her grasp.

He harbored no pity for Mammon. The man was a fool. He'd let his delusions of grandeur consume him, until in the end he'd been weak. So weak.

Leviathos wasn't about to make that mistake.

He watched Keegan drive away. Now was not the time for the book, but that time would come. He would find a way to retrieve it. To use it. Now, thanks to Mammon, he knew it didn't work as they'd expected. But it was still invaluable. The heir could control the army, and he would find a way to control her. But unlike Mammon, he'd do it slowly, take his time, and make no mistakes.

His attention shifted to Taeg, who stood guard at the entrance to one of the pyramids. His mouth tightened. Taeg was no doubt strutting around like a rooster, thinking he'd won. He'd always thought he was the shit. And true, for many years, he was. Winning at sports. Winning Ana's heart. But Leviathos had learned to not desire those things anymore. Not until he was in a position to make them his by right.

Good riddance to Mammon. Without him, Leviathos was free to act as he wished. He'd use what he learned from him to his advantage, leaving all of his old master's weaknesses behind.

One thing was certain: Taeg and his brothers hadn't seen the last of him. Not yet.Leviathos stepped back and turned to leave…when he noted the profile of a man standing no more than a few yards away. The tall, gaunt man wore a white linen shirt and pants that emphasized his thin form and the dark color of his hair. An aura of power emanated from him, raising the hackles on the back of Leviathos's neck. A prickle of foreboding traveled down his spine, bringing with it an involuntary tremor of fear.

The man didn't acknowledge Leviathos's presence, but rather kept his eyes on the moving car, now a tiny speck in the distance. However, there was no doubt that the man was aware of him. Tendrils of power, pulsing with almost visible energy, snaked off the man toward him.

Finding his voice, Leviathos addressed him. "Who are you?"

A hint of a smile tugged the man's lips upward, and he turned to face Leviathos full on. Something about his face seemed familiar, and with a start he realized the man's nose and mouth somewhat resembled his own. This was no lost relative, however. He wasn't even a demon. But whatever he was, he was powerful.

"I'm somebody who can help you."

Annoyance at the man's presumptiveness lent Leviathos's voice steel. "What makes you think I need any help?"

"You want power. You *deserve* it. I can help you get it." The man nudged his head in the direction of the car. "I can even help you get your hands on the object in that vehicle."

Paranoia set in, warring with the fear coursing like lightning through his veins. "How do you know about that? Who sent you?"

The man laughed. "I know a lot of things, and I come of my own accord."

Somehow Leviathos believed him when he said that. The man started forward, approaching him, and Leviathos resisted the instinctual urge to back up. "So what's in it for you, then? You don't expect me to believe you're just some sort of Good Samaritan, do you?"

That elicited a chuckle from the man. "Not in the least. I surmise that the object would be helpful to me, too."

Leviathos stiffened. If the man thought he was just going to back away and relinquish the prize, he had another thing coming.

The man must have noticed Leviathos's body language, because he held his hands up. "Relax, I don't want the book for myself. I want you to have it."

Leviathos stared blankly at the man. "Well, then, what do you want?"

"Your loyalty."

Despite the aura of danger the man put out, a laugh still bubbled out of Leviathos's throat. "I just rid myself of one 'master.' I'm not about to sign on with another one."

"I don't want to be your master. I just want your assistance on a one-time basis, once you have hold of the book and retain its powers."

Huh. Just one time? Sounded like an interesting prospect… *if* the man could do what he said. But somehow, given the power pulsing off him, Leviathos believed him.

"What's your name?"

A slow grin lit the man's face. "It's Belpheg."

⁎)(⁖

"You dare seek our council?" The Councilman's monotone voice echoed inside the chamber.

Brynn held her ground, doing her best to ignore the creepiness of the Councilman's eyes, which was all she could see of him. "Yes, I dare."

"Don't forget that she's the reason you have Mammon *and* the book," Keegan said from beside her.

Taeg and Ronin had stayed behind, guarding the zombies she'd ordered into one of the pyramids while she and Keegan stood before the Council with Mammon and the book. The whole trip had been worth it, especially when she got to see the look on Mammon's face as one of the Council's prison guards carted him away with the dagger still embedded deep in his chest.

"She's a danger to us all," the Councilman said to Keegan. "And you were ordered to kill her."

"Yeah, well, I didn't."

A creepy chorus of indecipherable whispers echoed all

around the Councilman. "You deserve to be tried for this—"

"Save it," Brynn snapped. The indrawn breaths from the black space told her she treaded on thin ground, but she really didn't care. She already hated these beings for what they'd allowed Mammon to do to Keegan and his brothers, and to the women who had birthed them. She wasn't about to treat them like gods. Not even close. "You have a shitload of zombies packed into a pyramid. They're dying to get a bite of human flesh and I'm the only one who can stop them."

"Do not make idle threats," the Councilman hissed. "We know you would not abandon your fellow Earth dwellers to a fate such as this."

Brynn fought a tendril of fear. "You don't know anything," she said coldly. "I don't have any family left on Earth. I don't care what happens there. The only way I'll call the zombies off is if you honor my requests."

"You insolent—"

The Councilman broke off, and his eyes darted sideways. The chorus of whispers grew to a loud crescendo as his eyes grew wider. "C-Councilwoman," he stuttered. "What an unexpected surprise."

"Give it a rest." The voice was unmistakably feminine, angry, and strangely familiar. Out of nowhere, another pair of eyes appeared next to the Councilman's, but these were human-looking. "Council members, you dared try to keep this incident a secret from me?"

The whispers erupted.

Keegan chuckled. He leaned toward Brynn. "It appears that Earth's Grand Council member has just discovered what's been going on behind her back."

Brynn gave him an incredulous look. "You mean they

never told her?"

"Silence," the Councilwoman spat, her tone brooking no argument. The chorus fell silent. Her gaze moved to Brynn. There was something so familiar about it. Almost like she'd seen those eyes on television before. Wait, was that...could that be—?

"Speak, madam," the Councilwoman said to her. Her tone, far kinder that that of the Councilman's, filled Brynn with hope. "What requests must be honored in order for you to call off the army?"

Brynn tried to calm her racing heart. "I want your word that I won't be harmed."

"Done," the Councilwoman said.

"I also want Keegan and his brothers to live on Earth."

Keegan sucked in his breath, and Brynn clasped his hand. He held on tight, as if every nerve in his body was tightly wound in anticipation of what the Council would say.

The Councilwoman's eyes twinkled, possibly with amusement. She glanced back and forth at the invisible Council members until finally she turned to Brynn. "Keegan and his brothers are valued employees of the Council. Would they be willing to continue as *Detainors* here on Earth?"

Keegan gulped. "We would be honored to do so."

The Councilwoman nodded. "Then it's done."

"One more thing," Brynn said. Maybe she was pushing her luck, but she was going for it.

"Yes?" the Councilwoman asked, definite amusement in her tone now.

"They get to keep the New York apartment."

The Councilwoman answered with a hearty laugh. "Agreed. Now, the counterspell."

Trying not to smile, Brynn lifted the book and read from it.

When the counterspell was complete, the Councilwoman nodded. "You may go."

"Thank —"

Keegan grabbed her hand and abruptly dragged her to the portal. Once inside, he pulled her into his arms. "You really have balls of steel, don't you?"

Brynn stared at him, a mass of emotions overwhelming her. They hadn't discussed what would happen between them if he stayed on Earth. He'd never told her he loved her. But maybe, just maybe…

She shot him a flirtatious glance. "What are you going to do about it?"

"I'm going to love you. Forever and always." He gave her a kiss that stole her breath.

Her heart nearly burst with pride, with happiness. Keegan was hers. He was totally hers now, and she would never let him go.

"That's a really long time," she teased. "Are you sure?"

"Oh, I'm sure," he said. And from the sincerity in his eyes, she didn't doubt it.

She laughed, unable to stop the happy sound from bubbling forth.

"I love you, too." She yanked his head down for another kiss, then broke away long enough to say, "You know, that Councilwoman, I think she was —"

"Shush." Keegan laughed, placing a finger to her lips. "Don't say it. They depend on anonymity."

Before Brynn could protest, Keegan kissed her again. Then again, until she completely forgot what she had been about to say.

EPILOGUE

"You're insatiable," Brynn murmured.

Keegan ran his hand down the milky-white flesh of her thigh. "Look who's talking, love."

"True, I think I could do that all day."

He laughed and buried his face in her neck. "Let's try it and see."

"Mmm…how much longer before your brothers come back?"

"Hopefully another week at least," he said, the sound muffled against her skin.

"Stop." She giggled. "This apartment is more than big enough for all of us."

"True, but it becomes much harder to make love in every room when they're here." He pressed a kiss to her breast, and she arched up to meet him. "Besides, we *are* on our honeymoon."

"Yeah, it was nice of them to give us some time to ourselves."

"Mmm." Keegan traced his tongue around her nipple,

delighting in the way it puckered at his touch. It was sweeter than any berry. "I'm sure they're off having fun."

Brynn sighed. "Except for Taeg."

"Hmm?" he said absently.

"Taeg." She pushed on his shoulders, and he reared back. "I know he's out there looking for Leviathos."

"As he should. The man is insane and dangerous."

"I know, but I'm afraid it's becoming an obsession to him."

Keegan didn't say anything. What could he say? That Taeg was convinced Leviathos would try to come after her? That Keegan thought it might happen, too? No, she deserved to live happily, without fear. That was why Taeg worked so hard to find Leviathos. And Keegan loved him for it.

"He'll be fine," he finally said.

"I know. I just worry about him."

"Well," he said, "I know of a way to take all your worries away."

His hand drifted between her thighs until he found her warm center and stroked inward, reveling in the way she shuddered beneath him. She let out a little gasp and moved under his fingers.

Before Brynn could do more than utter a laughing protest, Keegan slid down and showed her just how adept he could be at making her forget.

ACKNOWLEDGMENTS

First I must thank my family for putting up with my countless late nights of writing, excessive pizza ordering, and general brain fogginess as I've mapped out this series. You inspire me to be a better person, and that makes you all heroes in my book!

My deepest gratitude to publisher extraordinaire Liz Pelletier for believing in and taking a chance on my story.

To Heather Howland and Libby Murphy, you ladies rock! What more can I say? And to Suzanne Johnson, who is utterly amazing *wink*. I couldn't ask for a better editing team than this.

And much appreciation to my critique partner and friend, Mary Abshire, for supporting my vision, even through those craptastic first drafts.

"WEST OF WANT is steamy, spellbinding, and a
must-read for all romance fantasy fans."
- Elisabeth Naughton, author of *Enraptured*

HEARTS OF THE ANEMOI

BOOK TWO

WEST
OF WANT

*Betrayal is all he's ever known,
but in her, he'll find a love
strong enough to be trusted…*

LAURA KAYE

Keep reading for an excerpt from
WEST OF WANT
book two in the Hearts of the Anemoi series
by Laura Kaye

Betrayal is all he's ever known, but in her, he'll find a love
strong enough to be trusted...

When Marcella Raines' twin brother dies, she honors his request to be buried at sea, never expecting the violent storm that swamps her boat. Though she's gravely injured—and still emotionally damaged from her recent divorce—Ella fights to survive.

Zephyros Martius is the Supreme God of the West Wind and Spring, but being the strongest Anemoi hasn't protected him from betrayal and loss. Worse, he's sure his brother Eurus is behind it. When Zeph's heartbreak whips up a storm that shipwrecks a human, his guilt forces him to save her.

Ella is drawn to the vulnerability Zeph hides beneath his otherworldly masculinity and ancient blue eyes. And her honesty, empathy, and unique, calming influence leave Zeph wanting...everything. When Eurus threatens Ella, she and Zeph struggle to let go of the past, defend their future, and embrace what they most want—a love that can be trusted.

CHAPTER ONE

Ella Raines knelt on the varnished deck of the sailboat's cockpit, her dead brother's ashes in her hands, and stared out at the dark green chop of the Chesapeake Bay. The cold March breeze kicked up sea spray and rippled through the sails, but all Ella could feel was the metal urn turning her aching fingers to ice. She had to let him go—she knew she did—but with everything else she'd lost, how could the world be so cruel as to expect her to give up her twin, too?

She twisted open the urn's brass lid and stuffed it in the pocket of her windbreaker. Sailing had been the passion over which she and Marcus had most bonded, not just as siblings, but as best friends. A day spent cruising on the bay, blue skies overhead and warm winds lifting the sails, had been Marcus's favorite thing to do. He wasn't a religious man, but said he most believed in God when he was out on the open water. So a burial at sea made sense, and it was time. When she'd woken up this morning and seen the clear forecast, she resolved today was the day. After all, it had been two months, and the first day of spring seemed a fitting time for starting over.

Leaning over the stern, Ella tilted the brass container by slow degrees until fine ashes spilled out, swirled on the wind, and blew away in a sad gray ribbon that blurred from her silent tears. Choppy waves splashed against the transom, soaking Ella to the elbows, and the boat heeled to the starboard. She braced herself on the backstay. The fixed steel cable bit into her hand but steadied her enough to empty the urn.

"Good-bye, Marcus. I love you." She barely heard herself over the sudden gusting of the wind that roared through the sails.

Ella locked down the grief and despair that wanted to claw out of her chest and climbed to a standing position. The boat heeled again, hard, the forty-five-degree angle nearly catching her off guard. She stumbled. The urn dropped with a brassy clang to the deck of the helm and rolled lopsidedly as the sloop tossed.

She turned, her brain already moving her hands and body through the motions of furling the mainsail and tacking upwind. A bright flash caught her gaze and a gasp stuck in her throat.

An enormous dark cloud sprawled low over the water to the southwest. Mountainous black plumes protruded from the top, creating a tower through which brilliant explosions of yellow-orange streaked. Inky fingers reached down from the storm's edge as the squalling winds lashed at the sea.

Where the hell had *that* come from?

A long growl of thunder rumbled over the bay. Ella felt it in her bones. The boat tossed and heeled. Waves pounded the hull, sloshed over the sides, and soaked her sneakers. A spare glance at her instruments revealed thirty-knot winds. Thirty-five.

A four-foot wave slammed against the port side. Ella slipped on the wet deck and went down hard on one knee. She grasped the wheel just as the boat lurched sideways. Thunder crashed above her, the sound vibrating through the whipping wind. Bitter cold rain poured down over the boat in a torrent. Tendrils of Ella's hair came loose from her long braid and plastered to her forehead and cheeks.

She needed to turn the boat and reach shore if she had any hope of escaping the wind. Ella wrestled the steering wheel hard to windward, the rudder fighting her every turn. Damn, how could she have been so reckless, so unobservant? Storms like this didn't just develop out of nowhere. A sailor never trusted the weathermen over her own eyes and ears. How long had she been kneeling on the deck giving in to her woe-is-me routine, anyway? And here she was, in the literal eye of a storm, sailing single-handed without life jacket or tether on. She locked the wheel into place. At least she could remedy *that* problem.

Ella reached for an orange vest and slipped her arms through the holes. A final glance at her instruments revealed forty-knot winds now. Dread threatened to swamp her. She disconnected the electronics, leaving only the compass to guide her. Her mast was a forty-foot lightning rod, so she did what little she could to combat the likelihood of a strike.

The windward course was a short-lived pursuit as the wind direction changed again and again. Eyes on the compass, she adjusted to the wind as best she could. She couldn't see squat through the deluge, and the hovering gray sheets of rain and spray and six-foot waves obscured the horizon. She'd have to ride it out. With shaking, bone-cold fingers, she connected the bottom of the three buckles on her vest. Small *clicks* sounded from overhead, got louder, more frequent. Hail pelted down the size of dimes, then nickels. Ella crouched against the wheel and shielded her head with her hands and arms. The falling ice ripped into the plastic of her jacket and bit into her knuckles.

Thunder crashed right above her and the storm-darkened sky exploded in ferocious jags of electricity. Rain and hail lashed her body, and wind and waves battered her ship like it had a personal vendetta to settle. With her. A tremendous wave crested over the starboard side, shoving her head against the metal spoke of the wheel. Spots burst across her vision. She cried out, the sound swallowed by the wind.

When she could focus again, her gaze settled on the lidless cremation urn wedged fore of the wheel pedestal. Marcus. What she wouldn't do to have him with her. She reached around the huge wheel to grab the container, just grasping for something, anything to make her feel less alone. She couldn't reach. Shifting her hold on the wheel, she stretched, her fingers straining, yearning to feel the cold brass. Not quite.

She lunged for the urn, grabbed it up, and hugged it to her chest.

Thunder and lightning blasted the sky above her. A wall of wind shoved at the side of the sailboat. It lurched. Spun. An ominous crack reverberated from below. A wave pounded Ella's shoulders and back, flattening her atop the urn onto the deck of the cockpit, holding her hostage with its watery weight. Seawater strangled her, stole her breath, and receded.

The boat reared over a peaked wave and bucked. Ella slid into a free fall.

Not releasing her death grip on the urn, Ella's right hand shot out and clutched the steel backstay. The ligaments of her shoulder wrenched apart in a sickening, audible pop just as her lower body whipped over the transom and hit the frigid water. The jolt stole her scream, allowed her only to moan long and low. Icy wetness soaked through her heavy clothes and the drag tugged and pulled at her destroyed joint.

Triple bolts of lightning illuminated the gunmetal sky in quick succession. Shaking nonstop from cold and pain and adrenaline, Ella stared up at her hand clutching the metal cable. One strike and she'd be done. Her mind laid out the choices. Ship or sea. Urn or ship. Drown or fry. Life or death.

A wave swamped her. And another. She choked and gagged. The next slammed her head against the fiberglass transom.

Her hands flew open from the impact. She plunged into the storm-tortured water, sucked down nauseating mouthfuls. Her body whipped feet over head, side to side. Impossible to determine which way was up. The violent churning of the sea ripped the lifejacket off one arm, but the orange padding held just enough to finally guide her head to the surface.

Despite her daze, survival instincts had her gulping oxygen, precious oxygen. Her successful fight against the urge to vomit left her shuddering, the sour bile almost a welcome respite from the cold salt. No matter. The next cresting wave forced her to drink more.

Panic jolted through her body, shook the drunken haze from her mind. Kicking and paddling, she spun around and around, until she'd done several three-sixties. The boat. Gone.

As her body crested the top of wave after wave, she strained to see some glimpse of white in the thick, dark gray. At thirty-four feet, the *True Blue* was not little, but the sea was too rough, the wind too forceful.

No. No, no, no. Not their sailboat, too. Not the last place

that truly felt like home, the last place filled with memories of laughter and love and honesty.

Deafening thunder rumbled over the world. Jagged electricity flared over the monstrous seascape.

Ella tilted her head back, squinted against the blinding rain, and screamed. "Is that all you got? Well, fuck you! Fuck you and the cloud you blew in on! I've got nothing left to lose, so take your best shot!"

A wave smacked her in the face. She gagged. Coughed. Laughed until sobs took over.

Exhaustion. Pure and utter. Like she'd lived a thousand lives.

Debris thudded against her ear. She howled as the jarring hit rang through her head.

Please don't let it be pieces of True Blue.

Her eyes focused on the sea next to her. Nothing. She propelled herself around. The urn. Ella gasped and irrational joy filled her chest.

She half-swam—a nearly impossible feat against the thrashing waves with one useless arm. Each leaden stroke sapped what little energy she had left.

She grabbed the urn. Held it in her numb hands.

"I knew you wouldn't leave me," she whispered against the brass, all she could manage. "We're true blue."

Together, the churn carried them up one side of a wave, then plunged them down the other. Ella's head slumped against the flat base of the upside down container. Her eyelids sagged.

And everything went black.

CHAPTER TWO

A life force was fading.

The sensation tugged at Zephyros's consciousness, embattled as it was as he raged over the sea. Caught up in his own thoughts, his own pain, his own loss, he writhed and tossed, howled and lashed out. The wind and rain—nature's very energy—were his to control, even when he was out of control. But, still, the wrongness of the sensation tugged at him, demanded redress. In his elemental form, he felt the call of life and birth and renewal most strongly. He could ignore it no longer.

He forced himself to embrace the calm that had once been the truest manifestation of his nature. Around him, the clouds dispersed, the rains thinned, the winds settled to a bluster. The sea, black and roiling a moment ago, eased into the early spring chop typical of the bay.

Zephyros allowed the tranquility of the open water to fuel the return of his composure. He focused. Scanned for the soul decrying its unnatural end. Commanding the West Wind to carry him down from the heavens, he soared on the gentle gusts.

The only thing nearby was a lone sailboat, floundering in the wind.

He glided around the fine boat. No life resided on its decks or within its hull. A sour pit formed in his gut as he began to suspect what had happened.

Rising up to gain a broader view of the sea, Zephyros searched, the dwindling life a beacon he latched onto. Pursued. The thrum of its force vibrated within him. Closing in, he descended toward the surface, the waves passing under him in a blur. There! A flicker of orange upon the dark gray-green.

Flashing into corporeality, Zephyros assumed the form of a giant water kingfisher.

Slate-blue wings exploded twenty feet out on either side of his body. He plunged head-first toward the bobbing figure, the wind ruffling through the crown-like crest of blue feathers atop his head. Rarely did he ever have the need to shift into his sacred animal form, but it was a power all the Anemoi possessed.

Glaring down at the water, Zephyros braced himself. Extreme temperatures pained and weakened him, and he'd be lucky if this water was in the fifties. He skied into the water's surface, spread wings gentling his landing. No such luck. Mid-forties if it was anything. But this wasn't about him, was it?

Just ahead, the human bobbed face down, tendrils of long hair floating in strands of silk like a halo. He smelled blood. Best hurry. His senses told him time was short.

Zephyros plunged his regal, avian body into the water, came up with the dead weight draped over his neck. With a shove of a wing, he pushed the legs of the body up, resituating the length along his back. He took flight.

Frigid water shook off him in a fantastic spray as his

massive wingspan flapped and lifted them away from the bay. His gaze lit on the sailboat and he banked in its direction. He circled the boat once, twice. The metal cables connecting the mast to the deck would not accommodate his wings. He couldn't land on the boat.

Taking extra care not to jostle the victim, *his* victim, Zephyros landed behind the sailboat. Instinctively, he commanded the change and shifted into his human form. The biting chill of the water tormented his naked flesh, but more important matters demanded his attention. Grabbing onto one delicate hand, he ensured his hold on the person draped across his back before turning and cradling the body into his arms.

He sucked in a breath. Mother of gods. A bruise mottled the whole left side of her face, from cheek to eyebrow. A nasty gash along the cheekbone oozed a thin line of blood. Her bottom lip was busted open, swollen. But even the severity of her injuries couldn't hide her beauty.

That sour pit in his stomach grew, suffocated. He'd caused this. Damn it, could he never do anything right? Ancient turmoil roiled through him, threatening to turn him inside out. No, of course he couldn't.

Zephyros adjusted the woman's weight in his arms and reached up over the transom. His fingers searched for and found the release, and the swim platform folded out toward them. He lifted the woman above his head and settled her on the glossy wooden surface, then hefted himself up beside her. With solid footing beneath him, he gently lifted her again. He stepped around the massive wheel to the seating area to the fore, and laid her out on a long bench.

Her head lolled to the side. Wheezes morphed into a weak cough. Her whole body seized. Water expelled from her throat.

Zephyros supported her shoulders, held her up until she quieted. Her eyelids creaked open, revealing the rolling whites of her eyes. They sagged again, and her whole body went limp.

Zephyros released a breath as unexpected relief flooded him—followed quickly by guilt. His suspicions about what had happened to her were confirmed by an imprinting on her life jacket. The words "True Blue" matched the dark blue calligraphy painted on the back of the boat. She'd been thrown overboard in the storm. *His* storm.

He shivered, a combination of guilt, shame, and the wind against his wet body. Well, the latter problem he could address. He materialized jeans and a T-shirt and made himself decent.

Like a magnet, she drew his gaze. He reached out and stroked his fingers over the reds and purples coloring the side of her face. Her hair appeared deep brown, but he suspected the darkness was an effect of the water still drenching her.

Shaking his head, Zephyros debated. He should leave now. The Coast Guard would find her. The bay had patrols. He could even command the current to carry the boat, with her upon it, to shore. Even as he agreed with himself, agreed leaving her would be for the best, he searched the boat for information he could use to help her. Storage lockers filled the space beneath the bench seats. Empty. His gaze scanned. He'd look below.

Down the companionway steps, he descended into the cabin and stepped in a few inches of sloshing water on the galley floor. All warm wood and white accents, the space was surprisingly spacious and bright. Far forward there appeared to be a berth. Aft of that bedroom, a large sitting area centered round a table. To his immediate left, a small galley kitchen, and to his right, a chart table. Compasses and instruments hung above it on the hull wall.

Zephyros stepped to the desk and opened the top drawer. Maps and paperwork sat in skewed stacks. He flipped through the pages until he found a name and address. That the name was male brought an unexpected frown to his face, but at least he had a lead on where to take her. Surely someone so physically attractive had a significant other, someone who would care for her and see her mended back to health.

As he moved to return above deck, a small aft berth caught his eye and he reached in and yanked a blanket from the bed. Up top again, he tucked the red comforter around the woman. The loose strands of hair around her face had air-dried to a light golden-brown. Peaceful in her unconsciousness, her face appeared delicate and young, unmarred by cruelty or pain— except for what he'd done to her, of-fucking-course.

Ignoring the rock of guilt in his gut, he considered the problem of actually getting the boat to harbor. Sailing was a foreign language to him. He had no need for the knowledge. He could soar on the wind, even glide on the currents for short times. All he knew was a sailboat with furled sails wasn't going anywhere.

No matter. He stepped around the wheel and down onto the swimming platform. The clothing would just be a drag, so he disappeared it and jumped. The cold water sucker-punched him. He gasped and willed his muscles to cooperate. How long had the woman suffered with the freezing waves battering her damaged body? He bit down on his tongue to keep from roaring out. The pain focused him.

Arms extended beside him, he closed his eyes and called the current. As a wind god, Zephyros was most at home in the sky, but marshaling sea currents worked on the same principle.

The rush of water pushed behind him, just as he directed, and scooped up the boat's hull in the grip of its gentle forward motion. One hand on the platform, he floated behind the boat, guiding its heading, adjusting as necessary, shivering until he thought his bones might snap. Luckily, the storm had chased away other maritime traffic. The bay was wide open and empty. Nice to have one thing going for him. Occasional gulls cried out high above, their pale bodies nearly camouflaged against the gray-white sky.

Within an hour, they were in sight of Annapolis. Above the town proper, a large steeple and a tall domed cupola framed the colonial seaport. But Zephyros's destination was a bit closer. The address he'd found should be on the neck of land just south of the town.

An inlet emerged up ahead. All along the shore, clusters of masts stood up together, sentinels on the water. He guided the boat toward the creek. A sailboat with a large blue mast sail glided past. Zephyros submerged into the cold, but not before noticing the confounded expression on the other captain's face. Of course. The boat he guided moved without aid of sail or motor.

He resurfaced long enough to see the other boat coming about, the captain on the radio. Damn it all to Hades.

This situation was about to become shit meets fan. For gods' sake, he currently didn't have clothes, and until he warmed he'd be lucky to hold a conversation. Naked, nearly incapacitated, with no ability to dock the boat, and with a gravely injured woman on board, he had little likelihood of contriving a convincing story about how they'd gotten that way.

His presence was a liability here. He was useless. Again.

As the blue-masted boat neared, the captain called out, asking whether the *True Blue* was in distress. No one answered, of course.

And it was time for him to go.

Zephyros released his grip on the platform and eased the created current until it dispersed altogether. He sank beneath the surface, shaking nonstop, and hesitated just a moment. His gut clenched. He hated the idea of not seeing her to safety. Okay, in truth, he'd done that. But what he *wanted* was to see her to health—awake and conscious and warm and happy.

Happy? What did her emotions have to do with anything? Fluttery panic ripped through his chest. The fact he was even thinking about her feelings was a major get-the-hell-out-of-there red flag. Getting involved was the last thing he needed. Hadn't he learned that? Again and again and a-fucking-gain?

No more.

The rescue sailboat came alongside the *True Blue*. A man's voice rang out above the water's surface. There. *He* would make sure she was safe, cared for, got everything she needed. The thought had Zephyros grinding his teeth in frustration. In self-defense.

In want.

No.

He wanted nothing and no one. And, in truth, no one wanted him either. So didn't that work out just perfectly, thank you very much.

Zephyros turned and, without looking back, swam to the opposite shore.

He broke the icy surface gasping for breath and shaking so hard his bones hurt.

"Job well done, Zephyros. Very good. And on the first day

of your season, too," came the last voice Zeph wanted to hear in that moment. Or any moment.

Zeph wiped the water from his eyes and climbed the small embankment opposite the marina where he could hear a small crowd gathering. The clothes he materialized didn't begin to compensate for the consequences of over an hour of exertion in a forty-degree sea. Grinding his teeth together to keep them from chattering, he faced his younger brother Eurus, Supreme God of the East Wind and Harbinger of Misfortune. Evil in a pair of $900 dress shoes. Zeph ignored the comment intended to pluck at his guilt and rile him up. "You have no business here, Eurus. Leave. I don't have anything to say to you."

Standing on the shore in his I'm-dark-and-mysterious black leather getup, Eurus stared across the water through the black wraparound sunglasses he always wore. His lips twitched. "Be that as it may, I have something to say to you." He turned away from the drama unfolding across the inlet and faced Zeph, but didn't speak.

Striking a careful indifference as emergency vehicles poured into the marina parking lot, Zeph glared at his brother. He'd paid his debt to Eurus, and then some. Not that Zeph truly believed he owed that fucker anything, but he'd wanted to make nice, keep the peace. Problem was, Eurus didn't agree. And never would. "For the love of the gods, Eurus. What do you want? I'm freezing and don't want to stand here arguing with you."

Eurus laced his hands behind his back. "Fine. I'll get right to the point. I plan to submit a petition."

Gods, he hated how Eurus made everything so damn dramatic. "About?"

"I will propose that, lest you beget an heir by the end of

your season, my son Alastor be installed as your heir." Zeph gaped as Eurus plowed on. "Only Boreas and I have addressed issues of succession." He shook his head and tsked. "And it's very dangerous, Zephyros. Very dangerous indeed not to have an heir in place."

Maybe Zeph's ears were frozen and the words had gotten garbled. No way his brother had just proposed— "You can't be serious."

Eurus arched an eyebrow.

"You're out of your mind." As if that wasn't stating the obvious. "A god of the East could never do the job of a god of the West." Not to mention the fact Alastor was a complete recluse and, more importantly, Zeph would never trust anyone of Eurus's line with…anything.

"Alastor could."

Zeph turned away and climbed the rest of the way up the embankment. "Whatever. I'll get around to having an heir when I'm good and goddamned ready." When that might be, he had no idea. After all, someone had to stick around long enough first. "Besides, Father would never approve an eastern god as the heir of my line."

"He would if he had the blood of spring in his veins."

Going stock still, Zeph heaved a breath. Icy fingers crawled up his spine. He schooled his expression and turned on his brother. Glared, but kept his mouth shut.

Eurus's smug expression went glacial. "Oh, come now. I know you want me to explain."

Despite the way his skin crawled and his gut squeezed, he'd freeze out here before giving Eurus the satisfaction of asking.

Leaning forward, a smile that could only be described as wicked curled the edges of Eurus's lips. "Your *wife*, Chloris," he sneered, voice dark and satisfied. Then he was gone.

The words cut through the air and crashed into Zeph so hard he couldn't breathe.

CHAPTER THREE

Words disconnected from meaning. Sounds out of context. Numbness like floating. And always the darkness.

Sometimes she surfaced. Nauseating light played behind eyelids she couldn't force open. Shooting pain accompanied the smallest shift in her position. A world-spinning ache throbbed beneath her face and ear. An odd, distant keening sounded in those moments, bringing a rush of relief through her veins that would pull her under into merciful oblivion once more.

Consciousness returned in the quiet of night. Ella blinked her dry, crusty eyes again and again. The dim room took shape before her. Sage-green walls. A mounted television. A movable tray. Gentle, rhythmic beeps entered her consciousness. Rolling her head just a little, she found the source of the sound. Monitors and medicine drips on metal stands lined the side of her bed. A hospital, then.

She opened her mouth, but knew instinctively she wouldn't be able to talk. Her tongue lay thick and unused. Her lips burned with dryness. She tried to lick them.

"Here. Take a sip."

Her gaze tracked the new sound, setting off a wave of dizziness. Her lips found the straw first, held right where she could reach it. She sucked the life-giving water into her mouth. It was the best thing she had ever tasted. She could've cried.

"Welcome back," the deep voice said.

Ella had almost forgotten someone was there. She released the straw and with effort made herself look up.

The nurse stood next to the side of her bed. She blinked and squinted. Focus slowly returned. He towered above her. His hair was short and dark, unruly curls just at the ends. Close-trimmed facial hair set off an angled jaw and lips pressed in a concerned line.

"More?"

She frowned. The straw stroked her bottom lip. She opened, eagerly drank more of the water. Her throat rejoiced.

"Thank you," she mouthed, no sound emerging.

"Don't try to speak. Just rest. And be well."

She sighed. And slipped into nothingness.

In the early morning gloom, she awoke again. A man, all broad shoulders, stared out through the slats in the blinds. Green scrubs. Her nurse again?

"Water," she croaked.

He was at her side so fast, she must've blinked. A couple of times. She hadn't seen him move.

This time when she offered her thanks, she could manage a rasping whisper.

His lips curved up, the smallest bit. "You're welcome." Intense slate-blue eyes stared down at her. "How are you feeling?"

"Dunno." She licked her lips. "What happened?"

His brow furrowed. "You don't remember?"

She closed her eyes and concentrated. A lump formed in her throat and swelled. "Marcus." Flashing images of a ferocious storm joined the memory of her brother. "Dead." She swallowed hard, the sound thick and tortured in her own ears.

"He died?"

Something in his voice begged her attention. She blinked up at him. He'd gone totally still next to her, his expression grave and alarmed. Ella frowned. "Yeah."

"When this happened to you?"

She opened and closed her mouth. The hair on her arms raised, the air taking on a warm, electrical quality. Obviously, some good drugs dripped into her veins. Still, his intensity did seem weird. Why was he so upset?

He grasped her hand. "Ella, did he die when this happened to you?"

Her gaze fell to his engulfing grip on her fingers. So warm. Her skin tingled where they touched.

The big man leaned across the path of her vision to capture her attention. "Gods, woman, answer me."

Her head swam. From the effort of remembering the question. From exhaustion. From the roiling power behind his piercing blue eyes. She shook her head once. "No, not then."

His whole body sagged. The air in the room cooled and calmed. He stood up and turned away, lacing his hands on top of his head. Ella missed the warm connection immediately, but was equally consumed with watching him. For a moment, he muttered and paced along the length of her bed, roughly scrubbing his palms over his face. He had the slightest sprinkling of gray at his temples.

His every movement radiated power. The green scrubs

pulled across the muscles of his shoulders, back, and thighs with each step. His very presence took up the whole side of the room in which he paced. He exuded a raw masculinity her body recognized, even if she was in absolutely no position to respond to it.

"You okay?" she scratched out.

He whirled on her, eyes guarded, muscles tense.

The movement was so unexpected, she gasped. Her heart raced, unleashing a series of throbs in her shoulder, neck, and head. She groaned.

"Damn it!" he bit out. He rushed to her and pushed a button on the side of the bed. A big hand smoothed over her forehead. "I'm sorry."

Ella's eyes clenched shut against the pounding torment rooting itself behind her eye and ear. But his touch helped. How amazing the power of human touch.

Then it was gone.

Her gaze scanned the room. Empty. A ball of panic bloomed in her gut. Where had he gone? And why had he left?

The door to her room pushed open and a woman with brown skin and pink scrubs breezed in. "Well, welcome back, Ms. Raines. It's good to see you awake."

Ella could only manage a drawn-out moan. The nurse was pretty, her smile open, and she wore her black hair in a curly natural style. The woman made pleasant small talk with her while she checked her vitals and entered her findings into a computer on a swivel stand.

"Don't you worry, now, we'll get you feeling better in no time. Can you tell me your pain level on a scale of one to ten, with ten the worst pain of your life and one pain-free?"

Licking her lips again and forcing herself to focus, Ella considered the question. How did one judge pain? Her shoulder was a good solid six. The throb vibrating through her skull, a seven. But her heart, oh, her heart might never recover. A ten for sure. But Ella supposed that wasn't the kind of pain the nurse was asking her to describe. "Maybe a seven," she rasped.

"Okay, honey. Let's see what we can do about that." The woman inserted a needle into the IV. Cool solace slid into her veins and tugged at Ella's consciousness. She almost gave in, before she thought to ask. "The man? The male nurse?" she slurred.

The woman smiled and shook her head. "Musta been a good dream. Only us ladies on this unit." She went right on, explaining procedures to Ella in case she needed anything, but Ella's attention drifted away, stolen by the pain medication and the memory of a man who didn't exist.